TALES IN FIRELIGHT AND SHADOW

Edited by Alexis Brooks de Vita

TALES IN FIRELIGHT AND SHADOW

DOUBLE DRAGON

DEDICATION

For Our Readers,
old tales casting light in dark places

Table of Contents

Prologue

In the dark night of the human soul, a fire is lit and a tale is told, stirred from a chthonic pottage of dirt, blood and terror: the folktale. The flame that simmers our earthly supper does double duty as light through black hours toward the brave sun of day. We feed the body and the faltering spirit with hearth fire, campfire, candlelight, and electricity: flames promising that we are not alone.

Like those flames, the following tales edify and terrify as they cast light in flickering contrast to the encroaching shadow, beginning with the deceptively beguiling tale of Mary Turzillo's "Pigeon Drop." The magic tale, the enchantment, we realize with a start, is a terrible illusion. Or is it, asks Jason Parent's tongue-in-cheek "Moody's Metal," a talisman clutched against witches, curses and despair?

Oh, but where is that folktale world so fondly recalled from childhood? Right here in Patricia Stoltey's sun-spattered "Three Sisters of Ring Island," a familiar story scraped to its bare bones-so to speak. In this skeletal frame, if we look around, we will discover that we live poised on the sea-sprayed cliffs of Joseph Michael's "Nuckelavee," immersed in the realm of fairy, fear and chaos, in Tenea D. Johnson's "Sugar Hill."

Or, in the small hours, might we prefer to face the unknown worlds within ourselves? Then welcome to master fantasist James Morrow's excavation of the secrets of the furrowed-brow philosopher in "Spinoza's Golem." Certainly, the intrepid reader thinks, foot on the brink of a precipitous plunge, this tale carves a face on our wordless grown-up anxieties. For is it not precisely our ache for both profound meaning and unbreakable belonging that renders Christina St. Clair's "Green Cat" a universal cameo of pathos and pity?

We reach out a hand to stay the destruction, to say, "Turn back; take back those words and all that pain."

For, none of us wants to be-or see-that disillusioned soul for whom it has all ended too soon, that one made up of shadows and whispers for whom there will be nothing sweet, nothing else, nothing more: Alfonso Arteaga's "*La Planchada.*"

How we dread to come across those doomed to endure the lessons of what it all meant, too late to mend or make amends: T.J. Weyler's "Keepers." So much of our suffering comes with the discovery that we are neither who nor what we think we should have been-as Ceschino's "Tailed" brings, quite literally, home.

Had we not better take these chances, live these enchantments, do exactly as Alexandra Dairo-Brown's "Mercy and the Mermaid" so triumphantly do? Surely the folktale exists to indulge our desire for life filled with love and joy-and to show us our fears that perhaps our lives will not be so idyllic.

To show us how to bear up under the grinding down, as in Novella Serena's "My Bogeyman."

If living has deprived us of the love we need and the meaning we seek, montage asks from the depths of "*Sans* Lake," can we not reach out again to the world one last time from that spiritual place that surely is to come?

We who peer through an opaque lens at the dark side of the moon watch as A.J. Maguire's "The Nano-Fisherman's Wife" shakes her head and cautions us not to risk our one sure chance at happiness, for we never know if it is our last: the thought that troubles F. Brett Cox's "See That My Grave Is Kept Clean" and Jennifer L. Julian's "Dance."

For, as sun shreds night with returning opportunity, we must each answer that question we can only resolve for ourselves: what do we make of this folksy knowledge gained from those who've gone ahead and reached back with a cautionary tale like a friendly flame, torchlight that reminds us in our blindness that daylight is always coming, just ahead?

Closing this volume, we may consider that our folktales, braided of firelight, song and shadow, have taught us to see the darker side of right, a faithful kind of insight.

We read, dream and forge on, knowing we shall wake in a larger world, braver for our sojourn in sightless times and wiser for patience learned through old lessons enjoyed anew.

- Alexis Brooks de Vita

PIGEON DROP
by Mary A. Turzillo

A cat told me this story. I was looking up
relatives who I had heard lived somewhere in
Campbasso, and during my search I encountered
this ancient feline hunting voles on the wall of the
Borgo Antico in Termoli. He was walking on the
wall, which was almost vertical, picking his way,
very sure-footed. I believe this cat's name was
Massimo, but he mentioned it only once and after
would not repeat it.

He told of Puntino, a half-grown kitten,
perhaps a relative of his. This little Puntino knew
no magic himself but lived with Cagliostro the
Mage of Venice, along with a pigeon named
Semiramis. Puntino was entirely black except for a
white diamond on his chest. His mother had been
feral, and perhaps the rest of his litter remained so,
but he picked scraps of meat from the *cacciatore*
left over on Cagliostro's plate, and he purred at the
magician's feet.

Cagliostro traveled the circuit and during high
season never spent more than three successive
nights in the same bed. The mage was ambitious,
always striving to create new tricks. The pigeon
Semiramis was the star of his current finale.

Puntino at first played too rough with
Semiramis the pigeon, but after a while, he grew
gentler and considered the bird his friend. However,
every morning, the bird would shriek in terror, until
Puntino calmed her by catching her and letting her
go several times. She seemed to settle down and

even show guarded affection to both cat and magician during the off-season, when Cagliostro retired to a villa in Rodi Garganico.

"Why so nervous?" Puntino meowed at the bird sometimes, but Semiramis never answered. She couldn't talk, he decided, only coo in that soothing way cats like.

For one engagement, the magician's lodgings were directly above the theater where he performed, and so Puntino slipped down and draped himself on the back of an unsold seat in the balcony to watch. A pianist played bits of Puccini overtures and also Tartini's "The Devil's Trill Sonata," to build suspense for the magician's tricks, music Puntino found almost as delightful as his lost mother's purr.

At the finale, Cagliostro crowed, "And now I present my longtime avian companion, the honorable Semiramis, a dove of noble birth and intrepid spirit!" The magician always referred to Semiramis as a dove, since it sounded more elegant than "pigeon." Cagliostro invited children in the front rows to offer the bird crumbs, and Semiramis pecked at these warily.

With a flourish, the magician placed Semiramis's cage on a table at the front of the stage. He made a show of demonstrating that there was no hole in the tabletop, and nothing underneath the table. He even asked a small boy in a sailor suit to come up and crawl underneath it. The boy did so, waving shyly at his parents in the third row.

Cagliostro then clapped sharply, and a massive safe, half as big as a steamer trunk, descended from the fly space. The safe, suspended on a rope, dangled ponderously above Semiramis in her flimsy cage on the table.

The bird hopped about as if having a presentiment. Puntino's ears perked forward and his green eyes glistened with interest.

Cagliostro mounted a stepladder and drew out a sword which he'd used in a previous trick. The pianist leaned into the ivories, rumbling forth arpeggios in a minor key.

Then the magician slashed the rope that suspended the safe. It fell! The audience gasped.

Crash! The massive safe utterly smashed the cage. The table rocked, but did not collapse. Feathers swirled in the air. Was that a spatter of blood? Exciting. Frightening.

The audience tittered and shifted in their seats, but Cagliostro descended to the stage floor with a triumphant smile. He reached into the pocket of his silk waistcoat and with a flourish produced a slip of paper. He perused the message and then twirled the dial of the safe. The minute he had opened the door, Semiramis, uncaged, unharmed, fluttered out.

Cagliostro nimbly caught the bird's legs. She cooed, obviously unhurt.

How had the magician done this? Puntino was only a nine-month old kitten, but he knew that the magician's other tricks were all bogus-devices purchased by mail order or made by his own clever assistant, a dwarf girl named Lucrezia who lived near Termini.

Puntino padded back up to the magician's digs, settled on the soft rug at the foot of the bed and thought about this.

When the show moved to a new theater, Puntino followed Cagliostro to see if perhaps he had made a deal with a minor devil. Perhaps some of the magician's magic was real.

The magician set out for the theater, only a few blocks away. As always, he wheeled his gear on a cart, with the safe strapped securely in front and the bird cage dangling from his arm. But instead of going directly to the theater, he detoured to a verdant piazza. Puntino pussyfooted after him, curious as only a green-eyed black kitten can be.

Cagliostro opened the door to the safe easily. Aha. The magician had the combination memorized, and the consultation of the slip of paper was all just for show. Then Cagliostro squatted on his heels in the grass and strewed bread crumbs about his feet.

After a time, the pigeons pecked closer to the magician. Cagliostro's quick hand whipped out and grabbed one by the feet. He stuffed it into the safe and snicked shut the door.

Now the magician had two doves, two Semiramises. He dusted off his hands and headed for the theater.

A ticket-taker shooed Puntino away at the door, so he hid under an awning that had blown down. He waited until two dancers in the previous act came out through the stage door to escalate some lovers' spat. Then he slipped inside, like a wraith.

The pigeon act went as it had before, but this time, Puntino was sure he saw blood and possibly even, with his alert cat senses, heard a pigeon shriek.

16

***

When scraps of meat from the *cacciatore* appeared in a dish on the floor that night, Puntino refrained from eating them. "Not hungry, kitten?" said Cagliostro. "I'll give you a special treat if you help me create a new trick."

Puntino had no way to tell anybody the secret of his master's pigeon trick. But he tried valiantly to warn the new Semiramis. *Pietosa*! She listened and then tried to fly away, but the windows were closed, and the magician let her flap around until she lay exhausted on the wooden floor. Then he put her back in her cage.

One day, Cagliostro came home with another black cat in his arms. This one was entirely black, with no white diamond on its breast. He put the cat down in front of a plate of leftover *cacciatore,* and it ate the meat bits avidly.

Puntino hissed a warning, but the new cat only licked its whiskers and dove into the plate to lick the sauce.

When the magician opened a bottle of ink, Puntino was gone.

***

So said this ancient cat, this Massimo (if that was truly his name). But how can you trust a cat of Termoli? Cats are all liars, and particularly those of the Borgo Antico of Termoli.

I did find the descendants of my great-grandfather, Giuseppi Antonio Torzillo, but my Italian was laughable, and I never got to tell them the story of Puntino. And anyway, I don't think they liked magicians.

17

The End

Mary A. Turzillo's novelette, "Mars Is No Place for Children," won a 1999 Nebula Award, and, along with her novel, *An Old-Fashioned Martian Girl*, is recommended reading on the International Space Station. She has been nominated for the British Science Fiction Association Award for "Eat or Be Eaten, a Love Story " and the Pushcart for *Your Cat & Other Aliens* (vanZeno). She won a third place for long poem in the 2011 Rhysling awards and has recent and forthcoming work in *Asimov's, Analog, New Myths, Strange Horizons, Bull Spec, Stone Telling, Magazine of Speculative Poetry, Ladies of Trade Town, Aoife's Kiss, Star*Line*, and *Fantastic Stories of the Imagination*, plus an authorized Philip Jose Farmer sequel story, "The Beast Erect," in *The Worlds of Philip Jose Farmer 2*, Meteor Press. Her latest book is *Lovers & Killers*, Dark Regions 2012.

MOODY'S METAL
by Jason Parent

Samuel Moody didn't care much for inane superstitions. He placed little stock in his hometown's folklore, tales ranging from the diabolical to the downright bizarre. Salem had more than its fair share of legends, often making it difficult even for its natives to separate fact from fiction.

A quaint town with a rich but sordid history, Salem attracted all sorts to its Commons. Some came to see the turning of the leaves, fall foliage only New England could offer. Others came for the eclectic shops, seeking out unique gift ideas or strange and wondrous novelty items. More came to learn from the lessons of Massachusetts' past, to hear historical renditions of the town's true claim to fame, the notorious Salem witchcraft trials of 1692, naively believing that society had advanced beyond its potential for repetition.

But most came for a good scare and some Halloween flair. The more sensational the witching tale, the more tourists it attracted. Having been born and raised in Salem, Samuel thought he'd heard them all. Tales of sorcery, tales of darkness, tales of the Devil-Samuel secretly scoffed at the legends behind a veil of sincerity even as he told them to his customers at The Star and Moon, a novelty shop specializing in witchcraft paraphernalia. And the fools came in droves. They scarped up pentagrams and pointy hats, spells and scrolls, runes and rites as though they were in fashion. Dyed-water potions sold like snake oil to jackasses who wanted to ace their midterms, repair wounded friendships, bless certain business ventures, or ensnare the persons who captivated their dreams. Pimply-faced and broken-hearted teenagers were Samuel's dearest patrons. Their coin filled his pockets long before the mad-craze days of October. Cynical and greedy, young and ambitious, so Samuel would have happily and ignorantly continued had he not fallen victim to a dark tale of his own.

Samuel had been accustomed to telling a particular story, one handed down by his ancestors for more than three centuries, from a time when New England was a colonial hodgepodge of towns. He liked the story because his distant relative was a crucial character in it and for its basis in truth.

The year was 1666, more than two decades before the witchcraft hysteria in Salem. Samuel had thought the year to be another storytelling gimmick until he looked up the tale's origins and found it to be true. The setting was Newbury Plantation, located approximately twenty miles north of Salem.

There, one Goody Chandler fell ill, the cause of her sickness unknown. Doctor after doctor called upon Goody, each unable to determine the cause of her malady. A pariah named Elizabeth Morse lived nearby. Without science to explain the sickness that befell her, Goody turned to the supernatural to find a scapegoat. She fingered Morse as a witch.

As everyone in-the-know in 1666 knew, hanging a horseshoe over the doorway of one's home was the best way to prevent witches from entering the property. Long before America's colonization, horseshoes had been considered a source of luck by much of Western Europe. When placed over a doorway, making sure the opening faced up, a horseshoe would collect luck for those living under it. Turn it upside down, however, and all the luck would pour out of it. Many believed the horseshoe would repel evil spirits. Seventeenth-century Massachusetts farmers believed it would repel witches.

So when Goody hung a horseshoe over her door and Elizabeth kept her distance, it was small wonder that Goody's health improved. It didn't seem to matter that Elizabeth might not have wanted to visit one who called her a witch. The proof of her witchcraft and of the horseshoe's magic was in the coincidence. At that time, it was enough that her supposed spells had been kept at bay.

But being the Puri-tyrannical sort that seventeenth-century Massachusetts folk were, no spells were tolerated, not even those designed to ward off evil. One particularly dogmatic sort, William Moody, took offense to the horseshoe. He took it upon himself to remove it.

The sacred talisman removed, Elizabeth was free to enter Goody's house again. She did, and not surprisingly, Goody's health began to deteriorate. The term "relapse" may not yet have been part of American vocabulary. Goody replaced the horseshoe, and again, William confiscated it. She died soon after. Morse was jailed for witchcraft.

Samuel found the entire story absurd, yet he repeated it, and repeated it often. Members of his family had moved south to Salem decades ago, and they'd been cashing in on it and other tales ever since. In a place like Salem, with its well-known history, the stories were magnets attracting suckers to purchase his grossly overpriced wares.

Among all his petty gifts and cheap trinkets, Samuel had one item that never sold: an authentic iron horseshoe allegedly blessed with a protective aura by a long-forgotten witch. Despite his embellishment of Goody Chandler's ordeal and his ancestor's part in it, Samuel couldn't give the damn thing away. So there it hung, high up on a wall in Samuel's shop, its opening pointing up throughout the years.

Unlike most of his other goods, the horseshoe was authentic. Samuel was certain some steed out in the world had spent most its life walking slightly lopsided. But who knew? Maybe it was the same horseshoe William had stolen from Goody Chandler. Samuel didn't know where it came from, but, to him, the horseshoe was just a piece of metal that had long lost its polish.

So when Jared Clemons charged into his store one late summer day looking whiter than milk and rambling on about how a witch was after him, Samuel saw only an easy mark and a chance to unload his ancient inventory. Fear was a powerful sales agent.

Jared had the wild-eyed look of a man gone mad. His clothes were disheveled, a wrinkled plaid jacket and stained jeans over hiking boots, one of which was untied. Under normal circumstances, Jared was a handsome young man of no more than thirty, close shaven, strong jawed, with striking blue eyes and sandy blond hair pulled back into a ponytail. He always walked with a cocky swagger that rubbed Samuel the wrong way.

On that day, Jared had lost his swagger. He looked older, too, as if the years of his life had ganged up on him all at once. Dark circles raccoon-masked his dull blue eyes. The vigor of youth had betrayed him.

Jared owned Salem Spirits, a liquor store on Derby Street, only a few blocks from Samuel's shop. According to Jared, he'd gotten into a boundary dispute with his neighbor, Gloria Winters, the proprietor of a sophisticated bookstore filled with lost and forgotten tomes. Gloria had moved into the building two years prior. A mature woman in her early fifties, Gloria's looks had not left her, yet she kept to herself. No one seemed to know much about her. Jared was the first person Samuel knew of, besides her customers, who had spoken to her.

Jared explained the nature of the dispute, something to do with his placement of dumpsters encroaching on Gloria's parking spaces. Samuel only half-listened. It sounded boring, and he didn't understand why Jared was so animated. The matter seemed more appropriate for discussion in court, not in his shop.

The short of it was that both Jared and Gloria claimed ownership to the same sliver of land, and both were willing to fight for it. Words turned into argument. Anger became hostility. Threats were made, with Jared threatening legal action, and Gloria threatening action even less savory than lawyers.

"She claimed to be a witch, well versed in the black arts," Jared said, throwing Samuel a curve. If he weren't so taken aback, he might have laughed at the proposition. But Jared seemed deathly serious. "Of course, I didn't believe her, but . . ." Jared's voice shook as he spoke, each word an effort. "She backed it up with theatrics. God, it was awful. Her eyes rolled back until they were cloudy white. She spoke in some incomprehensible tongue. I could swear the sky darkened above us as she chanted. When she had finished, Gloria fell to the ground as though her spirit had left her. And on the ground, that's where I left her, too. I didn't bother to check if she was okay."

Samuel eyed Jared as he recounted the events. His hands shook. Every now and then, he'd glance over his shoulder as if some unseen whisperer lingered there casting spiteful and malevolent words into his ears. Nevertheless, Jared pressed on with his story, his altercation with Gloria clearly having a lasting impact. Samuel thought only of how to profit from the man's duress.

"I found the entire meeting with Gloria utterly disturbing," Jared continued. "It left me with the most dreadful sensation, but I was quick to discount it-too quick. I returned to my store immediately following the incident to find these big black ants crawling all over my porch and my door frame. They looked as though they were trying to burrow into my store."

"No doubt the witch's familiars," Samuel said, purposely lending false credence to Jared's superstitions. Biting back his laughter, his words came out as serious as a sermon.

"Yes," Jared replied. "But I didn't know it then. I just thought that maybe someone had spilled some of the honey mead I sell compliments of the local profiteers. But other weird things, worse things, started happening right away."

"Like what?" Samuel leaned in. Sure, he was skeptical of Jared's story, but that didn't mean Samuel didn't enjoy a good old-fashioned fairytale.

"It started with noises in my shop at night, shadows lurking after closing. At first, I thought it was just some customer who had lost track of time. Then, a bottle of wine would crash on the floor or a six-pack would tumble from an open freezer door. I'd seek out the sources, expecting to see teenage punks playing a trick on me, but I'd never catch them. Looking back, I'm not sure I would have wanted to catch whoever . . . ."

Jared's voice trailed off. His uneasiness seemed to increase as he relived the events of the past week. His collar captured the sweat that began to drip down his temples. His eyes darted from wall to wall.

Samuel's followed, not knowing what they were looking for. He watched as Jared's knee bounced incessantly and knew that Jared was more than just spooked. He found himself suddenly intrigued by the man's predicament.

Jared slid his forearms across the counter, closer still to Samuel. He stared through Samuel as if he couldn't tell if the shop owner were real or another one of his hallucinations. It made Samuel uncomfortable. It made him afraid.

"Last night, I saw it," Jared continued, biting on the nail of his thumb.

"What?"

Jared swallowed hard. "A shadow cast on the back wall of my store. It was shaped like a man but massive, nearly eight feet tall. When I moved, it didn't. It was watching me; I could feel it. I was terrified. I know it was that witch who sent the Beast after me. And when it spread its wings, huge and like a bat's, I ran. Sam, I've never been so scared in my life."

Jared took a deep breath. His face was flushed. Samuel thought he could see his heart pounding out of his chest.

"I hurried home. As I got closer to my house, I started to calm, thinking my imagination must have been playing tricks on me. But as I was walking toward my front door, I heard footsteps. They weren't human footsteps, more like hooves on cobblestone. They were moving fast, getting closer. I rushed to the front door, fumbled for my keys. Once inside, I slammed the door behind me. I peeked through the window but saw nothing."

Samuel found his own heartbeat had kicked up a notch. Though he was enjoying the tale, part of him worried that Jared might be dangerous, that perhaps his sanity wasn't entirely intact. Jared seemed intent on conveying his ordeal, not noticing Samuel's doubt.

"I went about my usual nightly habits, thinking maybe routine would calm me some. I crawled into bed, my heart still racing." Jared lost control and shrieked, "That's when I saw it again. I was lying in bed, Sam. In bed. The witch sent a demon into my house!"

For Samuel, the story had hit the point where Jared's fears had become sadly comical. He held his breath, trying to maintain his poker face. But Jared saw through it.

"You don't believe me? You would if you saw those eyes," Jared said, the words snapping. "They were yellow like a cat's, the pupils like black crescent moons. I was so scared, sure that death had come for me. I shuddered beneath my sheets, hoping, praying those eyes would go away. There I stayed, under those covers, sleepless and horrified, until the sun was high in the sky. Then, I came here."

Samuel didn't know what to say. He let Jared settle. A twinge of guilt came over him, inspired by his thoughts of exploiting Jared's fear for his own commercial gain. He gave Jared an opportunity to escape his hook.

"Fear does strange things to the psyche." It was the wrong thing to say.

"I know what I saw. When I finally got to work today, Ms. Winters was on her doorstep, leering at me like a tiger does its prey. She was sweeping the leaves off her step with her broom. If I had a bit more courage, I'd have gone over there and shoved that broomstick up her-"

"Okay," Samuel interrupted. His guilt was but a fleeting memory. "I believe you. And now you're here. My friend, you've come to the right place. If the spirit she's sent to haunt you is as you described,

27

then it's only going to get worse." *A true believer*, he thought, a smirk hiding beneath his blank expression.

Jared leaned over the counter, his eyes pleading. "What do I do?"

The hook was in deep, and Jared was dangling on it. Samuel moved over to a drawer, weighing his options.

"Most of the stuff here is for tourists. But having the significant Wiccan population that we do, plus the sinister sorcerers who hide in plain sight in what is now a witch-friendly community, I'd be remiss if I didn't keep the real deal in stock."

Samuel pulled some painted rocks from the drawer. "These ancient runes are said to emit an aura that keeps spirits away. Plant them in every room of your house and in your store, and they'll repel lesser spirits, like the witch's familiars."

He plopped the magic-less stones, likely dug up from someone's backyard, onto the counter. "Of course, Gloria's sent a much more powerful fiend your way, one that threatens your very existence. In all my days, I've only heard of a demon like the one you've described twice," Samuel lied. "And neither time ended well for the cursed individual. You're going to need something much stronger than these runes. Do you have a doormat?"

"No."

"Get two of them." Samuel walked to where various metal pentagrams hung. He grabbed two, the two most expensive, and returned to the counter.

"Place one of these under a welcome mat set

before the front door of your home and another at your store."

"Pentagrams? Aren't they supposed to be symbols of the Devil?"

"Only in the movies. Damn, Jared, how long have you lived here? Under Wiccan tenets, pentagrams are generally used for protection. They are holy symbols, and they should be strong enough to prevent the shadow spirit's entry. Of course, they will only go so far against Gloria herself. Witches have all sorts of horrible spells."

Jared gulped. The ebb and flow of shame washed in and out of Samuel before it could have any lasting effect. He was a predator first, a human being second.

"Isn't there anything else I can do?" Jared asked.

"Well, there is one thing, but . . . never mind."

"What? What is it?"

"It's not for sale."

"What's not for sale?"

Samuel pointed over his shoulder to the horseshoe hanging high on the wall. "That horseshoe has been in The Star and Moon since it opened and with my family for centuries before that. You know how people say horseshoes are lucky? Well, there's a reason for that. Long ago, a spell was cast on that one. It's well known that a witch cannot walk beneath a horseshoe. Ask anyone here in Salem, anyone who knows about these things. That very horseshoe helped save a woman up in Newbury for a time before it was taken down, back when those accused of witchcraft were accused with good reason, years before this whole Salem nonsense began."

"How much?" Jared asked. His voice didn't sound the least bit skeptical.

"I told you, it's not for sale. That horseshoe is a family relic that has blessed my kin with its luck for generations. Its sacred metal not only nullifies witchcraft, but it brings with it good fortune."

"Please, I must have it," Jared said, his fingers flipping through his wallet. "I have $436 on me. Is that enough?"

"You want me to sell you a priceless family heirloom for $436?" Samuel feigned shock and anger.

"Please," Jared begged. "That witch is after me. I know she won't stop until she's taken everything from me, even my life. I'd be forever in your debt."

Samuel huffed, secretly pleased with his acting, thinking it Oscar-worthy. "If what you say is true, then I have a moral obligation to help you. I'm not happy about parting with the horseshoe, but if something should happen to you, I doubt I'd be able to live with myself. Put the money on the counter. I'll get the shoe."

"Thank you," Jared replied, noticeably relieved.

Samuel grabbed a stepstool and a hammer. He carried them over to the wall beneath the horseshoe and used them to yank the nails loose that had held it to the wall. When he had finished, Samuel stared at the horseshoe with pretend reluctance, doing his best to appear hurt by its departure. His face stern and stoic, he placed the shoe next to the other items on the counter.

Jared eagerly snatched it up. Samuel could see plainly that Jared thought the old contorted iron shoe would be the solution to all his problems. *The $436 will go a long way, too*, he thought. He considered whether the other items should be included in that price and was swept over by uncharacteristic generosity, undoubtedly brought about by his sudden influx of income.

"Take the other items, too," Samuel said, bagging the rocks and pentagrams. "Remember to place the pentagrams as I instructed. As for the horseshoe--and this is very important--place it over your door, the opening pointing up. Otherwise, it's useless. And Jared," he said, pausing for dramatic effect. His customer hung on his every word. "Good luck."

With that, Jared hastily exited, looking deliriously happy, many shades brighter than when he had entered. Samuel laughed quietly. He'd just turned one hell of a profit.

A few weeks passed with no word from Jared. Samuel wondered if the horseshoe had subdued his fears of witches, demons, and whatever other nonsense plagued his thoughts. He had plenty of time to think about Jared, his own life falling into a haze.

Illness struck him, mild nausea at first, followed by occasional fever. Samuel's business suffered, in part because he'd spent more time in bed and in other part due to the scarcity of customers. It was nearing the end of September. The fall crowd swelled into Salem as usual, but it

31

seemed blind to his store. Halloween was his shop's Christmas season, and the season was off to a dismal start.

On the walk home from work one night, Samuel decided to make his way through the tourist hotspots instead of travelling his usual route. When he turned onto Derby Street, not far from his shop, he was surprised to see it bustling. Witches and skeletons and all sorts of strange, new-age costumes mingled over open beverages Samuel assumed weren't sodas. People lined the streets, locals and tourists alike enjoying the season.

The main attraction didn't seem to be one of the haunted houses or the theaters, but a building located near the end of the road, unimpressive in appearance and unadorned by any trappings of the season. *I don't believe it*, Samuel thought. He gaped at Jared Clemons' liquor store as people hustled in and out its front door. On the archway above the entrance, a horseshoe was nailed.

A coincidence, Samuel thought, scoffing at Jared's luck. He grumbled about his own misfortune. True, it had coincided with his removal of that horseshoe, but he wasn't about to chalk it up to some silly folk tale. He made his way through the crowded street, heading for home.

As he approached the end of Jared's property, a voice called out to him from beside the dumpsters. He turned to see a man whom he didn't recognize, standing there and smoking a cigarette.

"Sam? Is that you?"

Samuel didn't respond, instead choosing to examine the individual who professed to know him.

He took a defensive pose as the man rushed toward him. As he stepped beneath the streetlight, the man's features became familiar.

"How are you?" Jared asked, looking energetic, full of life. Samuel could hardly believe he was the same guy who had visited his shop, hysterical and terrified, only a few weeks prior. Jared looked better, healthier than Samuel remembered him even before his witching woes had arisen. He wondered if the lighting was complimentary.

"Good," Samuel muttered, not sharing Jared's enthusiasm.

"Really? You don't look so good. I hope you've been taking care of yourself."

Samuel grunted. He found Jared's chumminess off-putting and his beaming smile sickening. He showed no interest in small talk, expecting Jared to take the hint. Jared didn't.

"How's business?"

"Oh, you know." Samuel shrugged. "It has its ups and downs. I see you're doing well, though."

"I am. Business has never been better. It's all thanks to you."

Rub it in, Samuel thought. He insisted to himself that the success of Jared's store and the decline of his own were merely coincidental, sure that things would turn around for him by the following week. *That horseshoe has about as much luck in it as a four-leaf clover, a rabbit's foot, or a found penny. Nothing but superstitious nonsense*, he thought.

"And what an investment," Jared continued. "The amount I paid you for it I got back tenfold the very next day. Plus, Ms. Winters won't come anywhere near the place."

"I'm happy for you," Samuel lied. "Maybe you'll return the favor and send some of your customers my way tomorrow."

"Will do," Jared said, patting him on the shoulder as if they were solid pals. "Well, I'd better get back inside. I had to hire seasonal help to handle my increasing sales. Half of them have no idea what they're doing."

Jared dropped his cigarette onto the pavement and ground it out with the sole of his sneaker. He hurried into his store, greeting customers as he made his way inside.

Samuel couldn't be happy for Jared. He was too wrapped up in self-pity to care about anyone else. The sound of a door shutting distracted him from his bleak thoughts for only a minute. Gloria exited her bookstore and locked the door closed for the evening. She turned, and her eyes met his. They stared at each other until her lips curled into a frightful grin. The hairs on Samuel's arms and neck stood on end. A chill ran down his spine. He turned away, continued home, collapsed onto his mattress, and closed his eyes, exhausted but unable to sleep.

When his alarm sounded at 8:00 a.m., Samuel felt as though he'd spent the whole night in a trance. He rubbed the crusts from his eyes, splashed some water on his face, brushed his teeth, put on a clean shirt, and headed off to The Star and Moon. This time, he took his usual route, having had his fill of Jared and Gloria.

The air seemed to get heavier as Samuel

34

approached his store. It was almost fog by the time he turned the corner onto Essex Street. Immediately, he noticed the fire truck parked in front of his building. Smoke arose from it. "No," Samuel mouthed as he ran to his store.

The Star and Moon was gone, reduced to ash and smoldering wood by an overnight fire. The firefighters were dousing the last of its flames. The surrounding properties were untouched, but nothing was recoverable from his.

A crowd had gathered. From among it, Jared Clemons emerged. "It looks like you need a new horseshoe," he said, shaking his head. "That's some nasty business right there."

Jared was the last person Samuel wanted or expected to see. To make matters worse, he couldn't tell if Jared was mocking him or trying to comfort him. He lacked the stomach for either.

"I don't understand," Samuel stuttered. "What could have done this?"

"I don't know. A freak electrical thing, perhaps? I overheard some of the firemen talking. They didn't find any evidence of arson."

"Everything I had was invested in that store."

"Cheer up, Sam," Jared said, hugging his arm around Samuel's shoulder. Samuel didn't protest, his shock distracting him. "Your insurance will cover this."

Insurance? Samuel couldn't remember the last time he'd made a payment. He swore right then and there he'd kill himself if he'd let the policy lapse.

"Or," Jared continued, "you could sell me the lot. I could use a bigger place with the rate my liquor's been selling. I'd offer you a fair price, the least I can do for a friend."

Samuel shot Jared a cold, unfriendly look. He was beaten, unable to offer more in response. With heavy feet and a heavier heart, he turned around and walked straight home. For a second time in two days, he took the side streets, not really paying much attention to where he was going.

As he approached Jared's store, he spotted the horseshoe. A bitterness rose within him until he was completely consumed by it. He blamed Jared for all that had happened. The parking lot was empty, it being only 8:45a.m. The liquor store wasn't due to open until noon.

The horseshoe seemed to be taunting him, gleaming in the morning sun, mocking his ill fortune. Blood swelled into Samuel's head until his face was fiery red. The vein coursing through his left temple pulsated as though it might burst. Anger seized control of his wits. *Looks like you need a new horseshoe*, Jared's voice repeated inside his mind. *The least I could do for a friend*. The next few minutes were a blur.

When he regained his senses, Samuel remembered charging toward that horseshoe, his pocket knife in hand, its blade exposed. Despite having to reach up for the screws, Samuel had an easy enough time loosening the two that had affixed the prongs to the building. He could tell they had been placed hastily. Samuel unscrewed them the rest of the way with his hand and tore them from the wall. Then, he dropped them into his pocket.

Samuel's anger subsided, but his bitterness

remained. The horseshoe also remained, held upright by the one intact screw at the center of its base.

"Your insurance will cover this," Samuel mimicked, his spite uncontainable. He cursed Jared. At that moment, no matter how unfair it might have been, Samuel hated him.

"Everyone's luck runs out eventually," he said, tapping on the horseshoe. It slid clockwise 180 degrees, swinging a bit until it finally came to rest upside down.

Samuel's caution returned. He looked around to see if there'd been any witnesses to his brief bout of madness. There had been one: Gloria Winters. With broom in hand, she swept errant leaves off her doorstep. A black cat kissed her legs, weaving figure eights around them.

Gloria looked up from her sweeping as if she could sense his stare. She gave Samuel a nod and a smile. He looked away, ashamed. Darting off, Samuel sprinted back to the safety of his home.

He poured himself a stiff drink and fell into a chair, a thousand thoughts running through his mind. Samuel hadn't been home more than fifteen minutes when he heard the sirens go by. "Where's the fire?" he called out to them scornfully, nearly spilling his glass of whiskey in his uproar. The sirens' sardonic melodies jeered like bratty bullies. Why did it have to be his store that burned down?

Fifteen minutes later, the whiskey was already taking its toll. Samuel turned on the television, flipping aimlessly through the channels. *There's my store*, he thought as he came across the local news channel. *What's left of it, anyway.* He wondered why the police hadn't stopped by yet. He prayed the reporters wouldn't be knocking on his door for comment. If they did, Samuel had two words prepared for them; they weren't "no comment," but they'd have about the same effect.

"Tragedy struck twice in Salem today," an attractive newscaster said as images of the burnt structure that used to be Samuel's store were depicted for all of Essex County to know his pain. "First, The Star and Moon, a novelty shop owned by Samuel Moody that was popular among tourists for its witchcraft-related items, fell victim to fire in the early morning hours. No one appears to have been injured. The cause of the fire is unknown, but authorities have ruled out foul play."

"Here, here," Samuel said, raising his glass.

"Not more than thirty minutes after emergency crews had put out the fire, they returned to a nearby block where Jared Clemson, a local who owns the neighborhood liquor store, was struck and killed by an alleged drunk driver. The driver, Thomas Rudd of North Andover, does not appear to have been injured and has been taken into custody by Salem Police."

Samuel shook his glass, surprised to see it only half empty. He couldn't believe what he was hearing. Jared was dead? He'd just spoken with him before . . . *before I vandalized his horseshoe.*

That was it. The so-called coincidences were too many for Samuel to ignore. He didn't feel guilty. He had no remorse. Instead, Samuel burned with envious desire, a maddening need to put the horseshoe back in his own shop.

"So did he?" a young man in his late teens asked. He'd been mesmerized by Paul Moody's story since he walked into The Star and Moon. His elbows rested flat on the counter, his palms pressed against his cheeks, holding up his head as he listened.

"My father was no fool," Paul said. "That night, he hung the horseshoe over the door of his home until the insurance money came in and this store was rebuilt. Then he returned it to its rightful spot on the wall behind me." Paul gestured beneath the sloped ceiling where a scratched and unpolished horseshoe was presented like a prized Picasso. "And there it's been ever since."

The teenage tourist's mouth dangled open in awe. "Do you believe all that stuff about witches and evil spirits?" he asked.

"I don't know, kid. The power of faith can make anything true in the mind of a believer. But I'll tell you this; my father sure as hell did."

"All right, you've sold me. How much?"

"For the horseshoe? I haven't thought about it. Make me an offer."

"Twenty bucks."

"The metal alone is worth that much."

"Forty."

"Sold."

Paul removed the aged horseshoe from the wall. It had been propped up with nails small enough so that it could be easily slid off them. He placed it in a plastic bag with The Star and Moon logo, rang up the sale, and handed the horseshoe over to the tourist, who left his store with a gigantic grin spread across his face.

Brent Hewitt, Paul's friend who often visited the shop but never bought anything, stood nearby, thumbing through a copy of *The House of the Seven Gables*. After the tourist left, he approached Paul at the counter. Paul was beaming with pride.

"Your dad's name is Bob," Brent said.

"Samuel sounds better."

"Yeah, well, Samuel, then, would have sold that horseshoe for ten times more than you just did."

"I guess it's a good thing I've got a lot more than ten of them," Paul said, sliding a box out from beneath his counter. Inside it lay more than fifty horseshoes with the same used and rustic look as the one he had just sold. Paul picked one up, placed it on the wall, and waited for his next tourist.

Author's Note: Accounts of Elizabeth Morse's imprisonment for witchcraft can be found in Richard Godbeer's book *The Devil's Dominion* and in Samuel Gardner Drake's *Annals of Witchcraft in New England*, which was published in 1869. A special thanks to Peter Muise and his New England Folklore blog for the information he provided.

The End

Jason Parent's fiction is born from darkness, finding its home everywhere from the supernatural and surreal to the all-too-real iniquity of the human condition. His debut novel, *What Hides Within*, a mystery/horror blend, was published by Double Dragon Publishing in February 2013. It was an EPIC finalist in "horror," runner-up in the "Best

Horror" category in eFestival's Independent eBook competition and has been named to several "Best of 2013" lists for horror. His short stories can be found in several anthologies, and he has several more in the works; he is finalizing four novels. Information can be obtained on his website at http://www.authorjasonparent.com/ or by visiting him on Facebook at http://www.facebook.com/AuthorJasonParent?ref=hl

THREE SISTERS OF RING ISLAND
by Patricia Stoltey

The Norwegian folktale Three Billy Goats Gruff *tells of a trio of happy goats determined to outsmart the vicious troll living under the bridge that leads to greener, tastier pastures. The goats succeed in their mission and live happily ever after.*

But what if the three seekers of a more satisfying life were human, and what if those humans were three sisters?

Snappity-snip, say what you will,

This tale begins upon a hill...

Ring Island was a lovely place to live, as secluded islands go. The temperatures were mild, the storms gentle, and the breezes sweet with the scent of lavender and rosemary.

Even so, the three sisters who lived on Ring Island were miserable. Their father, a minor Norwegian king who had attacked and pillaged his way to great fortunes in jewels and gold, moved his wife and family and all their servants and possessions to the island by boat when the three girls were very young. Bounded on three sides by a wide, fast-moving river and on the fourth by the shark-infested sea, the king felt safe from those who would steal his riches or his daughters. He intended to keep them on the island forever, subject to his every whim, and on whom he counted to care for him and his wife as they grew older and perhaps even succumbed to illness or insanity.

One day the three sisters sat on a grassy knoll overlooking the raging river and the bridge that led

42

from the island to a great forest on the mainland. Beyond the forest stretched fields, verdant pastures and a village. Even farther away, on a hill, sat a castle at least three times as large as their father's mansion.

Helga, the oldest of the three, listened to the complaints of her sisters as she had for as many years as the girls pined for those things they could not have.

"I can't understand why no young man has come to ask for my hand," Solveig said, as she said at least once a day. Now eighteen and long past the age when she should marry, she drove Helga crazy with her relentless claims that someday she would leave Ring Island and reign over the even more beautiful kingdom on the other side of the river. Gazing at the castle in the distance, she sighed and wiped a tear from her eye.

Helga grunted and shifted her ample rump to a softer patch of ground near a tree where a cushion of moss relieved her aching hip.

Purdy, the middle sister, who was a lovely young woman in her own way, although not nearly as petite, repeated her daily response. "It's not that young men deny your beauty and your fortune, Solveig. They fear the troll our father commissioned to live under the only bridge that connects us to the rest of the world. The cracked and broken bones of many a young man are strewn about the mainland side of the bridge."

"Still," insisted Solveig as she fluttered her eyelashes and smoothed her golden curls, "one would think the prize worthy of greater effort."

43

Purdy shook her head and threw up her hands. "You simply will not face the truth, will you? There is no way a suitor will ever ask for your hand, or for mine. It is hopeless."

"Balderdash," said Helga. "Enough is enough. Mother should never have told you those stories about princes and love and the pleasures of life on the mainland. If Father knew how she corrupted your minds with wishes and dreams, he would be very angry. I've been listening to your whining and moaning for years. Neither one of you has the courage of a mouse or the imagination of an ant. Getting off this island would not be so hard. Our father has been very clever, but there are three of us. If we put our heads together, we can come up with a plan."

Solveig jumped up with excitement, clapping her hands and dancing about on the grassy knoll.

Purdy glared at Helga. "Not so fast, dear Solveig. Helga never has a plan that doesn't put herself first and the two of us last."

Solveig stopped dancing and listened as Purdy and Helga bickered. Finally, she sighed and pushed her two sisters apart. "I want to hear what Helga has to say."

Helga put her arms around her sisters' shoulders and drew them close. "We need to trick the troll," she said. "We need to use bribes to convince him to allow one of us to cross the bridge at a time."

"I have no defenses against a troll," said Solveig. "I'm not fast enough to outrun him, nor am I good enough with a sword to kill him. I cannot go

44

first."

Purdy was quick to add her doubts. "I'm stronger than Solveig, but slower and even less skilled with weapons. I cannot go first."

Helga poked each of her sisters in the side with a pudgy finger. "See what I mean?" she said. "You have no imagination."

"What do you suggest, Helga?" asked Purdy.

"Well . . . suppose Solveig approaches the bridge and calls out the troll, inviting him to join us for dinner in the mansion, if he will only let her pass for a brief foray into the woods for berries, which, of course, she agrees to share with the troll upon her return. We could even throw in the haunch of an elk to show our good faith."

Solveig and Purdy looked at each other and then back at Helga. "But Solveig would not return" said Purdy. "Wouldn't the troll be very angry and tear you to pieces when you try to cross the bridge?"

"Not me, Purdy. The next one to cross the bridge would be you. You would call the troll out and claim you needed to search for your younger sister who was presumed lost in the woods. To show good faith, you would take one of our old cows to the bridge and promise the troll two fine dinners at the mansion. And, of course, a share of the berries when you return with your sister."

"But, when I failed to return," said Purdy, "wouldn't the troll be so outraged he'd storm up the hill, snatch you off this grassy knoll, and drag your body beneath the bridge to chew on your carcass at his leisure?"

"Not all all," Helga said. "The troll dares not leave his lair under the bridge for long without permission. Father will not tolerate that kind of insubordination. As an incentive for the troll to let me pass over the bridge to search for you both, I'll invite him to an elaborate feast at the mansion. Trust me, he will let me pass."

"Won't father be very angry with us?" said Purdy.

Solveig shrugged. "Will that matter? We'll be long gone by the time the troll shows up at the door. I don't really care, anyway. Father hasn't been a bit kind to me and has been known to curse at me when I burn the meat."

"I guess I don't care, either," said Purdy. "He threw a leg of lamb at my head yesterday when I told him there was no pudding left for his dessert."

Helga merely shrugged.

"When should we go?" said Solveig. "I can be ready by tomorrow morning."

Helga nodded. "Tomorrow morning is fine. I'll help you carry the elk haunch to the bridge and remind you what to say. Purdy, you stay behind and make sure Father and Mother are unaware of our plan."

The next morning, Solveig pounded on Helga's door at first light. She carried a basket for gathering berries and a small leather flagon of water. Near the edge of the river, Helga transferred the elk haunch to Solveig's shoulder and urged her to step onto the bridge as she reminded her about what to say. At the troll's roar, Solveig tried to turn back, but Helga pushed her forward. The troll reached one long arm from his lair, grabbed the haunch from her hand. Two huge eyes peered over the railing. "Who are you, and why are you on my bridge?"

Solveig trembled and stammered and finally burst into tears. "Helga," she called out. "Help me."

Helga merely watched until the troll's hairy hand grabbed Solveig by the ankle and snatched her off the bridge. She stayed for a moment, listening to Solveig's screams and the crunching of bones. As the troll tossed bits and pieces of bloody corpse onto the bridge, Helga smiled. One down, one to go.

Purdy was pacing in front of the mansion door when Helga returned. "Did the plan work? Is Solveig over the bridge?"

"Of course. When did a plan of mine not work?"

"When is it my turn, Helga? May I go now?"

Helga patted Purdy on the shoulder. "Patience, sister, patience. Let's give the old troll a chance to digest his little snack and build up an appetite for the next meal. He'll be even more eager for the cow we'll take from the barn and offer as payment for your crossing."

Purdy reluctantly agreed, but was up at the crack of dawn, pounding on Helga's bedroom door. "I'm ready to go," she said. "I'm taking nothing but a walking stick and a flask of ale to prevent the troll from getting suspicious."

Helga had no reason to delay. As a matter of fact, she was eager to send Purdy on her way. They went to the barn, placed a lead on the oldest cow of the herd, and lured her down the hill to the bridge.

Negotiating with the troll from the edge of the river did not intimidate Purdy, as she was by far the smartest and most businesslike of the three sisters. Convinced the troll would let her pass safely, Purdy led the cow onto the bridge and started across. The troll reached up with his long arm and yanked the cow out of sight. Immediately he peered through the railing, his big eyes on Purdy and her flask of ale. Purdy froze in terror. The troll grabbed her by the ankle and pulled her into his lair. The roaring and growling was intense, Purdy's screams even louder than Solveig's had been. Soon Helga heard nothing but the crunching and cracking of bones, and saw nothing but bloody bits and pieces of flesh tossed from the darkness below the bridge to land along the river's bank.

Helga had never been happier. She would own the mansion and the island when her parents were gone. She would be rich beyond her wildest dreams, no longer forced to share the wealth with her sisters..

She climbed the hill to sit all alone on the grassy knoll and look down on the wild river and the rickety bridge, reflecting on her cleverness. Below, the troll emerged from his lair and stared up the hill toward the mansion. He used his claws to scratch at his head, almost as though combing and smoothing his hair. He started up the path, saw Helga sitting on the knoll, and bowed in her direction as though to acknowledge her as master.

Helga got to her feet and brushed the twigs and ants from her skirt. It was time to prepare her parents for company.

Snappity-snip, and please don't pout,
This little tale has been told out.

The End

Patricia Stoltey is the author of two amateur sleuth mysteries published by Five Star/Cengage in hardcover and Harlequin Worldwide mass market paperbacks. *The Prairie Grass Murders* and *The Desert Hedge Murders* are now available for Kindle and Nook. Her standalone suspense novel from Five Star, *Dead Wrong*, is scheduled for release November 2014. Visit her website http://www.patriciastoltey.com) or blog http://patriciastoltey.blogspot.com) for more information. She can also be found on Twitter as @PStoltey and on Facebook as Patricia Stoltey.

NUCKELAVEE
by Joseph Michael

The boy stared out into the sea from the safety of his room. His house lay near the layered sandstone cliffs of Stronsay, overlooking the full moon hanging over the waves that crashed against the wall of rock. Even through the glass of the window and the brick walls, the gently thunderous rolls of the sea could be heard in a strong, soothing lullaby.

The boy's room was lit only by the light of the shining white orb in the clear, dark sky above that ebbed through his window. It was a simple space, occupied only by a bed, a desk, and a sparse bookshelf, but it was his space. His life as the son of a farmer taught him to cherish that which belonged solely to him. His most prized possession sat in the wooden box on one of the shelves, hidden away by lock and key. He would show no one, for it was his and his alone until the day he took it where it was meant to go.

That evening was to be spent losing himself in the steady crash of the waves, the soothing light of the moon, and the firm cushion of the bed underneath him. His eyes began to drift shut as he kneeled there, lulled into drowsiness by nature's lullaby. Soon he would be nearly asleep, and then he would sink down into the bed and settle into the warm embrace of slumber.

That is what he did every night. That night, however, was the night that another sound broke through the peace.

Scraaaaaaape. Scraaaaaaape. Scraaaaaaape.

The boy's eyes opened suddenly, their blue reflecting the light of the white moon in the brief moment before it was obscured by a sickly green cloud that rose in a pillar from behind the cliff, spewed as though from the smokestack of some great engine far below. His brow furrowed as he leaned closer to the window, pressing his nose into the cold glass.

Scraaaaaaape. Scraaaaaaape. Scraaaaaaape.

A giant arm like the branch of a great tree swung over the edge of the cliff and dug skeletal fingers into the grass. The boy's eyes widened with fear even before the sinewy muscles of that arm strained to drag its mass over the cliff's edge. A shoulder. A stubby neck. Jagged spikes like curved fangs.

A thrill of terror jolted his body into action before anything like a head could rise out of the sea. In a second, the curtains were drawn shut to throw his room into darkness, and his body was buried under the sheets of his bed without even a strand of matted brown hair to poke out and betray his presence. He trembled, and his breath came and went in rapid gasps. His eyes were wide as he stared into the shadows under his blanket, his imagination running wild with memories of old tales and warnings.

Thum. Thum. Thum. Thum.

Something carried itself with methodical, pounding steps to his window. The tension ate at him until his eyes squeezed shut and his body curled in a protective fetal ball.

The pounding stopped just outside. He could not see the beam of baleful scarlet that pierced his curtains like a searchlight, slowly trailing this way and that in detailed examination. He could smell, however, even through the walls and the blanket, the stench of rot as though a pile of decomposition had dragged itself out of the sea and collapsed in a heap outside his window. Sickly, pungent, salty. The smell of illness and death. Just when he felt as though he could bear it no longer and pleaded for a breath of fresh air, the pounding began once more, moving around the house and deeper into the mainland until it was gone.

The boy did not sleep that night.

***

"Never seen the likes of it before."

The boy's father stood outside the house the next morning. The larger man dragged the boy out of bed as always, exhausted though he was from his restless night. The farm required prompt and diligent care, after all, and the boy had to do his part for its upkeep. "You'll nap after your midday meal, Cailean," his father had said after a moment of concern. "I don't know what's gotten into you today, but I need your help. I'm sorry."

Work had not started yet because Cailean and his father found the footprints that appeared overnight. At least, his father called them footprints because he did not want to admit just yet that something had appeared which walked on massive skeletal hands big enough to pick up a cow as if it were a child's toy.

The pair stood among the prints embedded in

the grass, the man's brow furrowed as he stroked his scarlet beard, the boy's eyes bloodshot and ringed with darkness from his sleepless night. "Looks like it came up from the cliffside," Cailean's father commented finally as he pointed off toward the start of the trail. "Then it went right up to our house and walked around it deeper into the island. No prints back, so I guess it went back to the sea from some other part of the coast." He paused. His arms crossed over his chest and his eyes narrowed slightly. "Or else it's still hanging around out there," he finished, a note of concern in his voice.

Cailean's gaze traced the footprints along their path. He paused on the fairy ring beside the barn that the being had walked by in its journey inland. A ring of mushrooms broken only in one place. One place large enough to fit a single fungus.

The odor from the night before still lingered in the air. The sky was overcast with faintly green clouds that blotted out the peaceful blue.

"...father," Cailean asked with some hoarseness, "do you remember the stories about the Nuckelavee?"

The man froze. A chill ran up his spine, as his blood seemed to have turned to ice. "That's not a name you bring up lightly, boy," he replied in a tense voice.

***

The work was long that day. It was not more difficult than any other day, though many of the crops were wilted, and one of the cattle had died of illness. It was the tension that hung in the air with the jade clouds and the lingering odor that drew the

53

day on far longer than it should have gone. Cailean was exhausted once he finally retired to the house in the middle of the day, his shoes drawing a *scraaaaaape, scraaaaaaape, scraaaaaape* across the wooden floor along his path to his room.

Despite the allure of the bed's pillow, he could not rest just yet. He had to check on his precious box and the contents within, as he had the night before.

Wearily, he drew the key from his pocket and opened the wooden box, revealing the large mushroom inside. Even here, he could feel the energy it gave off. The fungus had a spirit of its own, a strength, a power that could only be described as magical. He knew he could sell it in town for heaps of money. One single mushroom, but with so much strange potential within it. Who knew what sort of potions or remedies one could create from such a thing?

His fingers caressed the cap as if in quiet reverence. This was it. This was their ticket to a better life, one where they would not have to scrape for money or live off their meager crops. He was tired of working for so little, of being hungry and weary, of *wanting* so badly.

The boy chewed his lip and closed the lid. The journey to town was long. He would have to make sure to go with his father the next time he went on his errands. Such trips were uncommon, but worthwhile, in this case.

Finally, with a sigh, he found his bed and collapsed into it, asleep only moments after he felt his body hit the firm mattress.

His dreams of an arm of muscle and sinew crashing through his window to drag him into the sea plagued him in those hours. When he awoke for work again, he had slept, but he had not rested.

***

The day drew longer until the sun fell from behind the oddly green clouds and plunged into the sea. Darkness overcame the island of Stronsay, magnified a dozen times by the inky vapors that never retreated. There was no moon that night, nor could the carpet of stars shine through. The treeless plains were obscured in permanent shadow that refused to be broken.

Cailean attempted to sleep. He turned in his bed that night, curled up under the blankets. The waves did not bring him the comfort they usually did. The gentle, rolling rush came to him in heavy crashes as if they were right against his window. He could feel the sea straining to break through the walls of the cliff and tear it down, raking at it like giant, clawed hands. The cacophony formed words.

WHERE IS IT?

His breath caught in his throat. The boy threw the covers off and tumbled out of bed in his dash for the door. The darkness caused him to trip and falter before he fumbled for the handle. Something in the room fell with an abrupt *bang* that drew a skittish yelp from Cailean. Finally, the door gave way and allowed him passage to dash from his room into the kitchen and get away from the searching, pounding waves.

He stopped only once he reached the window by the stove. His chest rose and fell rapidly

55

alongside the heavy throbbing of his heart, his back slumped with the exertion of panic and fear. The boy hunched over the windowsill in a cold sweat, gasping for air. At least now he no longer heard the waves pounding at the cliff in a desperate bid to claim him or something he possessed.

As his wide eyes adjusted to the dark and his breathing slowed to quiet, tense sighs, he could see flashes of light from the corner of his eye. All too familiar scarlet rays flickered and weaved through the window. For a moment, a chill grasped at his heart. Slowly, his head lifted, and he glanced outside.

The sky was even darker than before, the clouds a sickly green of infection and disease. A thin sheen of similarly colored fog hung over the ground, carrying with it that intolerable stench of salty rot. The grass, once lush and verdant, had turned yellow and dead.

It was the shadow lumbering in the distance, however, that drew his attention. Its form was vaguely like that of a horse and rider, but that is where the similarities ended. The horse's legs appeared to end in webbed claws whose membranes continued up to the first joint. They also dangled in the air as it walked, for it strode on two lanky, muscular legs - no, not legs: the rider's arms.

It walked on massive hands like some kind of predatory bird, and the oversized head of the rider lolled uselessly on its shoulders, spewing that noxious smoke from its gaping maw without a lower jaw.

The horse's tail swung behind it, long and thick like a dragon's with a serrated fin at the end and another on the back. Branching tendrils hung off the tail and neck like dangling veins, and at the end of the neck was a head that resembled an equine skull. It was from that head that the beam of bloody light pierced through the fog as though from some infernal lighthouse, weaving along with the serpentine motions of the neck.

Cailean was frozen in place, hardly able to notice the stench assaulting his nostrils or the distant thunder of the angry waves. He stared at the shadow long enough that he was certain he was not seeing a tree moving in the wind or a piece of machinery that was active in the evening. It was a massive, breathing *thing*, a blight on the island, a force of pure evil that Cailean had once relegated to myth and fairy tales.

The scarlet beam of light suddenly swung around to shine directly in Cailean's face, and all at once, as his vision was filled with blinding red, his mind exploded with a shrieking, ringing chaotic noise.

EREISITWHEREISITWHEREISITWHE

***

When Cailean awoke, he found himself lying on his back, staring up at swirling, pestilent smog. His eyes stung and his throat ached, eliciting a brief coughing fit to purge the toxic fumes from his lungs. Distracted as he was by the disgusting taste of disease, it took him a moment to realize that he was lying on the dead grass outside.

A massive hand slammed into the ground

beside him, startling him to his senses. It was big enough to crush him with little effort and completely lacked any sort of skin to hide the white bones, red muscle, and green veins beneath.

Another hand crashed down on his other side, followed soon by the hulking body of the shadow. Its muscles rippled, and its veins pulsed and throbbed as they carried thick blood through its body.

A webbed, skeletal claw came down to press into the boy's chest, shoving him onto his back against the ground. The thin coating of sticky slime that covered it stuck to his clothes.

Cailean was trapped. He trembled with primal terror as the serpentine neck - those tendrils *were* veins, dangling like seaweed - carried the horse skull down to linger in front of his face.

Spiked fins like gills flared out along the back of its jaw as it took in a breath that filled a thin sac in its throat with plague-ridden fumes. Trails of putrescent smoke ebbed out from between interlocking teeth like oversized needles. Its tongue lolled out from the bottom of its closed mouth, slick with saliva and weaving like a predatory serpent.

The boy barely noticed all of that, however, for it was the single baleful red eye that caught all his attention. It stared at him, a black pit of a pupil in a shape Cailean had never seen, surrounded by rippling crimson like blood that gave off that paralyzing scarlet beam.

WHERE IS IT?

The voice was not heard so much as felt. Noise like a ringing in his ears grasped at his mind, not forming words but forming an understanding of a concept, a meaning. "...what?" Cailean was almost embarrassed by how high and hoarse his voice was.

MY RING HAS BEEN DISTURBED.

The eye finally closed with the sliding motion of four black lids. The head slowly rose to look up. The eye opened once more to cast its light down on something. Cailean, after brief uncertainty, followed its gaze. He realized that he was inside the fairy ring near the barn, and that searching light shone down on the spot where the ring was broken. The spot that was just the right size to hold a single large mushroom.

The monster lowered its head again to shine its light into Cailean's face.

I WILL NOT REST UNTIL IT IS FOUND. WHERE IS IT?

"I-it's...in my room," Cailean stammered. "On the bookshelf. I was-"

WHAT WAS YOUR INTENTION IN DISTURBING MY RING?

Cailean wished that he could move the webbed claw holding him down. It felt as though it was squeezing him tighter, crushing him. "I...I wanted to sell the mushroom in town-"

SELL IT?

The needle-filled maw parted as the throat sac expanded. A gurgling growl not unlike that of a crocodile rolled from its throat. Cailean could feel saliva drip onto him. "I'm sorry," he shouted, his voice rising in panic as he squirmed underneath the heavy claw that grew tight around his body. "I didn't mean to disturb your...your home. I just wanted my family to be all right, to not have to keep scrounging up whatever we could find to survive. People are superstitious even back in town, so I thought they would pay a fortune for a fairy mushroom!"

The maw closed as the behemoth's anger seemed to subside. The skeletal head retreated somewhat, and the claw loosened its grip on him.

Cailean gasped for a welcome breath, a breath that he quickly regretted as his lungs filled with rancid smog. He coughed and gagged for a few moments before his lungs were cleared again. He stared up at the creature through watery eyes. "Then...why don't you want anyone to disturb it?"

I HAVE LINGERED THROUGH THE PASSAGE OF TIME LONG ENOUGH. HUNDREDS OF CENTURIES HAVE PASSED. THOUSANDS, MILLIONS HAVE DIED BY MY STRENGTH. VILLAGES HAVE CRUMBLED. FARMS HAVE WITHERED. ISLANDS HAVE BEEN STRIPPED OF LIFE AND RENDERED DESOLATE AND BARREN. WHOLE SPECIES HAVE CHOKED AND BEEN SNUFFED OUT.

The muscles on the creature's skull tensed as it let out another growl. The emotion of bitterness came through its communication, but so too did a sense of honor and resignation.

YET NATURE AND LIFE CONTINUE. GRASS RETURNS TO ISLANDS THAT WERE DEAD. NEW ANIMALS APPEAR AND THRIVE. TIME PASSES. THE WORLD CHANGES. I HAVE FINALLY REALIZED

THAT I HAVE BEEN DEFEATED, FOR I DO NOT CHANGE. I AM DEATH, I AM DISEASE, I AM PLAGUE AND HATRED. YET I CAN NEVER TRULY DESTROY LIFE BECAUSE IT WILL INEVITABLY RECOVER, BE IT IN A YEAR OR A CENTURY.

Cailean was silent as he stared into the light of that single eye. Finally, he spoke again. "So...what? What does this ring have to do with it?"

I WILL JOIN THAT WHICH I CANNOT DEFEAT.

The eye shifted along the circle. Red light traced the mushrooms of the ring before returning to glare into Cailean's eyes.

AS THIS BODY FADES, MY SPIRIT WILL RETURN TO THIS CIRCLE. I WILL BE REBORN ACCORDING TO NATURE'S RULES. I WILL BECOME PART OF IT AND LIVE ON AS I SPREAD AND GROW. THE WORLD REQUIRES ME TO CHANGE, AND SO I SHALL.

The fanged maw snapped in front of Cailean's face. The boy gave an undignified scream, recoiling as much as he could from the sharp points far too close to his face. Even as it threatened him, however, the webbed claw slid back to dangle underneath the demon's horse-like body.

NOW GO. BRING THE MUSHROOM AND RETURN IT TO ITS PLACE. ONLY THEN WILL I RETURN TO THE SEA AND ALLOW THIS PLAGUE TO FADE FROM YOUR ISLAND. HURRY, LEST I

RELINQUISH THIS RARE OFFER OF MERCY AND SIMPLY TEAR YOUR HOME TO DUST.

The boy had never run so quickly in his life.

Within a minute, he was back with the mushroom in his hand. The creature stood beside the fairy ring when he returned, lashing its heavy, finned tail against the ground as its limp and jawless human head belched pestilence into the sky. Its single eye remained fixed on him as he dashed to the circle and placed the mushroom back in its rightful spot.

The fungus gave off a brief, faint glow of blue light that ebbed around the rest of the ring. Then, just as quickly as it had appeared, the light was gone, and the mushrooms sat as if they were completely natural.

The skinless leviathan blinked once more and turned toward the cliff behind Cailean's house. Heavy strides carried it along the dead grass to the layered sandstone cliffs, and once it found the edge and looked upon the crashing waves, the embodiment of death and disease leaped off and dove into the sea without another word, disappearing into the rolling depths once more.

Cailean stared after it for several long, bewildered moments.

Finally, the boy's legs found themselves unable to hold him upright much longer, and he slowly carried himself to bed for a long and peaceful rest.

***

The next day, the sickly green clouds that had appeared overnight were dispersed by a sudden, heavy downpour of surprisingly pure rain. While the abrupt loss of crops and livestock around the island of Stronsay was a severe blow, the many farmers banded together to share their resources and help each other rebuild and recover. With quite a bit of help, Cailean's father's farm soon became much more prosperous than it once was, and the two of them were able to live comfortably and happily.

A few months after that fateful night, a new and strange species of scarlet toadstool grew in the center of that fairy ring beside the barn. It soon became a native species, and despite its incredible toxicity, its rarity led the locals to let it be and simply avoid it.

It was not long after the toadstool appeared that a strange carcass washed up on the shores of Stronsay. It was heavily decayed by the time it was found, but a cursory examination revealed a serpentine neck and tail, a sturdy body, and webbed legs designed for swimming. It measured fifty-five feet from the nose to the severed end of its tail, and those who came to examine it were puzzled by its bizarrely prehistoric form and the strange branching of the spine that suggested it had had another neck or even a whole body attached to the back.

The corpse created quite a stir on the island, but when confronted with the news, Cailean merely shrugged and commented on the wonderful weather and the lush crops.

The End

Joseph Michael is the pen name of Joseph Brooks de Vita, a computer whiz and major in English Literature at Rice University whose interests are the comparative literatures of the uncanny and the critical analysis of video games. Joseph Michael is the author of "Lullaby of a Hated Person" published in *Love and Darker Passions* by Double Dragon/Blood Moon.

SUGAR HILL
by Tenea D. Johnson

There are six rats for every person in New York City. There are also three fairies, two Hathors, and an indeterminate, but increasing, number of haints. Lan Ts'ai-Ho is the only Immortal of ancient China. Though tonight may be a bad night, she lives in the city for the pleasure of it, and to watch moments like this, free from the pesky interference of clouds.

A blackened stage, six inches above the dance floor. A tight spotlight lifts one image from the dark: silver-purple polish pressed into cocoa toes floating beneath black straps of sandal. The image catches Ts'ai-Ho and holds her there, halfway between the club's entrance and the restroom. She inhales slowly, her eyes narrowed in appreciation. Slow Spanish guitar begins to roll from the speakers. The spotlight widens and reveals Ms. Tique perched on a barstool, her lips just beginning to hold the first notes of Annie Lennox's "A Thousand Beautiful Things." Ms. Tique looks splendid. Her dark skin glistens beneath the eggplant evening gown that hugs her narrow waist, dives down her chest and comes to a point under the deep cleft of cleavage. Even in this club, it's hard for the crowd to believe Ms. Tique is pre-operative and thus, by the crudest definition, still a man.

Ts'ai-Ho knows better. She's lived hundreds of years dressed as a woman and sounding like a man. Still, the diva's performance is so stunning that

Ts'ai-Ho almost forgets about Doren and why she came here. Then Doren's clear voice echoes in her mind, *I'm through, sick of this world* and Ts'ai-Ho continues toward the bathroom to seek out the haint, Carl, who spends his days haunting his descendents on 149th and St. Nich and his nights peering up from the floor drain in this club's restroom.

When Ts'ai-Ho finally waits out the line and enters one of the unisex bathrooms, it smells like Carl, old and piss-soaked. Ts'ai-Ho stands near the corner of the small room, hands clasped in front of her. She whispers the haint's name until he slides up from the floor, his body bottlenecking out of the small drain.

"Well, if it ain't La Dee Da," Carl says, his head cocking with each syllable.

Ts'ai-Ho turns the corners of her mouth up a centimeter, stares at Carl until he's uncomfortable.

"Well, what you want? I know you didn't come for the scenery," he says.

"Where's Doren?" she asks. Carl jumps slightly at the sound of her voice, still shaken by its bass tones after all this time. He recovers quickly.

"You don't know where your friend's at?"

"Do you know or not?"

"Did you try Brooklyn?" he asks.

"All the fairies are gone from the gardens, botanical or otherwise. The museum's fetish dolls have taken dominion."

Carl turns his nose up. "Dolls? What kind of dolls?"

"The spirits inside them, I said."

66

"No you didn't."

"Carl," Tsai-Ho pauses, taps one finger, lowers her voice an octave. "Where is Doren?"

"Where you staying now?" Carl asks.

Ts'ai-Ho's lips purse slightly. She begins to repeat her question.

"Because," Carl cuts her off, "if you ever bothered to find out, you'd know he stays in Sugar Hill, just down the street from you, just down the street from here. He's been there for months."

Now it's Ts'ai-Ho's turn to jump. Could she and Doren have drifted so far apart that he could live so close without her knowing? A decade ago it would have been impossible, but time has deposited them on different shores. She, the ancient, gravitated to the present and he, a third generation city-born fairy, has hankered for a past only spied in the pages of second-hand books.

She almost hadn't recognized Doren's voice on the answering machine. *I'm through, sick of this world and its fucked up stressed to press issues. The convent fairies are useless, well, fairies, sand blind them and god blast them. And I Doren of the Dell am Audi 5000 with big ups to the Boogie Down and Ballyheighe Bay.*

Yes, they could have drifted that far.

Sharp raps on the restroom door.

Carl sidesteps into the wall and is gone before she can thank him or say anything at all.

She exits the restroom, glaring at the young man who rushes past her. Outside the show continues, but the diva has left the stage. Her replacement is unremarkable.

***

The moon meets Ts'ai-Ho at the top of the stairs. The dim streetlights that line St. Nicholas Avenue resonate the same pale yellow. Merengue rolls down the block, its epicenter a polished SUV in a line of double-parked cars. Teenagers gather around entranceways. Two bodegas blast bright light onto the sidewalk where a few gather and many more pass. Ts'ai-Ho moves confidently through her neighbors, a rare Asian face on a Black and Brown block. Traffic flares in intermittent eruptions of horns; tail and headlights flash. While Ts'ai-Ho hurries to save her friend, Saturday night keeps rolling down Sugar Hill.

As she nears Convent Avenue, the night grows quieter, darker. Even before she rounds the corner to Convent, she squints, looking for fairies.

Though the street has the singular distinction of being the only stretch of green through the busy neighborhood, it's still a far cry from a glen or even the botanical gardens that fairy bands have inhabited in recent decades.

She stands still in the relative darkness, searching with her gaze. There, near the closest stoop: a glimmer of iridescent wings against denim. Ts'ai-Ho walks over, crouches at the edge of the sidewalk.

"Doren?" she asks. "Is that you?"

The fairy walks a few steps towards her, clothed in denim swatches from head to foot. It's not Doren.

"'Sup, Mami?" He's been drinking; his cheeks are so rosy that he almost glows in the dark.

"Have you seen Doren?" Ts'ai-Ho asks.

"You after that back-to-nature *trick*? For real though, Doren ain't shit. You need to bring that over here." He sweeps his right hand towards his crotch, nods on the last word.

Ts'ai-Ho clenches her jaw.

"I don't have time to play with you, fairy. I need to find Doren. Now."

"Damn, it's like that? You faded? I get horny as hell when I'm high."

Ts'ai-Ho sucks her teeth and stands up, looking for a sane fairy to speak with.

"Where is everyone?" she asks, already stepping away from the drunken fairy.

"Shit, it's Saturday night. They out getting they life."

As Ts'ai-Ho crosses the street, the fairy yells: "Yo, you ever want some real love, get at me!"

***

Ts'ai-Ho takes the steps up to her apartment two at a time. She mounts the landing outside her door, unlocks it, and enters. The door closes loudly behind her.

Ts'ai-Ho flips her shoes off in the hallway; they land cockeyed, close to the low shelf where they usually rest. She walks past the kitchen and the second bedroom, straight through to the back of the apartment where the answering machine sits atop an antique table, filigreed by Doren's light touch. Though she sees she has no messages, Ts'ai-Ho walks closer to the answering machine, willing the red light to blink. It does not.

Outside a siren wails past, leaving an undertone

of merengue in its wake.

For the first time, Ts'ai-Ho misses the gods, who, for a song, might do her bidding. Her songs are so strong that the gods themselves granted her forever life just so they could hear her play. She looks to the dusty case in the corner that holds her flute. She knows if she opens it she will find the wood smooth and glossy from use, the mouthpiece shaped to the contour of her lips. She knows if she opens her mouth that the song will be just as strong, strong enough to take her out of this moment. But she doesn't open it. Instead, she sits on the couch and tries to decide what to do.

On the chest against her bare feet, a shard of yellow catches her eye. Ts'ai-Ho moves the piece of paper covering it and a slight hush of wind escapes her lips. She's nearly forgotten the small yellow box with its runes and etched lid. She removes the lid and pulls the delicate dolls out by the tips of her fingernails.

Doren gave her the worry babies a year into their friendship. Even after he told her the name she didn't understand what to do with the small thread-covered figures inside the bright box. He explained that she should pull one out when she needed it. When she asked why, he answered, "So you don't have to worry, baby."

As Ts'ai-Ho places each one of the dolls on the edge of the chest, she sings a soft song to Doren, hoping that he hears.

***

In the four years since she has seen Doren-the actual Doren: thick black hair, dreaming blue eyes-

Ts'ai-Ho has never believed that she would not see him again. This new possibility hovers over the worry babies and seeps into the thread.

When she heard his message this afternoon, Ts'ai-Ho thought Doren was just throwing glamour. Once, glamour had dazzled her.

On the day they met, Ts'ai-Ho sat in the conservatory of the Botanical Gardens, playing her flute in solitude. The other patrons had deserted the building as closing time drew near. Ts'ai-Ho and her best friend, the flute, made the most of the quiet. Doren interrupted their solitude. He trundled in, a giant red tortoise that dragged its shell across the ground in long, loud scrapes. Ts'ai-Ho had stopped and stared. The tortoise Doren stared back, inclined his head and explained: *Fairies front and call it glamour.* She had laughed into her flute-tickled as much by the sight of the widening grin on the tortoise's face as by the thought of fairies calling their shape-shifting glamour at a time when humans did the same.

That night Doren introduced Ts'ai-Ho to the deeper layer of life pulsing through the flora. She saw Asrai transform from water trapped in petals to tiny women with long limbs calling to each other from the edges of flowers; watched as *trows* danced; heard the soft plop of water fairies lighting across the stream.

"This is New York City," Doren told her as they walked. The moon lit him up like an earth-born star. "There are as many secret places as there are secrets and beings to keep them. Fairyland is just one. And only in the Bronx. I hear they got some sick shit in Brooklyn."

For years, Doren and Ts'ai-Ho watched the city change. From rooftops, park benches, and tree lines they saw whole nations emigrate from one borough to another. They picked up Nigerian and brogue in the streets, dusted them off and exchanged them for Bangladeshi. Ts'ai-Ho's forty years in the city had been as exciting as four centuries on the Penglai where the same seven immortals made for limited change. She'd found exactly what she wanted in New York. When she found Doren, she had someone to share it with. For a time, he and Ts'ai-Ho were so close that they ran right up to the edges of each other. Little wonder then that Ts'ai-Ho didn't understand when Doren began to covet the 'purity' of the old world.

***

The argument started when Ts'ai-Ho asked what Doren meant by 'pure'.

"Untainted, of course. Take fairies, who you see when you come to visit me-those aren't fairies," he said.

Because fairies are tricky and Doren in particular had a philosophical bent to boot, Ts'ai-Ho listened, expecting a punch line or at least a sharp turn away from idiocy.

He continued. "Fairies live in glens. Not in subway tunnels or the projects you call botanical gardens." He puffed up in anger. "They make mischief; they don't get wit' bitches."

Doren grew larger with each sentence. "*Fairies* don't live in constant fear of rats or have to negotiate with them to take a fucking piss in the

72

bushes!" he said.

Ts'ai-Ho cocked her head and hummed. "Doren, I think perhaps-"

"No Tsai, I'm telling you. I've got this-"

"All figured out?" Ts'ai-Ho said.

Doren, now half her height, turned to Ts'ai-Ho, changed his tone to match the tinge of derision in her comment. "No, not all figured out." He paused. "Got an answer for everything, huh? This is *my* day in and day out. Trust, it ain't pretty and it ain't pure. This is what *I* know, Ts'ai. You know your 1500, 1600 years but I know these 500 blocks." Doren was pacing now, running a rut in the hardwood, as he grew ever larger. His eyes glinted when he faced Ts'ai-Ho.

"Humans don't even know we're here, and if they did, these thick-skinned bastards wouldn't miss a step," Doren said.

Ts'ai-Ho tried to lighten the mood: "And you love them for it."

A smirk died on Doren's lips. "I'm serious, Ts'ai. We're lost here."

"Perhaps you mistake your problem with that of all fairies," she said.

"I'm speaking on the plight of a people. Not some personal bullshit. Faerie *will* cease to be if we keep walking this path. We'll be fuppies with no soul. We'll start thinking remote controls are magic. That curses are just cusswords!"

Doren towered over Ts'ai-Ho now.

She stood, raised her chin to meet his gaze, and spoke. "Ah, I see. You don't want to be happy; you want to complain."

73

Doren blazed at her, his face turned a sepia tone that reminded Ts'ai-Ho of old temple photographs. Too late, she opened her mouth to speak softer words. Doren didn't give her the chance. He turned and ducked through the doorway, taking with him his dreaming eyes and handsome face, his open friendship.

After their argument, Doren only showed his glamour, coming to her in guise. Yet Ts'ai-Ho had enjoyed the blue fireflies gathered at her bedroom windows. She had smiled at the homeless men holding primroses with her name etched into the petals. Because she believed that Doren would forgive her and once more show his true face.

Ts'ai-Ho turns to the window on the far wall, hoping to glimpse a blue firefly. There's only a dark patch of sky and the fire escape zigzagging down the building next door. She stands looking at the mound of discarded bottles, diapers and trash at the bottom of the escape.

Glamour.

The worry babies vibrate on top of the chest. Lan Ts'ai-Ho sweeps past and toward the front door.

***

The moon keeps its distance, shining down on Sugar Hill from just east of the Harlem River. Ts'ai-Ho stands in the grass outside of La Jupía's lair waiting to be invited in. Tsai-Ho does not sit on the wooden bench just behind her or lean against the low, black fence in front. She stays alert, holding her flute case firmly in her left hand.

La Jupía's permission wafts up from beyond

the fence, a strong smell of oranges left too long in the sun. Ts'ai-Ho walks farther into the grass, stops just before the back end of Sugar Hill drops off into the dark.

La Jupía is there, little more than a shimmering, a Dominicana mirage that has been uprooted from the island and now patrols the caverns between tenement buildings from 139th to 155. If anyone on the hill has seen Doren, La Jupía has.

Ts'ai-Ho removes her flute from the case and places it against her mouth, fingers poised. La Jupía comes closer. Her colors cluster; she is almost a form. Ts'ai-Ho plays her urgent question, a series of triplets that end with high notes. The question flutters near La Jupía. La Jupía meets the sliver of spirit that Ts'ai-Ho and the flute have created, wraps herself around it. When her answer is ready, La Jupía pushes the song back into the flute. It has no more flavor than water: *No Doren, not today, not yesterday.*

Ts'ai-Ho plays another melody. It asks about the glamour Doren might be hiding behind. When La Jupía pushes the answer back into the flute, Ts'ai-Ho's throat burns with the spice of habanero. *Glamour? I see spirit. I see all.*

***

As Ts'ai-Ho leaves La Jupía's lair and rounds the corner back to St. Nicholas Place, the lights of Yankee Stadium burn bright behind her. But there are other reasons that she looks shadowed and small. Ts'ai-Ho can't think of anyone else who might know Doren's whereabouts. She passes a

75

pocket of people in front of her apartment building and stops at the phone booth near the fire escape. Ts'ai-Ho picks up the receiver and dials her home number. There are no new voicemails. She cues up Doren's message from this afternoon. When he starts speaking, she shuts out the street noise and focuses, trying to pick up clues from background noise. Her mind runs reels of Doren's demise while she listens: blood splattered across his fingers as he calls to say it's too late; the thump of his lifeless head lolling in her arms; the weak howl of anguish as Doren dissipates into the ether. She pushes away the images and plays the message again.

"My Ts'ai, it's done. I'm through, sick of-"

The worry babies drop into a shaft of moonlight at the bottom of the fire escape. In the second before each one passes from the light back into the dark, Ts'ai-Ho almost convinces herself that she has seen floating candy wrappers or some other mundane sidewalk flotsam. But standing single-file, close to the building, the worry babies are unmistakably extraordinary. There are half a dozen of them: red, blue, green, yellow.

They are so small Ts'ai-Ho can only see their color. The worry babies walk close to the building, just above the pavement, their magic hidden in the shadows where the brick meets concrete. When she recognizes them, Ts'ai-Ho stops listening to Doren's message and curses under her breath. She glances at her neighbors. Their conversations continue, uninterrupted.

Ts'ai-Ho places the receiver back in the cradle, following the worry babies with her gaze. They have hardly covered the distance of one of her strides. So, for now, she stands and marvels. Up to this moment, Ts'ai-Ho hasn't seen any hint of fairy magic in the worry babies; but now she is faced with a band of beings that bear little resemblance to the curios she thought she knew.

They head southeast, towards 155th street. As Ts'ai-Ho watches, they cross against the light and inch up the street's sharp incline. The C train station is at the top. As the worry babies go down the first stair, they drop out of sight. Ts'ai-Ho follows.

***

There are safer stations in the MTA than 155th Street. But few can compare with its entertainments: as Ts'ai-Ho descends onto the platform, a homeless man, dressed in tatters, shits a yellow load of last night and grunts to himself about the lack of privacy in subway stations. Ts'ai-Ho looks past him, searching the shadows.

The worry babies stand out among the dark spots of old gum on the ground. Ts'ai-Ho falls in behind them. A hot wind blows, signaling the arrival of the uptown train. Across the tracks, people trickle down in ones and twos, deserting the late-night benches to catch the train. Ts'ai-Ho follows the worry babies. She wonders what kind of fairy dust Doren spun into their thread to carry so much magic: life, invisibility . . . . teleportation.

Ts'ai-Ho feels the change before she sees it. Just as the train doors open for passengers on the other side of the station, an envelope of bottomless space appears in front of the worry babies. They step in. Before they can disappear, Lan Ts'ai-Ho is next to them, being sucked into a tight blackness that spits her out on the other side.

***

When she opens her eyes, the homeless man is above her, looking down. He wears a dark suit.

"You all right?" he asks.

He helps Ts'ai-Ho to her feet. As he does, concentric circles of lightheadedness radiate from the crown of her skull. Ts'ai-Ho realizes she hasn't eaten all night. Thoughts of food absorb the next few seconds. At the same time, the circles of Ts'ai-Ho's lightheadedness grow larger and the right half of each crashes into the wall beside her. Ts'ai-Ho stares off into the distance and pictures dim sum delights.

The homeless man removes a handkerchief from beneath his suit and brushes off the knees of her slacks. The semi-circles reach the beams that separate the local and express tracks. There, they break apart and ripple into oblivion. As they shatter, Ts'ai-Ho notices them for the first time.

Before she can investigate further, she must get rid of the homeless man, lest he be alarmed by the seams of the city. Ts'ai-Ho turns to him.

He holds a corner of the handkerchief in each hand, trying to snap the dirt out of it. His suit is shiny black. The suit does not move as he snaps the cloth in the air. When his arms move, the arms of the suit lag behind and Ts'ai-Ho can see brown sleeves moving where the black suit does not. Peering closer, she can see an entire set of ragged mismatched clothes beneath the suit. A strange veil of light glows between the two.

She decides that the homeless man doesn't need her protection.

"You sure you're okay?" he asks.

"Yes, thank you," she answers.

Ts'ai-Ho walks the length of the platform, checking the shadows for worry babies. The envelope of space still hangs in the air, a bit of not nothing that looks wetter than the air around it. But no worry babies. She walks back up to the street.

***

At first, Ts'ai Ho doesn't suspect the nature of the world she's crossed into. She stands on the corner of 155th and Amsterdam, looking for the worry babies in swatches of light on the sidewalk. A woman with curly dark hair and a burgundy messenger bag passes her, stepping off the curb. She only walks a few steps before a massive SUV squeals around the corner and stops within inches of hitting her. Its headlights spill onto her face. Burned rubber prickles in the back of Ts'ai-Ho's throat. After one tight breath, the young woman looks up at the driver and looses a burst of expletives, her fingers grasping the small silver cross on her chest. When the 'motherfucker' reaches the driver, his windshield explodes.

This is a first for Lan Ts'ai-Ho. In all her travels, from Penglai to Harlem and beyond, she has never been in a place where feelings have as much power as the ones who produce them. She immediately feels uncomfortable here and regrets it before she can stop herself. The regret beads up on her skin and slides down her arms. When it falls from her fingertips, regret crystallizes into a discomfort that pings against the sidewalk where it breaks.

The driver mistakes the sound for more of his own breaking glass. He starts to yell and in his blind rage, his own curses shatter the other windows. The young woman walks away, snickering. Ts'ai-Ho breathes deeply and avoids eye contact. She worries what will happen if she connects with his emotions.

Before she can call her worry back, the worry babies stand in a circle, facing her. They are as tall as the street lamps. This large, their faces are terrible. The simple lines and circles of mouth and eyes are now a swarm of dark dots bleeding into each other.

The one closest to Ts'ai-Ho teeters on spindly thread-covered legs. Its large rectangular head sits forward from the rest of its body. Behind it the other five worry babies sway on equally thin green and blue legs. Their arms stick straight out from their bodies.

Ts'ai-Ho clears her throat: "Did you find Doren?" she asks.

The closest one steps closer; the others hang back. The leader then. It has no mouth to open and so stares intently at Ts'ai-Ho. She tries to think of a way to communicate, remembers the flute. She opens the case and brings the instrument to her lips. Before Ts'ai-Ho can play the first note, the lead worry baby bends down, its sideshow body bowing, and chomps down on the other end of the flute. Ts'ai-Ho's flute, her gateway to immortality and thousand-year-friend, is lost in the dark maw of the creature's mouth. The worry baby steps back, closing the circle.

Ts'ai-Ho's shock knocks the wind out of her. As she tries to catch her breath, the worry babies vanish.

Ts'ai-Ho thinks that frustration will cascade from the sky and strike her down. It does not. Frustration, an electrical current, rivets her to the ground. It buzzes through her body, pauses in her teeth; then jumps into the nearest street lamp and blows it out in a shower of orange sparks. Helplessness scurries in shortly after and crawls up Ts'ai-Ho's back. It scratches, lightly, maddeningly at her scalp until she runs back to the subway station. She heads straight for the spot of Not Nothing that brought her here and doesn't stop running until she spills out the other side.

***

Sunday morning is bright, bleaching the ceiling a shade of white that makes Ts'ai-Ho close her eyes before she rolls over and raises on her elbows to look at the answering machine that blinks . . . blinks . . . blinks.

***

At the northernmost tip of Manhattan, a piece of the ancient remains. Lan Ts'ai-Ho sits in Inwood Hill Park, the last 200 acres of primordial forest on the whole island, waiting for Doren. The morning air is fresh; the neighborhood sounds of Inwood distant. Ts'ai-Ho sits on a bench with her legs crossed loosely as a light wind blows the stray hairs on the back of her neck. In the message, Doren said he would meet her near the caves. She glances in

81

the direction of their dark doors and wonders if he will leave her waiting for naught. Squirrels scuttle across the grass and climb up a gnarled maple; a painted lady butterfly stumbles through the air, comes close to Ts'ai-Ho's face, lands on the corner of the bench and stays there. A park ranger passes by, clipboard in one hand, bottled water in the other. When he leaves, Ts'ai-Ho is alone with her thoughts and the butterfly. She turns to it and speaks.

"You're well then?" she asks.

"Aye, I'm straight," it answers.

"Doren, could you-"

The butterfly's body bubbles out and joins together at the edges until it's a quivering brown sphere. It pops, raining a fine dust over Doren who now sits naked next to Ts'ai-Ho's shoulder, his mouth as high as her ear. Ts'ai-Ho blushes, moves her gaze to the empty spot just in front of Doren.

"I thought you had or were going to-"

He looks over, and his gaze stops the words. There is no glamour there, only a steadiness that makes Ts'ai-Ho wonder at its origin.

"I was worried," Ts'ai-Ho finishes.

"Trust," Doren's eyes brighten and he smiles. "I know. Came close enough, truth be told."

A knot forms in Ts'ai-Ho's throat.

"Doren-" she begins.

"But it was reminded to me, by some very rude little dolls I might mention, that I've got some unfinished business-a new flute that needs carving, a threat that needs mending."

"It was only frayed, Doren," Ts'ai-Ho says.

"What binds us can't be broken, like old world to new."

The End

Tenea D. Johnson is the author of the poetry collection, *Starting Friction*, and two novels, *R/evolution* and *Smoketown*, of which *Publisher's Weekly* wrote "the understated, lyrical prose makes even small moments feel triumphant." Her short fiction and poetry have appeared in various magazines and anthologies. In 2012, she had the great pleasure of reading with Jeffrey Ford at the Fantastic Fiction series. She's working on a fiction album as well as the next book in the *R/evolution* series. She is co-editor of the 2013 edition of the *Heiresses of Russ* anthology with Steve Berman and author of "Swell of the Cicadas" in Prime Books' *Shades of Blue and Gray: Ghosts of the Civil War*.

SPINOZA'S GOLEM
by James Morrow

As the curator of the Cambridge Museum of Philosophy Artifacts, a position I hope to retain until the end of my days, I believe I've developed a sixth sense for detecting a crank or charlatan out to sell us a fraudulent relic. I can unmask such mountebanks as readily as an expert poker player can spot a bluffer. A telltale catch in the voice, a characteristic trembling of the fingers, a revelatory canting of the eyeballs: owing to such signs, I've avoided acquiring Kierkegaard's alleged walking stick, Hegel's presumed sherry decanter, a purported rough draft of Schopenhauer's *The World as Will and Representation*, and the unpublished rules for an ontological role-playing game, *Daseins and Dragons*, supposedly authored by Martin Heidegger.

Our location is obscure but not arcane. An unmarked green door at 25 Mount Auburn Street, not far from Harvard Yard, is the portal to the CAMPA trove. We receive visitors by appointment only. Write me a letter, convince me of your scholarly integrity, and I shall admit you to our *sanctum sanctorum*. Here you will see not only the scale-model abyss into which Nietzsche stared until he found it staring back at him, but also the pickled remains of Descartes's failed attempt to ensoul an alley cat by transplanting a human pineal gland into its brain, to say nothing of the two-meter high translucent pyramid through which Leibniz clarified his *Weltanschauung*, each of its fifteen

84

thousand dice-size cubes representing a possible universe with which God might have blessed his creatures, our own supremely harmonious world sitting at the apex. Wonders are many, and in my twenty-year career I've secured an inordinate number of them beneath bulletproof glass.

Acquiring exhibits for CAMPA is rather like running an international espionage ring. We have agents in every European capital. By day these highly trained operatives prowl through antique shops and flea markets, looking for artifacts of such consummate oddity that they might very well have figured in the evolution of Western rationality. (A bazaar in Cairo once yielded the insectarium in which Hobbes kept two opposing armies of ants, their periodic battles serving to reify his notion of the *bellum omnium contra omnes*, the war of all against all, a touchstone of his political philosophy.) By night our spies eavesdrop in coffee houses and taverns, listening for clues to the whereabouts of mislaid objective correlatives. (A chance remark in a London pub led to our acquisition of Locke's sculpted celebration of the human sensorium, a crystalline female head complete with golden wires attached to the eyes, ears, nose, and tongue, each such filament soaring outward for three feet then looping back to the brain.) Of course, an agent need not spend all his waking hours amid demimonde dwellers and louche lizards. Sometimes he simply purchases a catalogue for an auction pending in some European country or other, discovers that the attendees will be bidding on a deceased philosopher's effects, and shows up

85

clutching a CAMPA checkbook. Indeed, it was through such a public sale that our museum acquired one of the holy grails of philosophy artifacts: the lost glass illustration of Benedict de Spinoza's worm-in-the-blood metaphor, formed and buffed by the master lens-grinder himself.

When the relic arrived in Cambridge from Amsterdam, addressed to me, Jacob Greenblatt, I immediately telephoned my daughter, Naomi, who teaches archeology at Boston University and occasionally goes digging in North Africa. She happened to have the afternoon free-professors enjoy more flexible hours than curators-so she hopped on the Red Line and soon appeared at my door. We carried the crate to the back room. Naomi got to work with a crowbar. (At age seventy-four, I am beholden to the whims of my arthritis.) With surpassing caution we removed the fragile treasure, and suddenly there it stood, shining forth like Excalibur in its granite sheath, a two-foot-wide glass cylinder blown to suggest a human vein. The interior housed a ceramic but philosophically inclined worm the size and shape of a baguette, plus free-floating glass beads representing the various blood-components-lymph, chyle, plasma-that the segmented occupant had selected as objects of contemplation.

"What the hell?" said Naomi.

"In this piece Spinoza has dramatized an important dimension of his worldview," I explained. "From a bloodworm's perspective, this vein is the entire universe. The tube contains parts and manifests causes, but it is itself neither a part

86

nor a cause-nothing exists beyond its confines."

"Some people feel that way about Cambridge," noted Naomi.

"When indulging in theological speculation," I continued, paraphrasing Spinoza, "human beings commit an error analogous to the bloodworm's delusion. They fail to appreciate that the one and only Substance must possess an infinite number of mental, physical, and, *nota bene*, unnamable attributes." I caressed the vermian habitat. "In truth there is a world beyond the vein wherein the worm resides, and a world beyond that world as well, an endless and axiomatically divine Nature that defies mere human imagination. Achieve an intellectually affectionate relationship with this impersonal Deity, and you will become a good and happy person."

"All you need is God?" said Naomi. "What about lovers and friends?"

"Spinoza appreciated human connection, but such fellowship was hardly the *sine qua non* of his existence." Absently I picked up the crowbar and hefted it in my palm. "He spent his days grinding lenses for other people's microscopes and telescopes, living on raisins and gruel, craving neither riches nor reputation."

"That puts him one up on me," said Naomi.

"Myself as well."

"If Spinoza's Deity is impersonal, how can I love him?"

"It."

"It."

I hugged my daughter and said, "Do you love the pottery you've unearthed in Ethiopia?"

"Yes."

"There."

"Perhaps."

As it happened, the ultimate value of the glass bloodworm lay not in the artifact itself but in its oaken base. A brass knob protruded from one side. Evidently the pedestal held a drawer. I yanked the knob. Protesting with squeaks and squeals, the compartment delivered its contents to my inspection.

My heart raced. A book. I gasped. A volume owned by Spinoza himself: no, better than that, I realized upon flipping back the cover, a volume *written* by Spinoza himself-the hand was unmistakable-a dozen or so pages penned in Latin under the rubric *Experimentum Philosophicum*. I bid Naomi goodbye, bore the volume to my office, pulled out my Lewis and Short, and got to work, soon discovering to my delight that the humble bloodworm had been guarding nothing less than Spinoza's private journal, composed in The Hague during the final decade of his short life.

***

22 April 1670

Although I am a man without a people, excommunicated by the rabbis of Amsterdam for observing that the Tanakh is entirely of human design, I shall never abjure my heritage *in toto*. Lately I've drawn inspiration from the Jewish legend of the golem-for next week will see the publication of my unorthodox and dangerous philosophy, *Tractatus Theologico-Politicus*, a circumstance that has behooved me to construct a

88

clockwork bodyguard.

As I child I was enchanted by the tale of Judah Löew ben Bezalel, the Prague rabbi who takes a shapeless mass, a *gōlem*, of clay and gives it humanoid form, subsequently suffusing his sculpture with the lifeforce by incising on its brow the Hebrew word emeth. (Translator's note: that is, "truth.") Although Judah Löew's brain-child proves a faithful servant and protector of the ghetto, the experiment entails a scriptural obligation: the golem must never labor on the Sabbath. Avoiding such sacrilege is a simple matter of periodically effacing, and later restoring, the first letter of emeth, the Aleph, leaving Mem and Taw, characters that spell meth. (Translator's note: that is, "death.") But one fateful Friday evening Löew forgets to disable his creature, and so it runs amok in the ghetto, smashing down doors, destroying wells, overturning horse carts, and torching the communal firewood supply. When Sunday rolls around, the heartsick rabbi dutifully grinds his beloved golem to dust.

Tonight I dressed my bodyguard in a woolen tunic and sturdy boots, then animated him for the first time. Unlike Rabbi Löew, I had no need of the Kabbala in achieving this result. The golem of the Paviljoensgracht lives not by magic but by springs and cogs, ratchets and escapements, in accordance with principles laid down by my fellow Dutch experimentalist, Christiaan Huygens. To be sure, Mijnheer Huygens's investigations are rather more physical than metaphysical, but he is nonetheless my brother in reason.

I have named the automaton Bezalel, in honor of Rabbi Löew's lineage. Doubtless my adversaries will say that in building the creature I committed an act of hubris. Certainly the rabbis back in Amsterdam will accuse me of "playing God," using Bezalel as yet another occasion to persecute me. I do not play God. The concept is incoherent. (Even God does not play God.) That said, I shall allow that the automaton has bestowed a certain clarity on my ruminations. Although I "created" him, my project cannot be analogized to any presumed gesture by the One Substance. The Deity that is Nature does not "create" anything at all, for Being is by definition sufficient unto itself.

At the stroke of midnight Benedict de Spinoza, proponent of the God of infinite extension, loaded his decidedly finite extension-this curious assemblage of bronze bones, leather tendons, and mother-of-pearl flesh-into a pony cart. Furtively I conveyed the golem to the Oranjeplein. Here in this windswept nocturnal park we would be immune to the prying eyes and meddling morals of our fellow citizens.

I dragged Bezalel free of the cart, standing him upright as I might a clothier's mannequin, then drew forth the silver key from my overcoat and inserted it in his neck, adjacent to the jugular pipe. Slowly, methodically, I wound him up, one turn, two turns, three, four, five. I stopped: a modest trial seemed best-I would animate my bodyguard in full another day, giving him comprehensive power to protect me.

Reaching toward the sternum, I took hold of

the function dial and switched it from modality one, dormancy, to modality two, vigilance. A rasping noise filled the air as the mainspring uncoiled and the wheels-within-wheels began to spin. The golem lifted his head, opened his eyes, and began marking time. He raised his left foot, then returned the extremity to the ground. He raised and lowered his right foot. Left foot, right foot, left, right, left, right. His arms swung back and forth at his side like pendulums.

Cautiously I twisted the dial to modality three, intimidation, then fled to the nearest tree, prepared to scale the branches if Bezalel proved more unruly than I anticipated. I looked back. The creature moved haltingly, advancing more through baby steps than confident strides, moonlight glinting in his glass eyes, wisps of fog coiling about his thighs like serpents. Eventually I would test modality four, belligerence, and modality five, the behavior I have not yet named. For now it was sufficient to observe modality three in all its menacing glory.

From the moment I saw Bezalel shambling toward me, I knew I'd brought forth not only a loyal bodyguard but also a faithful listener. He would be my eternally agreeable sounding board, the audience on whose steadfast sympathy I could always depend-even beyond the grave. I've already approached the one man I truly trust and instructed him in the disposition of both my corpse and my creature. (Translator's note: Spinoza is referring to his landlord.) "Bury me wherever the town elders see fit," I told Mijnheer Von Der Spijk, "but then, under cover of night, you must perform an exhumation and place the golem beside me in my crypt."

***

On only a dozen or so occasions in my life have I selected a destination from which nothing-not hell, high water, wild horses, mad dogs, Englishmen, nor the Great Wall of China-could deter me. I think immediately of Cambridge Courthouse. (I would get to my wedding promptly or perish in the attempt.) Massachusetts General Hospital also comes to mind. (I must deliver my wife, Hannah, to the obstetricians with great efficiency, so they could in turn deliver Naomi to the world). And then there was Nieuwe Kerk Den Haag in the Netherlands. For if in his journal entry of 22 April 1670 Spinoza spoke the truth-and his partisans argue that he never employed any other idiom-then his clockwork bodyguard lay in the same churchyard that held his earthly remains.

As you might imagine, I decided against contacting the mayor of The Hague and begging him to let me tamper with the philosopher's grave. He would probably say no-and even if the municipal authorities assented to my ambition, they would surely claim the golem for themselves. Bezalel must be displayed in my museum and nowhere else on earth.

When I proposed to Naomi that she accompany me to the Netherlands, she immediately arranged her life accordingly, canceling classes and posting on-line assignments. Digging for relics is in my daughter's blood. True, our planned plundering of Spinoza's bones and their accompanying automaton seemed less like an archeologist's dream than a ghoul's delight, but our motives were unimpeachable. If our adventure proved successful, the world would have yet another reason to esteem the seventeenth century's greatest philosopher (an assessment I am prepared to defend against devotees of Leibniz and Descartes). I dubbed our expedition the Raiders of the Lost Christian Consensus, an admittedly snide appellation, keyed to my conclusion that, when it comes to densely reasoned theological discourse, complete with quasi-geometric proofs, Spinoza's *Ethics* leaves the Church Fathers in the shadows.

And so it was that my daughter and I took an Aer Lingus flight from Logan Airport to Schiphol in Amsterdam. We checked into the Seven Bridges Hotel, rented ten-speed bicycles, rode around the Rembrandtplein, and, returning to Reguliersgracht 31, caught up on our sleep. The following morning we leased a minivan from Hertz and drove fifty kilometers southwest to The Hague. Our quest had begun in earnest.

Stage one, we decided, must be a pilgrimage to the great man's house. Although the Paviljoensgracht canal no longer exists, having been displaced by a lovely two-lane thoroughfare with a grassy median, we had no trouble locating number 72-74. We parked in the shadow of the philosopher's statue, a mass of bronze now green with oxidation, then approached the Spinozahuis, a modest three-story affair maintained by an antiquarian society that, we soon learned to our dismay, makes a point of keeping it closed to the

93

general public.

Our instincts lured us south, across a bridge spanning the extant canal. We found ourselves on Spinozastraat. The irony amused me. In his lifetime our lens-grinder could not venture this far from the Jewish Quarter without enduring the taunts of those who thought him a depraved atheist, and now the route in question bore his name. To all appearances the philosopher of The Hague had enjoyed the last laugh, and so had the One Substance-though neither entity would especially care, Spinoza being a man without malice and his God a divinity without emotion.

As the celebrated Dutch sun, muse to countless incomparable painters, arced toward the horizon, Naomi and I returned to the Paviljoensgracht, then motored into the business district. Beyond a pick and two shovels, our purchases included a tool kit, essential for disassembling Bezalel, plus two oversized suitcases, necessary for getting his components across the Atlantic by jetliner.

Having outfitted our expedition, we drove along the Spui toward the Nieuwe Kerk den Haag, paragon of early Protestant architecture in the Netherlands. These days the building no longer serves an ecclesiastical function, being a venue for organ concerts and student recitals, a fact that failed to assuage my guilt. Music hall or no music hall, we were about to perform an act of desecration.

We parked outside the gates and waited. Night came on slowly, almost bashfully, as if ashamed to deprive Holland's artists of their light. We proceeded to the churchyard. The grave we sought was clearly marked. terra hic benedicti de spinoza. The earth yielded readily to our implements. The Raiders of the Lost Christian Consensus, may God forgive them, had begun their unholy work.

**

11 May 1670

The estimable Mijnheer Von Der Spijk has permitted me to store Bezalel in a ground-floor closet, just off the front parlor. To thank the man for his generosity, I gave him a demonstration, winding up the automaton-I calculated that four turns of the key would be sufficient-then setting him loose in the stone alley beside the house. Bezalel ambled all the way from the gate to the garden, where he sat on a bench and contemplated the flowers with his glass eyes. Mijnheer Von Der Spijk gasped in delight-as a painter, he appreciates Bezalel's aesthetic sensibilities-then clapped his hands and informed me I was a genius, a diagnosis from which I did not dissent.

Just as I suspected, Bezalel has proved the ideal audience for my ruminations. Two days ago I shared with him my discovery that the mind is the idea of the body. To wit, the universe has never wielded, nor will it ever wield, a Cartesian cleaver separating human mental activity from those entities we call bodies. Cogitation and corporeality are in essence the same thing. Bezalel accepted my insight without reservation, which is more than I can say for most of the correspondents (notably Oldenburg in London and Leibniz in Paris) for whom I have described my system in detail.

During the first week following the publication

of the *Tractatus Theologico-Politicus* no untoward incidents occurred, though I knew that much of the Latin-speaking world was reading it. But then, last night, my heresy caught up with me. Torches in hand, pistols at the ready, an angry mob appeared at the front door, demanding that I render myself unto them. Mijnheer Von Der Spijk immediately rushed into the Paviljoensgracht and attempted to mollify the intruders. Their intentions, he now learned, included hauling me to the Oranjeplein and hanging me from an elm tree. Mijnheer Von Der Spijk countered that I was an irreplaceable tenant, and so they had best find a different Jew to torment.

As my landlord distracted the mob, I tore open the closet door, wound up the golem, and switched the function dial from modality one, dormancy, to modality two, vigilance, to modality three, intimidation. Bezalel awoke. His limbs creaked. His wheels whirred. He marched across the parlor and, traversing the portal, waded into the bloodthirsty horde. The blackguards dispersed instantly, and I had no cause to advance the dial to modality four, belligerence.

To all appearances, Bezalel, Mijnheer Von Der Spijk, and I have won the first skirmish in the War on Spinozism. The final outcome of the conflict remains in doubt, but my calculations tell me reason will prevail.

***

For two unbroken hours Naomi and I labored in the moonlit churchyard. My daughter, of course, did most of the digging, while her septuagenarian father supervised-for how scandalous it would be if

America's premier curator of philosophy artifacts dropped dead of a heart attack while violating Spinoza's grave. Suddenly Naomi's spade struck wood, inspiring her to furious effort, and in time a pair of dark oblong boxes, flecked with mold but essentially sound, stood revealed at the bottom of the cavity, bathed in the lunar glow.

Two coffins! A double grave! By the evidence of these twin receptacles, Spinoza's golem was no less factual than his worm-in-the-blood diorama. For eleven generations, master and mannequin had lain side-by-side in the sodden Dutch earth.

Luckily we were spared the necessity of disturbing the lens-grinder's remains, for someone had scratched *ossa sepulta*, buried bones, on one of the coffin lids. We turned our attentions to the unmarked casket. Naomi applied the pick, tearing the lid to pieces, and soon the automaton stretched before us, supine, his glass eyes burning with Selene's fire. Even in his decrepit state, Bezalel displayed facets more dazzling than I ever dared imagine, a creature at once *outre* and exquisite, his gleaming mother-of-pearl cranium harboring the clockwork equivalent of a brain, his strong bronze hands eager to keep his creator from harm, his bright bronze chest exhibiting both the function dial and the tattered remnants of the woolen tunic. A tarnished silver key protruded from the creature's neck, poised to tighten the mainspring.

The tool kit provided every implement we required. Working feverishly, determined to finish the task before sunrise, we systematically dismantled the creature, sketching each element and diagramming its relationship to the whole. After placing the detached head and orphaned torso in one suitcase, the pelvis and limbs in the other, we loaded our prize into the minivan, then turned our attentions to the grave. Carefully, ever so carefully, we replaced the grass tuffets like pieces of a jigsaw puzzle, smoothing the surrounding loam, until to our eyes the site appeared unmolested.

At dawn we drove back to Amsterdam and, wheeling our priceless discovery before us, checked back into the Seven Bridges Hotel. Sleep eluded me that night. As the moon rose over the city, I climbed free of my bed and, opening the appropriate suitcase, contemplated Bezalel's head. What gloriously abstruse notions Spinoza had set dancing through the creature's clockwork brain. *The mind is the idea of the body.* It made no sense. It made perfect sense. An exasperating, exhilarating, inexhaustible thought. I wondered if I would ever sleep again.

The numinous Dutch sun returned, limning its favorite nation. A taxi took us to Schiphol Airport. We entrusted our luggage, including the anatomized golem, to the care of Aer Lingus's baggage handlers, then boarded a flight to Boston.

And that is how the most astonishing relic in the history of Western thought came all the way from Holland to Massachusetts. After bearing the suitcases to the back room of CAMPA, I set them on the floor and nervously inspected their contents. Everything seemed intact. I laid my palm on Bezalel's torso, half expecting to sense a heartbeat, then contemplated the function dial. The mystery of

98

modality five-"the behavior I have not yet named," as Spinoza put it in his journal-taunted me. Mutilation? Dismemberment? Decapitation? One thing was certain. I must never activate that option, no matter how great my curiosity grew.

***

18 August 1670

Priests, pastors, and sages have responded to *Tractatus Theologico-Politicus* with all the vituperation I'd anticipated. Bishop Pierre-Daniel Huet, tutor to the Dauphin, recommended that I be "covered with chains and whipped with a rod." Dutch theologian Phillip van Limborch dismissed my effort as "defecated erudition and masticated critique." Still another defender of the faith has called me "the most subtle atheist hell has vomited on the earth." This last condemnation almost pleases me. I'm thinking of having it inscribed on my tomb (after changing "atheist" to "thinker").

Yesterday morning a sweating emissary pounded on the door of the Paviljoensgracht 72-74, flourishing an official summons from our local Council of Theologians. This pious fraternity expected me to appear before them that very afternoon to answer charges of sacrilege and sedition. I told the emissary that I should be happy to explain myself to this august body, but I must be permitted to bring an automaton to act as my advocate.

The tribunal convened in the Nieuwe Kerk den Haag. A bailiff swore me in using the famous Bible authorized by King James the First. After according the somnolent golem suspicious frowns and hostile scowls, my three fat and apoplectic accusers confronted me with the gravamen of the indictment. On the evidence of the *Tractatus*, I was an atheist and-a persuasion no less abominable-an anti-theocrat, bent on replacing Christian governments throughout Europe with secular states catering to the basest impulses of their citizens.

I retorted that anyone who read my *Tractatus* carefully would see that, far from being an "atheist," I am something like the opposite, a man who daily breathes, ingests, imbibes, and dreams of the One Substance. Concerning the label "anti-theocrat," I argued that ere long all rational men will come to share my critique of the Christian churches-namely, that they seek to consolidate their power by frightening congregants with the myth of a capricious and vindictive God. The sooner this fraud ends, I declared, the better.

My defense did not impress the Council of Theologians. After a brief deliberation, they agreed that I must be banished from The Hague forever.

So I wound up the automaton. One, two, three, four-fifteen turns altogether. I switched the function dial to modality four, belligerence. Bezalel reacted with admirable speed and breathtaking efficiency. He lifted a rotund theocrat from the bench, carried him sputtering through the portals of the Nieuwe Kerk, and hurled him into the Spui canal, then straightaway disposed of the remaining judges in the same fashion. A few moments later my three antagonists stood dripping and shivering on the banks of the canal. Thus did I win my case. I suspect I shall not be hearing from the Council of

Theologians for many months to come.

That night I rewarded my mechanical paladin for his heroic service, favoring him with my philosophy of immanence. All is in God. All lives and moves in God. The laws of Nature and the decrees of the Divine are synonymous. From God's infinite essence all things follow by necessity, as it follows from the eternal condition of a triangle that its three angles are equal to two right angles. What the laws of the circle are to all circles, God is to the world. It's really quite simple.

***

There was no question that Naomi and I would attempt to resurrect Spinoza's golem, though the odds were against us. After more than three centuries in the ground, Bezalel's internal workings were probably corroded beyond redemption. And yet I had faith that, if we reassembled the machine with sufficient care and a surfeit of lubrication, we might accomplish the miracle.

When it came to choosing a venue for our experiment, Naomi and I quickly reached accord. We would restore Bezalel in the basement of the museum. Capacious and warm, with track lighting and an ambience that savored of the macabre-jagged shadows, spider webs, fissured plaster, artifacts stored in mummy-like wrappings-this space would afford us the sort of seclusion that Spinoza himself so highly prized.

We lit a candle in remembrance of Naomi's mother, then began the momentous project. Working with our sketches from that anxious night in the churchyard, we pieced the golem back together over the course of four hours. The sight of Bezalel standing upright, arms hanging limply by his side, head lolling on his chest, brought a frisson to my aging frame.

Spinoza had dressed Bezalel in tunic and boots, and Naomi had come prepared to bless him with an equivalent sartorial dignity. Removing a down parka from her backpack, she slid the golem's arms into the sleeves, then activated the zipper. A *tallith* completed the ensemble.

"Go ahead," I told her. "A few rotations only."

Naomi reached toward Bezalel's jugular and turned the silver key-once, twice, thrice. She switched the function dial fromdormancy to vigilance. A rasping sound echoed across the basement, like the death rattle of a windlass. Bezalel lifted his head. His eyelids flickered open. He raised and lowered his left foot, then his right, then his left, then his right. His arms cycled back and forth as if attached to a brachiating ape.

"Eureka!" I cried.

"Shazam!" shouted Naomi.

Then the unexpected happened. For reasons that defied my understanding of Bezalel's brain, mind, and soul, he now exhibited a will of his own: an automaton grown autonomous. With steely deliberation, he groped toward his neck and clasped the silver key. Still marking time, he cranked himself up to full power.

"Bezalel, no!" I screamed.

The golem seized the function dial, twisting it to modality three, intimidation, then to modality four, belligerence, and finally to the ominous modality five. Good God, what had I done? Had I allowed my blind ambition, my overweening ego, to jeopardize my daughter?

Bezalel marched inexorably forward, arms outstretched, the track lighting turning his eyes to embers. Summoning all my resolve, I vaulted into his path, then turned to Naomi and cried, "Run!"

As my daughter lurched toward the basement steps, the golem and I collided. modality five. Strangulation? Evisceration? Defenestration?

No. Something else entirely. With infinite tenderness, the creature embraced me. He squeezed his parka against my bosom, the pressure transmitting amity and affection, just as he had surely comforted his maker over three centuries earlier. I hugged the golem back. It was the ethical thing to do.

"Yes!" declared Naomi, punching the air with an exultant fist.

For a full minute the bodyguard and I remained in each other's arms. My tears flowed freely. The golem's cogs sang sweetly. With manifest reluctance he seized the function dial and twisted it back to modality one. Eventually the mainspring ran short of energy, whereupon Bezalel's head tipped forward, and he returned to his inert state, a static extension of his dead creator, waiting to be recalled to life.

***

Needless to say, I've decided against exhibiting him in the museum. The golem boasts such subtlety that I could never bear to see him become an object of idle gawking and smug academic chatter. Naomi agrees with this judgment, and I imagine Spinoza would, too.

Last week I moved Bezalel into my office. We stare at each other across my desk. Since the night Naomi and I experimented in the basement, I haven't wound the mainspring, though I suspect that before long I shall require modality five, affirmation, as will my daughter, marked to inherit the creature, and her husband-Naomi recently announced her engagement to an art historian-and their children, and their children's children. Spinoza would be the first to understand. Although he was the most self-sufficient of men, there were obviously moments when he needed something other than his all-encompassing Substance. True, the philosopher had his intellectual colleagues, but few of them really appreciated him, and he had his circle of friends, though he couldn't rely on them for nurturance. His solution, Bezalel, in no way diminishes my regard for the man. Indeed, the Paviljoensgracht golem makes me admire Spinoza all the more.

Tomorrow I fly to Paris, where I shall ascertain the authenticity of Blaise Pascal's personal roulette wheel before authorizing our French agent to acquire it at Sotheby's. I shall leave you with a thought that sustains me as I continue my quest to comprehend Bezalel. "All happiness or unhappiness solely depends upon the quality of the object to which we are attached by love." I needn't tell you who wrote that.

Now permit me to add a coda: keep on the lookout for philosophy artifacts-not only tangible relics, but also verbalized wisdom. Should you happen across an idea that strikes your fancy, bring it here to 25 Mount Auburn Street. We'll sit in the shadow of the golem and engage in reasoned discourse. And if, on exiting my office, you find yourself in need of an embrace, that can be arranged as well. As Spinoza liked to say, it's all the same thing.

The End

James Morrow is the author of nine novels, three stand-alone novellas, and two short-story collections. Although his obsessions are wide-ranging, he frequently writes in a satiric-theological mode. His best known works include *Only Begotten Daughter*, *Towing Jehovah*, *Blameless in Abaddon* (a *New York Times* Notable Book of the Year), *The Last Witchfinder* (called "provocative book-club bait" and "an inventive feat" by Janet Maslin), and *The Philosopher's Apprentice* ("an ingenious riff on *Frankenstein*" according to NPR). He has twice received the World Fantasy Award and twice the Nebula Award, as well as the Prix Utopia, the *Grand Prix de l'Imaginaire*, and the Theodore Sturgeon Memorial Award. An anthology of his short fiction is forthcoming from Wesleyan University Press. James Morrow is Guest of Honor of the International Conference for the Fantastic in the Arts, 2015.

GREEN CAT
by Christina St. Clair

The plant in the window looked like a green cat staring into the horizon planning its escape. It had only just arrived in the mail, flattened in a box that was lined with soggy wet newspaper. The receipt suggested the recipient ought to recycle the packing materials since they had been carefully acquired from secondhand materials in the town of origin: Athens, Ohio.

Athens, now there was a town to visit in Greece, not Ohio, but perhaps Susan Solstice could go there after she established herself in Sedona. She loved her new name so much more deep than her real name, Marya Pokeroski. Obviously Polish. Not that there was anything wrong with being a Pole. She was an American first, though. The Polishness was mere ancestry. She wanted life, not death, like what had happened to her grandmother who'd been gassed in a concentration camp. She also fancied she could channel a great Guru, a real heavy. Indeed, every night when she said her prayers, she asked Paramahansa Yogananda to come through her to teach wisdom to others.

Of course, she would have to charge a fee in order to live in Sedona, which probably wasn't cheap. But she would only charge those who could afford it and offer her service free to those with no money. Or maybe she could barter for goods. But she certainly didn't want someone's old clothes or dirty shoes. It would have to be food, and not Big Macs, either.

"2012," she said to her husband, Ben. "I can't believe twelve years have passed since we entered this millennium. Remember 2000 when the world was going to end and we were all supposed to die? Or at the very least we were supposed to endure massive computer failures, black-outs and food shortages."

"Marya, I don't see what this has to do with your moving to Sedona," Ben said.

My name, she thought, *is no longer Marya. I am Susan Solstice, the famous psychic.* "I *knew*, don't you understand, I *knew* way before the millennium got here that all was going to be okay." Marya thought perhaps it had been Paramahansa who'd told her in her dreams not to worry about the future. She could not reveal this to Ben. He was a stubborn but steady mechanic. He simply would not understand. "There is more to life than what we see," she added mysteriously.

"There's enough to deal with in this life if you ask me without imagining you've got special powers."

But I do, she thought and smiled benevolently at him. *You're lucky I am wholly loving and good, or I might blow you away with my thoughts.* It wasn't only that she'd been completely aware that nothing bad was going to happen at the millennium. She'd also recently had an amazing contact from a Hindu, probably Paramahansa. He'd told her to chew on betel leaves.

It had all begun with her having a lot of stress-related digestive problems. Planning her move to Sedona meant a lot of changes, including leaving

107

Ben behind. She loved her significant other, but she couldn't possibly allow herself to be tied to his monotonous life when there was so much more she could be doing with her psychic gifts. No one said transitions would be easy. The thought of being on her own had felt like death to her: death of her relationship with Ben, death of her life in the small town where she'd been born and raised, and death of her income as a personal assistant in a lawyer's office. All these things had to go, but her stomach had churned and gurgled and been so fussy that she'd begun to worry she might have colon cancer. Then one night in her dreams, this Hindu guru tells her she needs to chew on betel leaves three times a day, and that will take care of her problems.

Marya had never heard of betel leaves. Never! In fact, she didn't even bother to record the dream in her journal until much later when her stomach acted up again, and then she couldn't remember what plant leaf she was supposed to chew. Betel popped right into her mind, and when she looked it up on the Internet, she discovered it was some sort of herb used by Indians in Ayurvedic medicines to treat many different ailments including digestive problems. Perhaps equally significant, it was used by Hindu people as an offering to the gods. Also, the first offering a child made to his guru was sheaf of betel-forty leaves folded along the middle and used like a chaw of tobacco.

Then-and this could not have been mere serendipity-she found a nearby grower and ordered a plant. It had cost her twenty-five dollars plus shipping for a small betel vine that came in a three-inch pot. She'd since repotted it in good soil and inserted a bamboo pole for it to wind upon. She didn't immediately chew on the leaves because there were so few of them on the plant, but she did add little pieces to some chamomile tea. Her digestive tract settled down, and sometimes she had a sense of peace. She wondered if the betel might be having a narcotic effect.

"I am going to quit my job today," Marya told Ben. "I'm going to leave for Sedona next week. I've found a B & B where I can stay until I get myself established."

He groaned. "Why don't you just go for a couple of weeks? Take a vacation. You'll probably want to come back. Then you'd still have your job."

"I won't be coming back, Ben," Marya said firmly. Her stomach rumbled like a volcano about to explode.

That night, Marya plucked half a leaf of betel to chew upon. It tasted strong and aromatic. But by the morning her stomach had settled down, and she felt deeply peaceful. She called into work and told her boss she quit. She purchased a one-way ticket to Sedona on the Internet. So confident was she in her plan, the paperless e-ticket didn't even worry her.

When Ben walked through the door all covered in the usual smelly grease, she was in the bedroom packing.

"Go if you want," he said. "I'm not going to try to stop you."

His lack of resistance felt like a fence falling down. She realized then that he'd always stood in the way of everything she'd ever wanted, like the

109

time she'd planned to quit her job and go to law school rather than remain a lawyer's flunky. He'd insisted it made no sense for her to give up her income to study a subject she despised. At the time, he'd refused to accept the fact that she'd find the job much more bearable if she were the one, rather than her attorney-boss, making the money for the tedious tasks she had to carry out on his behalf. Ben might now be setting her free, but it was too late. She'd freed herself.

In the night she slept on the couch away from Ben, but his presence intruded into her dreams. The two of them were in a black spacecraft flying around a starry universe. A large white nebulous cloud that at first she thought was the Milky Way appeared, but it turned out to be a storm. They had to extinguish three candles so there would not be a fire in their space capsule to destroy them. Suddenly, the ship descended and landed in a big lake where it floated and turned into an inverted bowl. The bowl became a boat and drifted down a river and got wedged between a sandbar and the shore. A voice similar to Ben's called out, "Marya, I love you." She hopped out of the boat and began to swim towards a city of light. But suddenly she wanted to know where the river might lead, so she managed to free the boat. It swirled past her on a rapid current. A hand reached over and grabbed her fingers and pulled her to safety.

In the morning, a little stiff from having been cramped onto the couch, she went early into the kitchen, put out a box of Cheerios and a bowl of blueberries. She brewed the usual ten cups of coffee and set out three candles on the table to symbolize the dream candles. She lit them, saying special prayers for guidance, for love, for hope, and she waited for Ben to come down.

When he made an appearance, predictably on time, his eyes looked red as if he'd been crying. She poured his cup full and set out his cereal, just like every day. She waited for him to make a dismissive comment about the candles, but he simply ate his food, drank his coffee and looked sad.

Usually, they chatted in the mornings about the day before or about the latest news. His silence unnerved her and she had a moment of remorse, of missing him already, but she gritted her teeth, determined not to give in.

"I wish you wouldn't go," he finally said.

When Marya said nothing, he got up and took her hands in his. "Marya, I love you." Then, still holding onto her, he blew out the candles. "Please stay, please stay, please stay."

It was the fulfillment of her dream! Now there would be no fire in the space capsule. Now there would be a safe landing.

Marya stared at Ben's gnarled hands with the grease still discoloring his nails. The man worked so hard. He always came home on time, usually took a shower and helped cook dinner, then sat in his easy chair in front of the TV to watch CNN and sitcoms. With her. She thought about the endless phone calls to her bosses' clients and the preparation of never-ending law briefs and the summarizing of billable hours.

She jutted out her chin. "I'll stay, but I'm not

111

going back to my old job!" She stared at him stubbornly. "I'm going back to school." The last words launched themselves un-beckoned from her mouth. Silently she said *thank you, Paramahansa*.

"You're fifty years old," Ben interrupted.

"So what?" Marya replied. She plucked the other half of the betel leaf and chewed it thoughtfully, feeling more and more relaxed and peaceful with every swallow. "Maybe I'll become a herbalist," she said and smiled to herself.

The End

Christina St. Clair, www.christinastclair.com, award-winning author, features family relationships and spirituality in her work. She has published essays, articles and fiction. Her fantasy novel, *Emily's Shadow*, released from Blood Moon Publishing, a subsidiary of http://www.double-dragon-ebooks.com/, is soon to be followed by a sequel. Anovel about the power of human connections for good or ill, *Ten Yen True*, co-authored with Amanda Armstrong, www.amandaarmstrong1974.co.uk/, was released Feb. 20, 2013.

LA PLANCHADA
por Alfonso Arteaga

Como hojas secas esparcidas por el viento, así se esparcen alrededor del mundo diversos mitos o leyendas, los que siempre causan la zozobra del oyente, al cual le queda la duda si sera verdad o mentira el relato que escucha. Existe uno en particular el que yo corrobore de cierta manera, el relato del fantasma de La planchada.

Empezare por contarles ciertos eventos o apariciones de este personaje que ya es parte de las leyendas urbanas, y como fue su tragedia, la experiencia que yo tuve al toparme de frente con este ser.

Resulta que a principios del siglo xx, había una enfermera de nombre Eulalia quien siempre se conducía tanto en su trabajo, como en su vida diaria, con mucha propiedad. El amor por su trabajo era muy conocido. Una peculiaridad de ella era que siempre vestía con su uniforme perfectamente almidonado y muy bien planchado, de ahí su sobrenombre de la planchada. Ella se hacía querer por sus pacientes, pues siempre estaba preocupados por ellos de tal manera que aunque no fuera su turno de trabajo, regresaba para ver si sus pacientes habían tomado sus medicamentos.

Había un lazo muy fuerte que la unía con los enfermos por el tiempo que durara la estadía de ellos en el nosocomio, y trascendía en una amistad despues que el paciente salía. Varios hospitales se acreditan el haber contado en su nomina de empleados a esta peculiar enfermera: el hospital

113

Juarez de la cuidad de Mexico, otro de la ciudad de Guadalajara, y uno mas en la ciudad de Monterrey, las tres ciudades mas importantes del país del mismo nombre.

En el hospital Juarez de la cuidad de Mexico, se cuenta que ella estaba enamorada de un medico residente de nombre Joaquín, y que un día, este salio para hacer una especialidad. Jamas regreso, lo que propicio que la enfermera cayera en una depresion misma que la llevo a descuidar a sus pacientes. Por tal razon, fallecieron algunos de ellos. Se comenta que ella se enveneno en el mismo hospital, pero que despues de su muerte, regresaba a cumplir con las obligaciones propias de su trabajo, haciendo rondas nocturnas a los pacientes y proporcionandoles sus medicamentos. Algunos pacientes aseguraron que esa mujer, la que los atendio, fue muy dulce con ellos y mencionaron su impecable uniforme de enfermera blanco y muy bien planchado.

Otra version es que en la ciudad de Monterrey, tambien al Mexico, en el octavo piso del hospital de especialidades del IMMS, ella, por descuido derivado de la pena de haber sufrido un desengaño amoroso, se le olvido suministrarle los medicamentos a un menor de edad que estaba bajo su cuidado, y que este murio. Se dice que el padre del menor la había matado y arrastrado su cuerpo por todo el octavo piso del nosocomio. Yo creo que esta, tal vez, sea la version verdadera.

Pues ahí precisamente en ese hospital, hace algunos años, fallecio un hermano muy querido. Unos días antes del deceso, otro hermano y algunas

114

personas estabamos afuera del hospital escuchando sobre la tragedia que le había sucedido a la enfermera en el octavo piso. Y esa noche a peticion de mi hermano enfermo, nos tomamos unas copas, y ya entrada la noche, nos adentramos en el elevador para verificar, envalentonados por el alcohol ingerido, que habría en ese piso que se sabía estaba clausurado. Pero, al pasar por el cuarto piso, se abrieron las puertas, y entro una enfermera a la que no le vimos el rostro pues, inmediatamente que entro, nos dio la espalda. Mi hermano empezo a tratar de entablar una charla con ella, pero no contesto al cuestionamiento del seductor de mi hermano. Y aunque usted, amigo lector, no lo crea, en el octavo piso, la puerta se abrio, y ella salio del elevador como flotando pues no se le veían las piernas. Mi hermano y yo nos miramos uno al otro y bajamos a la planta baja, bañados en sudor frio, y con nadie hablamos del tema, pero eso si, esa experiencia me seguira por el resto de mi vida.

Fin

THE WOMAN IN THE IRONED DRESS
by Alfonso Arteaga
translated by Alexis Brooks de Vita

Like dry leaves scattered by the wind, this is how myths and legends scatter around the world, so that the listener remains perturbed by doubts of whether the tale he's been listening to is true or made up. There is one in particular that I can corroborate myself: the Tale of the Woman in the Ironed Dress.

115

I'll start by telling you about certain events and sightings of this person still told as urban legends, and what her tragedy was, and my experience when confronted by this being.

Early in the twentieth century, there was a nurse named Eulalia who conducted herself very properly, as much in her work as in her personal life. Her love for her work was very well known, and even more so her peculiarly starched and ironed uniform, which is why she was nicknamed The Woman in the Ironed Dress. She loved her patients and was so concerned for them that, even when she was not on duty, she would do the rounds to make sure they'd taken their medications. She had such a strong bond with the sick in her care that it survived as friendship even after her patients were discharged.

Several hospitals claim to list in their roster of former employees this particular nurse: the Juarez Hospital in Mexico City as well as the one in Guadalajara, and a hospital in Monterey, the three biggest cities in Mexico.

In Juarez Hospital in Mexico City, they say that she fell in love with a doctor named Joaquín, and when he left to specialize and did not come back, she became so depressed that she began to neglect her patients, and some of them died. They say that she poisoned herself in that same hospital, but after her death she came back to take care of her professional obligations, making her nightly rounds and giving her patients their doses of medication. Some of the patients swear that this woman who takes care of them is very sweet, and they particularly mention her white nurse's uniform, so well-ironed.

Another version is that in the city of Monterey, also in Mexico, on the eighth floor of a hospital known as the Mexican Institute of Social Security, after suffering a betrayal of love, a nurse forgot to administer medications to a child in her care, and he died. The child's father killed her and dragged her body all around the eighth floor. I believe that this one, perhaps, might be the true story.

It was precisely there, in that hospital, that a well-beloved brother of mine passed away. A few days before his death, another brother and some guys were hanging around outside the hospital, listening to the tragedy of the nurse and what happened to her on the eighth floor. Urged by my sick brother, we downed some liquid courage, and, at nightfall, got into the elevator to find out for ourselves what was on the eighth floor, which we knew was sealed off.

But when we got to the fourth floor, the doors opened, and a nurse got on.

We couldn't see her face because, as soon as she came in, she turned her back to us.

My brother started trying to chat her up, but she didn't respond to his lady's man come-ons and questions, and anyway, reader, my friend, you won't believe me when I tell you that on the eighth floor the door opened, and she seemed to float out on invisible legs.

My brother and I looked at each other and got back down to the ground floor bathed in a cold sweat. We never told anyone about this. But, yes, this experience will haunt me for the rest of my life.

The End

Alfonso Arteaga is the pen name of a father and son pair of writers. Father Alfonso Arteaga Rodriguez was born in Rioverde, San Luis Potosí, Mexico and is a nationally-known poet and songwriter for Spanish-language recording artists. The published author of over 130 poems, father Alfonso Arteaga also co-authored *Emblema*, a children's story of Monarch butterflies and a desert eagle, with Víctor Guzman, published by Progreso Editorial. Son Alfonso Israel Arteaga Martinez is the author of several essays in English and Spanish on subjects as diverse as Alien/Nation and Tango; he works in Immigrant Protection for the Mexican Consulate in Houston, Texas.

KEEPERS
by T.J. Weyler

I was too little to remember the first time Cheryl dumped us on Lost-and-Gone Mountain. The way my brother Henry John tells it, she got worn out on the two of us dogging her steps behind the shopping cart, making moon eyes at every box and can, forcing her to feed three on tips and then still looking at her pitiful. One night, she just piled us into her car and drove, up one twisting switchback and down another, until she found some turnoff that suited her and wove through the trees.

Henry John says I slept through the ride, even through the racket her old rattletrap clunker made. Not him. He could tell Cheryl had hit one of her moods. She stopped, made us get out, then slammed the doors and drove off without a word.

My brother sat down at the edge of her tire tracks, cross-legged like they did at preschool. He let me curl up and keep sleeping in his lap. That's just how he was. Saved energy until something could be done, not wasting one tear or question. Sat there all night, just watching for Cheryl to come back.

She did.

In the morning, she pulled up and opened the door, still without a word, and drove us back to the sloping porch of the house left to her by her daddy, the only thing she owned outright. She used to say he'd roll over in his grave, knowing she was letting some other woman's bastards eat her into debt. She used to say it a lot, especially in the days coming up to and heading away from a paycheck.

Henry John told me once that Cheryl *was* our natural mother, but her daddy cut her out of his will until she lied about it. I don't know. I looked and looked, but never could see anything of her in either of us. Even sunburned almost to withering at the end of July, her skin was not the same kind of brown as ours. And her hair might've been dark enough that more people called her brunette than dirty blonde, but it was bone straight when she bothered with it. Ours was curly black, thick enough that I got her comb caught and tangled for sure the one time I fooled with it.

She never once tolerated so much as a nickname, let alone getting called our mama. But then, only Cheryl ever claimed us as anything at all. And never once threatened to turn us over to the county.

Maybe she didn't want the paperwork. Or the questions. Maybe she figured her daddy could still hear well enough in the grave.

I do remember the *last* time Cheryl got fed up.

She finally got talking-close to one of the other women on her shift. That's something, 'cause Cheryl did *not* like other people nosing in her business or looking for excuses to. We'd ride with Cheryl over to their house and "play" with the Johnson kids so the two of them could carpool down to work without Cheryl worrying we'd burn down her house, and the other woman could avoid going back to her mean drunk of a boyfriend who had a car.

Mostly, the six of us kids gathered on the floor

120

around the sofa, out of the way so as not to block the sightlines from the easy chair to the half-busted TV. Eventually, one of the woman's people-maybe a brother or cousin-would shuffle out. He never spoke except to cuss the reception for being fuzzy or us for being loud, and he stank of the mangled cigar stub he rolled from one side of his mouth to the other. Henry John sat with his books and watched the rest of us. He couldn't read much more than his name, but he wanted to something bad. He didn't get involved unless the Johnson kids tried to hit me like they did each other, or if it looked like I was forgetting the two rules.

Rule One said to be the best kind of guest anybody could think of. Since we almost never got invited anywhere, house or table, making sure we could come back felt like the most important thing. Rule Two said we had to look out for each other on account of how nobody else would, Cheryl included. The rules turned out fine for Henry John, but the Johnson kids thought I must be simple the way I didn't play most of their fool games. But my brother didn't make rules for no reason, and I knew I always turned out sorrier breaking them than I ever did keeping them.

Well, that night the Johnsons were letting me have it for being the worst, time-wasting not-hider they'd ever seen. They said they didn't even hardly look for old stupid anymore and that if I wasn't going to play why did I bother asking to and on and on. They always did that, calling names at people 'til somebody got mad enough to fight. Didn't much care who, or why, or who won in the end.

Seems stupid now, but I was little, and tired of hearing the lie. I did *so* know how to hide, I told them, better than any old *Johnson*, and I'd show them when their kids' kids still couldn't find me.

I hid about the best anybody ever had in that house, in a corner that looked too small and obvious, but that had some piled up rags and boxes that I could squeeze around without messing up too much. So I heard them tumbling back and forth through the rooms, shrieking and fighting when they found each other, and eventually calling out *Grace, Grace*. But I said I'd show them, and I would. After awhile, it got quiet.

I hadn't decided how mad to be that they'd forgotten me, whether to just stay hiding 'til Cheryl came or storm out into the living room and call them all the names I knew.

Then somebody said, "I see you over there."

I froze. The stink of that cigar seemed to follow his words, but I didn't let myself cough or sneeze. I didn't move a single muscle but my eyes to see that he'd blocked the door.

"Come on out here," he said, "and you can have a piece of gum. Don't have to share it or anything. It's peppermint."

I don't know what I planned on doing, but my brother busted through behind him right then and knocked him clean to the floor.

"Grace!"

That was all Henry John said, but I lit out of that corner faster than a stray cat hit by a BB, and the two of us ran for the living room and straight into Cheryl and her friend. Cheryl didn't ask, just

122

caught us both by the collars and started beating. By the time the Johnsons heard that man cussing, she had us in the car.

Henry John got it worse than me. But whereas I whimpered and sniffled as much about the scare as the beating, he just pursed his lips real tight and said, "Don't you break rules again, Grace."

Cheryl kept pushing both hands through her hair and pacing at their door, so riled up that the other woman forgot all about the relative and kept trying to soothe *her*. "Kids will be kids," she said, and "didn't mean any harm" and such. But she kept peeking over her shoulder out to where we sat in the car on the clay and crabgrass lot of her front yard.

Cheryl paced and cussed and paced, not really saying sentences but just being mad all over, like usual. Until that lady went and did it. "You know how boys are," she said. "Got to put them in school. Must be about bored to death with his little sister."

Cheryl went stock-still. The woman shut up real quick, said goodnight and closed the door. When Cheryl got in the car, she and Henry John stared at each other in the rearview mirror for a long time before she turned the key.

Truth was, Henry John was supposed to be in regular school already. The fall coming up was going to be his third time skipping. Not that Cheryl ever tried to register us in the first place. On his part, my brother refused to leave me: the preschool-kindergarten was a different building than the other grades, and only went for half-days besides. I knew Henry John wanted to read because of the way he carried around his books and stared at them all the time, and by the way he practiced writing his name over and over when he thought nobody was looking.

When we drove around the first sharp turn from the Johnsons', a fat yellow moon started eyeing us from over the ridge. Close, too, about as big as my hand against the window, turning everything shadow-black and silver-echo weird in that light. I was going to show Henry John, but Cheryl's muttering rumbled louder and then louder.

"I'd like to see that," she said, frowning into the rearview. "Like to see them try and force me." She swerved onto a gravel road weaving in some direction other than the house. The car stuttered over some of the bigger rocks.

"About starved myself," Cheryl said, still watching the mirror and not the road. "Daddy would roll over and die again."

She took another turn that left the oaks and pines pressing against the windows, turning my hand and the leaves almost the same shade of moon-color as we whipped by. Branches shrieked something awful rubbing against the glass.

Henry John didn't say a word. He kept his eyes on the woman taking us deeper in and higher up. Probably onto a horse trail by now, or even one of the bigger hiking paths, the way the car bucked and wobbled. The moon itself got hard to see as the trees closed in and then rhododendrons started crowding across the outside until those big leaves about swallowed us whole.

I think that's when I knew.

See, the Johnson's loved telling whoppers, the scarier the better. And their favorite one told about a spot up the ridge called Lost-and-Gone where people dropped their problems. Problems like whiny not-hiders nobody wanted, so deep in the woods only monsters lived there. Monsters that ate guts and bone, that ate those problems down to scrap, not a trace left to bury.

Cheryl stopped the car, and all the air in my body got stuck in my throat, too scared to go the rest of the way out.

Henry John wore his real serious face from when he got to thinking our way out of things, like when groceries ran short of the next bill or somebody sent the law up to Cheryl's house to see if she really did have a couple of truant kids living there.

My brother and Cheryl looked at each other for a long, long time. I still can't say if she had plans to.... *do* something to us. Don't have words for the expression on her face.

I thought they'd both forgotten me. But then Henry John unbuckled his seat belt, and mine, and took hold of my hand. All in silence, without breaking eye contact with Cheryl. He opened his door and leaned against it so it'd stay open for me with the rhododendrons pressing so hard.

As soon as the door clicked behind me, Cheryl threw the car in reverse and near squished us anyway backing out to the road, spraying rocks and mud the whole way.

I guess.... .I guess I didn't really believe it, that she'd gone through with it. But even while I stared at the churned up ground and broken twigs, the crickets and other night-things started up again. And then Henry John tugged my hand and started walking.

"Come on," he said.

Just his matter-of-fact voice, from when we had to clean up the dishes and broken glass Cheryl threw when she had one of her bad days. From when we had to figure out how to make one half-rusted can into dinner for the week.

I've never been as practical as my brother. I busted out crying. 'Cause if Henry John had gotten into his practical place, it meant Cheryl wasn't coming back, at least not for a good long while. Henry John didn't shush me like most people would have, or even yell about how I thought gibbering like a baby was any help to anybody. Instead, he just took real tight hold of my hand and led me on through the woods. Didn't say another word. He lifted up branches to keep anything from smacking my face, but he let me cry, and stumble as slow as I wanted, as long as I kept moving.

All the directions looked the same: pine trees silver in moonlight, rhododendron growing uneven up and down the hillsides that rose in lumpy, uneven waves in the darkness. Looked like a lot of forest to me. A lot of shadowy, same-looking forest. But Henry John had my hand, and he moved just like he knew where he was headed.

I've never asked about that. Not in all this time. I'm not sure which would bother me more: that he wandered out there pretending to keep his little sister calm, or that he had some inkling of what we might find.

The house shocked me out of the last of my hiccoughing.

Well, more like leftover bones of a shack the woods were busy claiming again. Most of the back wall was buried in stones from at least a couple of mudslides that nobody had tried to clean up. Little trees grew on top of the thickest layers. Beyond that, it didn't look so different from Cheryl's place. Same sagging porch, wood greyed down by years of weather. Lights inside, even when most people assumed such a place ought to be abandoned.

Unlike Cheryl's place, smoke floated up from the chimney in little curls like the end of somebody's cigarette, and it smelled like restaurants. Like the good ones downtown, where people got to sit at a table with cloth napkins, and they gave out free bread. A couple of flies hovered around, like proof of food inside.

For that smell alone, I would have been willing to go without asking too many questions. It had been a long time since we had actual meat on our table, for any meal, even kinds that came from tin cans.

But then there was also the singing.

Cheryl never had use for bedtime stories or lullabies. Waste of time. From what I gather, no one in her family ever sang to her either, so I don't guess she thought we were missing much of anything.

The sound carrying over the darkness, following the tickle of all those good food smells, made a liar out of her. It was soft, and friendly, and all those things that picture books with happy families ever promised.

Henry John kept hold of my hand, though. We walked up to the house real slow and deliberate, all the way up to a screen door that didn't sit quite right in its hinges, letting more smells and light spill out all around the sides. My brother knocked, same as if we were waiting at a neighbor's on those nights Cheryl didn't realize she'd locked us out again. Some of them let us in, to wait on their couches not touching anything. Some of them left us on the porch. Henry John treated both the same way. If he thought I wouldn't get into too much trouble, he looked over his books. If I got to fidgeting pretty bad, he'd just look at me until I felt too guilty to so much as slouch.

The old woman came to the door humming. Opened the door like she was expecting us. She had deep wrinkles in her old brown face, the kind made for those billboards that went up around holidays reminding you to buy special food. The kind of face that if she smiled the whole way, you'd nod and agree to whatever. Funny, because she also looked like smiling didn't come natural to her. Between that and the way her song made me feel, I almost said *yes* right then, even though she hadn't asked anything.

She looked each one of us over real careful, almost as careful as Henry John puzzling out the words in his books. Then decided something that made her nod quick and pull the door open wider. "Y'all call me Grandmother," she said. She wiped her hands on the apron tied around the waist of her faded flowered dress and waved us inside. "Food's about done."

Henry John tugged me along.

If the outside of the house looked like a cave-in, the inside looked a lot like a regular house. The fabric on the sofa had gone nubbly, and the dark color probably used to be bright enough to claim as brown or maybe green. The easy chair in the far corner had just about worn out where somebody rested their head and legs.

But the old things were cared for. The blanket laid over the back of the sofa folded up neat, edge to edge, and the color matched somehow, so it was probably more than a cheap cover for holes or stains. The pillows on either end showed careful lines of stitches instead of spilling stuffing out of rips. No dust bunnies clumped up corners; no stacks of old plates or cups sticky with undrunk coffee cluttered up the tables or shelves. I couldn't find one cigarette butt anywhere.

The old woman hadn't waited to see if we followed. She'd gone back to the kitchen to fuss with pots and pans, each sizzle and whiff of smoke adding to that wonderful smell that pulled me harder now.

"Hungry, ain't you?" The old woman's voice carried in the small house. "Wash up."

My stomach took that as all the invitation necessary to start gurgling. But I looked to my brother to make the final decision.

Just then, a man walked in from another room. Well-not quite a man.

Most of him looked about the same as the men

129

who filled up the stools at the bar where Cheryl served food for a couple of months, or the cousin of one of her work-friends who tinkered with the car and stopped it belching black smoke. What I mean is, hard thick-ish arms with short fingers stained colors that wouldn't wash off anymore. He didn't wear any shoes at all. Must have been walking outside a lot, anyway, 'cause the mud and gunk around his toes didn't seem to bother him anymore.

Up to about the neck, he looked like plenty of other people we'd seen. But there, he sprouted out fur, lots of it, and the face sure didn't belong to anybody I knew. It looked sort of like he'd made a hat-mask out of the head of some animal. A bear, a wolf, a deer? When I looked too hard, my eyes felt itchy, and by the time I blinked them clear, things looked all re-arranged anyway. Big horns sprouted out of the top, and if I squinted, I caught tiny peeks of a regular, human mouth below the furry nose. Plenty of kids wore plastic masks when they went door-to-door at Halloween. Not us-Cheryl didn't want us bothering the neighbors more than we already did, begging like that's all we knew how to do.

This didn't look at all like a costume. No edges or lines made a seam between neck and fur, between human mouth and animal face. I'm not sure they really *were* separate anymore.

Then that mouth grinned wide enough to show teeth.

All of a sudden, food didn't feel like such a good idea.

"You behave, Forest," the old woman said. She

130

hadn't looked up from her pot.

The man ducked his head, horns and all. "Sorry, ma'am," he said. "Just been awhile." He took a seat at the table.

The old woman turned around to us, humming that tune under her breath. Maybe she thought it would make us feel better, but Henry John eyed her as fierce as any grown up and didn't move. The way he held my hand, I couldn't have gone anywhere if I'd wanted to.

After a minute, the old woman quit, rocked back on her heels. She didn't smile, but it looked like she wanted to. "All right, then," she said. "You take your time deciding."

She turned and went back into the kitchen and pulled out a couple of plates. "Haven't had company around here in a long time," the old woman said. "Used to expect someone to show up every now and again, have a reason to put the other plates out."

Nobody who knew Cheryl ever used special anything for me and my brother, even if they did let us into their houses. Hearing our forks scratch around those matching designs drove Cheryl right up the wall, and she'd forbidden us to so much as say hello to the people who'd been stupid enough to let us ruin them.

Charity is what she called that, and spit whenever she said it. My brother didn't have to tell me that the real reason was it reminded her that she didn't have special company dishes, or anybody trying to come over to use them.

We stood in the front doorway of the house and let the old woman pass us by with steaming plates

131

of food. She settled in with the almost-man.

And then Henry John heaved a sigh so big it made his whole body shake, and led us to a bowl full of cold water with towels hanging in front. Seemed pretty old-timey to me, not even having sinks.

"Don't forget the Rules, Grace," my brother told me.

***

The food on the plate looked a lot more solid than anything that ever showed up in the cans Cheryl brought home: a whole piece of meat, not even ground up or shredded and floating in broth to make it stretch. Dark enough to be beef or pork, but round, in some kind of shape I'd never seen before.

The whole thing smelled like dreams I used to have on the last days before Cheryl's checks came in. In those dreams, the neighbors all had so much cooking that the food smells would seep in through the walls and the floor and the ceiling, would tangle up in each other so thick I couldn't decide if I liked the smell or not. Then my stomach cramping would wake me up, and I'd cry until Henry John shushed me or Cheryl yelled about how she'd *give* me something to cry about, I kept on whining.

The old woman put a serving of onions and mushrooms on each plate, along with a serving of that fancy meat and a helping of greens that smelled so much like the woods at night I'd swear if I closed my eyes, I'd probably see the moon.

Everybody sat down, settled in their chairs.

"Give thanks," the old woman angling to be our Grandmother said.

Henry John and I folded hands and ducked because the couple of times we got to eat anyplace else, whoever cooked spent a long time talking about how we ought to be glad we all weren't swallowed up in fire that very second, useless to everybody like we were.

But when the old woman started, she seemed to be talking not to us, but to the food.

"You did not expect death," she told the meat on her plate, "but we know that your trust was no small thing. Without you, we could not continue. So we remember and are grateful."

Before I could look to Henry John and see if we were supposed to say anything, she stabbed her fork down into the meat on her plate and swallowed.

I didn't see the food go in her mouth, didn't see her chew. But the meat was gone from her fork, and her throat worked.

It took all my manners not to say anything and mind my business. I cut off a little piece of what was on my plate and took a bite.

The meat didn't taste like tuna, or spam, or casserole. It tasted... .soft, kind of, and deep, like it was telling me something it took a long time to say.

"Don't like liver?" The man with the animal head asked in an old-rocks voice. Without eyebrows, or whites to his eyes, I couldn't tell if he was poking fun or suspicious.

I shook my head. Then I realized that didn't say what I meant. "Never tasted it before," I said. "Sir."

Liver? I remember a couple of the restaurants Cheryl worked in served it: liver and onions, chicken livers. But I didn't remember it looking anything like this. Mostly, they fried it, or served up flat slabs coated in gravy. Did all of it taste like this?

"The only part worth eating," the old woman said. "Holds the songs of all the things this one survived, of every experience it had to overcome and learn from." Each time her fork rose up full, I'd see her swallow, but not the moment she bit down or chewed.

The liver held the songs.

I decided I liked it.

***

"You're tired," the old woman said, and held out her arms.

She looked comfortable enough on the blankets she'd spread over the sofa for my brother and me to sleep on, but I froze. With Henry John gone to do his business, nobody could help me decide what to do. The only thing stupider than walking up to strangers was running out into a bunch of woods I didn't know. Freezing up could turn out worse; Cheryl wasn't the only grownup who got mad when I hesitated.

The old woman's face didn't change. Not a one of those deep lines shifted toward a frown or a grimace. She looked me over real good, though. And started to hum again, that song that had pulled us right up the porch stairs. The song that probably led us to the house in the first place.

I don't remember moving. Her lap rose up around me, warm and soft, and the rumbling murmur of the song ran down my back as she

134

continued to sing. As we sat there, the old woman started running her fingers through my hair.

When the Johnson kids tried that, they yanked and yanked and laughed at me for going around with such ugly tangled stuff on top of my head. Only they had ever tried. Cheryl never had much interest in doing things like that.

Before "don't" got all the way to my mouth, the smooth rhythm of the old woman's hands against my scalp made the jagged feelings settle back down. And she kept humming. Her thick fingers never caught in the curls because she took her time. The years of calluses made her skin feel almost softer, like pebbles worn down by streams.

In the drowsy place the humming made, only one thought intruded, like a snag in a thread. In the kitchen, I'd seen the old woman's hands, and she had nails like mine-short and blunt, not like Cheryl's sometime work-friend, whose flower-colored claws were all the time scraping when she jerked me around for back-sassing or being in the way.

I'd have promised all over that I'd seen the old woman's fingertips. But every now and again, I felt the whisper-scratch of at least one very long nail as it slid across my head.

No matter. I made up my mind then, before sleep caught me the rest of the way and lost my manners for good. Rule One. "Thank you, Grandmother," I said.

That singing felt like a hand smoothing down each eyelid.

"You been real decent to me and my brother," I

added, "and that's more than most."

Her hands stopped.

"No really," I said, and had to stop because my yawn got so big. I didn't want her to think I was poking fun. "I... well, I never had a mamaw before, and... well, just thank you, is all."

After a long minute, her fingers got back to combing. "Sleep," she said again.

***

I guess I recognized the sound of that old clunker before I really understood what it meant. What with the pan full of dinner smoking with the uneven heat of the old stove, my mind only noticed that something besides wind was moving outside. By now Grandmother trusted me enough to cook most of the meals, unless we had meat. Those times, she cooked alone, still trying to keep the secret.

And then Cheryl peeled out of that car in her usual way-annoyed and in a hurry-as if me and Henry John had cooked up this extra chore, making her come all this way to get us.

The groan and creak of the car door slamming brought Henry John to the edge of the doorway. Papaw Forest had him studying snakes and owls, to learn listening without being caught. To be honest, Henry John looked kind of silly with his neck stretched out and head titled.

Nothing about the look on his face made me want to laugh, though.

We both knew whose shoes clomped up the yard toward the porch. That our weeks of living up here ended as soon as Cheryl reached the door. I think I'm the only one who knew why, though. What Grandmother planned, and what I had to do.

"Mind that pan, Grace," my brother said. "It'll burn."

And just like that, he made everything simple again. Rule Two meant looking out for us, no matter what.

I switched the pan to a different burner and stirred the smoke away, then wiped my hands on the towel and went to answer the door. Henry John melted back out of sight.

Cheryl didn't look different. I think I must have expected her to be happier, or sadder, or *something*, that us being gone would have shown in her face somehow. But aside from makeup that ran a little too dark and bags that said she'd been working double shifts, Cheryl looked just the same as the day she left us. As the day before that.

"Supper's about ready." I said it real fast to stop her from talking. I didn't want to talk to her, didn't want to hear her voice. Then I stepped to one side and nodded toward the hallway. "Come on."

Grandmother made me wash up and set the table with an extra plate, just the same as when Henry John and I came. Just like we'd been two more guests, not a part of this place. I closed the cabinet on the tall stack of unused dishes and felt... more like I had when we first stepped up to the door.

Henry John had vanished faster than a rabbit down a hole. He didn't come back out until the last minute, behind Papaw Forest, who for once wore the face of some regular old man. I don't know how anybody could look into it without feeling the not-true of it. The bland, smiling wrinkled old face scared me all the way through, like his toothy smiles. What played dress-up as a regular person? Every time he shifted to see something else, and I noticed the whites of his eyes, my stomach turned over.

Henry John had been passing plates for a full minute, his mouth set and his eyes down, when Cheryl jumped like somebody goosed her. That got everybody's attention.

Cheryl didn't like our eyes on her. Her mouth worked, holding in what she'd planned to say. But she couldn't stay all the way quiet, 'cause she finally said, "You've grown."

Henry John's eyes got cold in a way I'd never seen. He shrugged and passed the plate in his hands.

Grandmother thanked the food, and we started eating. All except Cheryl. She used her fork to push the beans, corn and greens around on her plate, but never lifted any to her mouth. "Never were picky about food, at least," she told her plate.

Henry John clenched his jaw but didn't look up again.

And all of a sudden, I knew why I felt so funny. The fight going on between Cheryl and my brother didn't include me. My growing didn't shock her. She thought of me as Henry John's, only worth noticing 'cause I had something to do with him.

I thought about how hard I cried that night in the woods, about how I'd never felt so bad. How I felt as lonely and strange at this table as I'd felt at all those others.

And I wished Cheryl dead and gone.

We could go back to our lives then, our new lives. Henry John would not sit twisting up his mouth. He would tell stories at dinner, about the things he'd learned to read in the wind or on the ground. Papaw Forest could put his wild head back on and not have to pretend for a dumb lady too stupid to know her makeup didn't match. I could stop feeling like this.

Right on cue, Grandmother started to hum.

***

It wasn't more than a day before one of those county cars nosed its way up a trail that hadn't been around before.

I don't know what Cheryl told them, but the good mood from the singing had sure worn off by the time she told it, 'cause three big men in matching suits climbed out. So did a woman with a suit-jacket and skirt of the same color. They all frowned at the house. The woman pulled out a clipboard and started writing.

Grandmother had me husking corn for dinner, so I watched from the porch stairs while one of the men tromped up the yard to Grandmother and shoved some papers at her. I guess he was used to people being more scared when they saw him coming or heard what he had to say, or maybe just acting crazy. When Grandmother didn't back up from him, shout, or even change expression, he kind of stumbled and got lost in his speech. Grandmother looked him over real careful, in her way. When she shook her head, the man jerked back, and only just managed not to run back to the car.

Then it was the woman in the suit-jacket's turn. She walked up with her clipboard in front of her, frowning like we should all be sorry. She started a speech that seemed to get more unhappy as she went. She called me and Henry John "the minors" and only talked about us as a set. I still don't know if she bothered to find out our names. She never once looked me in the face, even though I was sitting on the steps not two feet from her. She talked at Grandmother like she had a certain amount of time to fill, shooting out more and more big legal words none of the suit folks expects anyone else to understand, only to recognize as important and bad news.

The crazy part was that during the whole time she shot those words at Grandmother, as if she were trying to saw down a big tree in her way, the woman in the suit-jacket held her hand out in my direction, flicking it at me like I'd just come to her same as a stray dog.

I kept shucking my corn.

Not getting a reaction from Grandmother or me seemed to agitate that woman pretty bad. As soon as she chomped out her last words, she kind of rounded on me-I guess to see what was taking so long-and then stomped over and snatched up my hand. Really, just like one of those greedy Johnson kids lunging for the last crumbs in a chip bag.

She jerked me so hard she made me drop the corn I was holding, and scratched me besides. She held on tight, clear enough expecting me to buck, or yowl, or start twisting to get loose.

I stood up, slow and careful. Then waited, like my brother would. Rule Two.

"These minors are wards of the state," the woman spat at Grandmother. "Their parent or legal guardian has authorized us to take them both into custody. You'll be notified of your court date."

Grandmother didn't even have to lift her chin to look over the woman and hold my gaze.

"Goodbye, Grandmother," I said and let them haul me to the car.

***

Well, they drove us back down the mountain, then away to a bigger city where I didn't even recognize the names of the stores. The whole time that suit-jacket woman spat her legal words as if no one ever gave her even one chance to talk. She went on all about how Cheryl had *defied reason* (messed up bad) by not having any papers proving we'd been to school or even had our shots, let alone to prove we'd been put in care of some mountain people of *dubious* (real suspect) character when they had no blood ties to support the idea and probably couldn't even read besides.

She talked at me and Henry John and the other men who sat on either side of us in case we tried to jump out of a moving car.

They brought us to this building that smells like cleaner and where all the stains are too worn into the floors and walls to ever go away. Where the kids are worn out, too.

Henry John got his chance to learn to read books. Not like he hoped for, though. He told me the words were hard to keep up with-sometimes he forgot what it was he tried to read, which alphabet, which marks, or maybe fingerprints or sounds on the wind. And besides, he said that the parts he could figure from the books here were most time just suit-nonsense, things that weren't true or useful at all.

The suit people said something's wrong with my brother. They said that Henry John's brain was wrong, or that everybody waited too long to try to teach him. They thought of him as broken and useless, just like Cheryl used to, because he doesn't talk all the time. Started to look at him with that same expression she used to, those days before she drove us out to the woods.

They didn't listen when Henry John did have something to say. So a couple of nights ago, he slipped out when they weren't paying attention.

All the suit folks are real upset because no one's found any trace of him. I know where he is because before he left Henry John told me he was going back to Papaw Forest. He'll finish learning the secrets that made Papaw Forest... whatever he is, and be one too. Henry John wanted me to know that he'll still be my brother.

I can't say I blame him. The mountain is the right place for him.

The woman in the suit, or other ones like her, keep making me sit in rooms, trying to get me to tell them about Henry John and about Grandmother. Seems like no one's been able to find the way back to force her to explain. They don't listen when I tell them *Lost-and-Gone*. They've told me that it's important, that I'm not in trouble, that if I know anything about my brother I better tell before something bad happens and it's too late to help him.

They tell me that if I talk, they'll help me find someplace else to live, and the other kids here will stop picking on me. They ask if I wouldn't like to live in a nice house with a family. Wouldn't I like to belong someplace?

They don't have the first idea about anything. Grandmother's not coming down here for any trial. In fact, even if everybody doesn't forget there *is* a Grandmother in the next day or so, they won't find her house ever again.

Yesterday, they finally told me that Cheryl died. She went into work like usual and before she got to her lunch break, she just fell over. They're saying cancer, tumor, alcohol.

I say, *liver*.

Grandmother, bless her heart, really couldn't keep a secret that big for long.

"I don't understand you," the latest suit says. She slaps that folder with all the typed-up words closed and frowns at me. "I tell you your only *mother* has passed, and you just sit there?"

Not my only. I knew what Grandmother planned. She was going to keep us. Henry John and I would have had a real home, finally. But Cheryl came back. So Grandmother thought she'd fix it for us, make it better. Take your problems up her mountain, and they don't ever come back, eaten down to scrap.

I love her for trying, but I couldn't agree to it.

Because Cheryl came back. That's the closest

she could come to being our mother. That's why I wrote the note they found in her pocket. The one that's making them search for Grandmother so hard. I said poison, 'cause who'd ever take the time to think about fingernails strong and fast enough to take an organ without somebody noticing?

I broke Rule One doing that, lying about Grandmother when she was only trying to help. Not much of a guest; still lost them both. Grandmother asked me if I understood what choice I'd made, the last question she asked me in that silent way of hers. I told her yes with my goodbye. Because I do understand how it has to be. I made my choice.

At least Henry John got back. I didn't break Rule Two.

"She was the only kin you have left in the world, now your brother's left you," the suit woman tells me. "Where's your heart, girl?"

Not where they think. Never where they expect.

Grandmother taught me that.

The End

T.J. Weyler is the author of the acclaimed story "The Neighborly Thing to Do," published in *Apex Magazine* and *The Book of Apex: Volume Three*.

TAILED
by Ceschino

The small storefront jumped out at him, an unseemly blight on an otherwise appealing stretch of narrow street somewhere in Hell's Kitchen. He had veered off of Eighth Avenue when a traffic signal impeded further progress. Lost in his Blackberry, he had not paid attention to the street number as he rounded the corner. He looked around. His surroundings were unfamiliar.

It was a warm spring day, but not hot, and a cool breeze danced through the quiet Midtown street, playing with freshly green leaves and carrying the scent of strong spices from the hole-in-the-wall he spotted up ahead. His stomach rumbled, and he felt glad to have left the office relatively early on this particular Friday afternoon. He had just received a glowing performance review at the beginning of the week and closed two deals in the following three days, and he had an urge to reward himself with something new. The small establishment with an odd air about it, dingy though it looked, piqued his sense of adventure, wafting scents he could not recognize and exuding an air of the forbidden.

As he drew closer to the eatery, he slowed down. Something pungent hit his nose in waves, offset by the smell of the savory seasonings floating in the air, but not completely disguised. It reminded him of something he hadn't had in a while and preferred to avoid-chitlins or *menudo*, perhaps-a strong smell, unpleasant to him, unsuccessfully transformed by a small army of appetizing flavors and smells into something intended to be delicious. The sidewalk dipped down into a shallow recess in front of the establishment. A small man in an apron, stationed at the level of the sidewalk to attract visitors, smiled stiffly at him and nodded in his direction.

He hesitated, but his desire for a change of pace won out. He was always the first among his friends and at the office to try something new or unusual if it was placed in front of him-although he couldn't identify what type of food seemed to be inside. There was no sign anywhere in sight to identify his discovery, or even a helpful menu taped to the door. A blank steel plate was bolted above the wide entryway, appearing once to have held a sign or to be waiting for one.

He smiled at the short man in the apron, and the man blinked at him and nodded again.

"One?" the man asked.

"Ah-what kind of food do you have here?"

"Good food." The man blinked again, emphatically, and smiled.

Kevin chuckled and shrugged a bit. "I'm sure it is good-but where is it from?"

"From?"

"The food-where does it come from?"

The man furrowed his brow and looked in the direction of the restaurant.

"What country does the food you serve come from?" Kevin persisted, wondering whether he should drop the issue.

"Ahhh", the man said, and smiled. "Not from

here."

Kevin decided not to pursue the question further. "One seat will be fine."

"Outside?" the man asked.

"Uh-" Kevin started, looking at the smoky silhouettes shrouded in shadows inside.

"No room inside. Outside better," the man declared, ushering Kevin to one of two small tables in the concrete alcove nestled below the sidewalk.

Something heavy seemed to hang in the air drifting out of the place, and Kevin decided that maybe it was preferable not to go in, anyway. The air made him feel drowsy.

A waiter, slightly shorter and visibly younger than the man in the apron, hurried out to greet Kevin. "Hello, sir. What's your name?"

"My-my name?"

"Yes, sir," the waiter said, bowing slightly. His voice was high-pitched and sounded constricted, as though someone was squeezing his vocal cords.

"I'm...Kevin," Kevin replied, uncertain whether he should divulge any information about himself. The place was making him more uncomfortable by the minute.

The waiter stumbled over his words. "You wan food? Want-you want food? Sorry."

"Uh-yes. May I have a menu?" Kevin responded.

"Uuhhhhh...no menu. Sorry. Only-uuhhhh..." The waiter wrung his hands.

"Only what chef makes," the man in the apron interjected from behind Kevin, smiling down at them with a broad grin and his eyes closed, nodding with a jerk.

The young waiter smiled. "Ahhh-yes, only what-chee-chef-make."

Kevin's jaw hung slightly ajar for a minute as he tried to understand. "Oh. A daily menu?"

"Just what chef makes, sir," the man in the apron said again, a little more tersely.

"Okay..." Kevin wondered how long the restaurant had been in business. The wait-staff seemed to have no training or experience. "Well, what's the chef making today?"

"Uh..." The waiter shrank into himself and chuckled nervously. "Tay-tayyow-taayyoooww-taaaiiiilll. Taaiill," he managed, with a great deal of effort.

"Tail?" Kevin asked.

The waiter's eyes widened as he looked past Kevin. His jaw trembled a bit. Kevin turned to look at the man in the apron, who had fixed the waiter with a hard stare. The man turned and nodded at Kevin again with a close-lipped smile and his eyes closed.

"Uh-uuhhh....hooox taaiill. Hox tail," the waiter stammered.

"Ox tail?" Kevin asked.

Both servers smiled and nodded, the waiter bowing to accentuate his nod.

"That's fine," Kevin said.

The servers blinked and nodded again, smiling widely, and the young waiter hurried back into the restaurant, pulling a drape across the shadowy entryway and smiling again at Kevin as he did.

Inside, away from the entrance, Kevin could

148

hear muffled voices and muted shuffling. A low, scratchy voice entered the conversation, but he couldn't make out what it or the other voices were saying. The sounds of movement picked up speed, and the voices whispered more stridently. Kevin squirmed uncomfortably in his seat. The sounds grated against Kevin's ears like metal on asphalt.

Suddenly, there was a loud thud and a gravelly shout, which was quickly muffled. Kevin sat up, startled, as more thuds and clatters came from behind the curtain. The man in the apron shouted into the restaurant in a language Kevin didn't recognize. It sounded to Kevin like a series of quick growls and clicks. The waiter's head peeked around the curtain and bowed at Kevin.

"So sorry, sir-we drop something-food getting ready," the waiter sputtered.

"I-maybe I should go," Kevin said and pushed his seat back so he could stand.

The waiter and the man in the apron rushed to Kevin's side, both talking at once.

"So, sorry, sir. Please stay. Food almost ready. Sorry for noise. Food coming," the waiter pleaded, his hands pressed together in supplication. The man in the apron had a hand on Kevin's shoulder and gestured toward his table, smiling, blinking and tilting his head. Kevin looked at both men, uneasy, but gave in to their pleading and reassurances and sat.

The waiter vanished and returned within a few minutes with a steaming bowl of stew. After a moment's hesitation, Kevin spooned up a piece of meat and took a bite. Somewhat to his surprise, the

149

stew tasted fairly good. All of the ingredients seemed to be fresh. The meat was tender and free of fat and gristle. It had an earthy taste, but it was not too heavy. All in all, had it not been for the odd aura of the place and behavior of the staff, Kevin probably would have enjoyed the meal. He ate the rest of the bowl's contents, wiped his mouth with a napkin and turned to the waiter, who had been hovering nearby since he brought the food.

"How much?" Kevin asked.

"Huh?" The waiter stared at him.

"How much?" The waiter continued to stare. "For the food," Kevin added.

"Oh..." the waiter said, looking down.

"Fifteen," said the man in the apron.

Kevin put a twenty on the table, got up and walked to the subway station.

Shortly after arriving home, he collapsed on his bed and fell fast asleep.

His dreams were restless. He drifted in and out of sleep; a haze clouded his thoughts throughout. He found himself wandering through dark, grimy corridors, looking ceaselessly for something that he sensed was important to him but unsure what, exactly, he needed to find.

His body ached and he felt nauseous, but a small voice repeatedly assured him through his stupor that he would find his goal soon, and he would be better for it. Trusting the voice, he kept walking. His body navigated the maze in front of him without input from his addled brain.

Darkness yielded to shades of blue and then a steady gray, and he moved more slowly, worried that someone-who, he did not know-might apprehend him. He did not know why he should wish to avoid detection-he could not think of anything he had done wrong-but he felt with a certainty that if he was caught, he would forever lose what he was trying to find.

Gray shifted to blue and back to black. Kevin eventually felt himself come to a stop, and he slept heavily, dreamlessly.

Kevin felt stiff and limp when he awoke. He lay in bed for what felt like hours, unable to move.

He eventually managed to sit up, but a dull, burning pain seared through every muscle and joint in his body when he did. His head ached, as if his brain had swollen and been knocked around in his skull. The nausea from his dreams returned, and a different burning sensation-sharper and more insistent-began to spread through his stomach, which growled as if to show resentment. Overcome, Kevin flopped back onto his bed and stayed as flat as he could until the pain and nausea subsided.

It took another two attempts before Kevin could stand and make his way, unsteadily, to the kitchen for something to calm his stomach.

He felt as if he hadn't eaten in days, and as the burning and sickness subsided, a ravenous hunger took their place. Kevin squinted at the clock on the stove, his eyes refusing to adjust. It was one o'clock. Kevin's head started to pound again, and he returned to his bed with some orange juice and a piece of toast.

He checked his phone. It was Sunday. Kevin nearly dropped the toast and checked again.

151

Definitely Sunday. He had slept through Saturday.

Kevin didn't feel well enough to go anywhere for the rest of the afternoon. He stayed in his apartment watching TV and poking around on his tablet before turning off the lights in the evening to go to sleep early.

Kevin woke up Monday morning feeling a bit groggy, but the soreness from the weekend was mostly gone. Triumphant over whatever had hit him-it must have been food poisoning, he decided-Kevin opted not to use up a sick day.

In his office building, riding the elevator, Kevin overheard two women who worked on his floor whispering loudly about someone seen in the lobby. "Did you see that guy?" asked Sofia, whom Kevin had known since they interned together.

"Which one?" the other woman asked. Kevin did not know her name.

"Some guy in a long coat. He had his whole face covered up-hat, scarf, everything."

"How weird. It's so warm today-it's like 80 degrees out."

"I know. But that's not all. He was just standing there. I actually got in earlier because I needed to do some work-another Monday morning deadline from your favorite person-"

The second woman rolled her eyes in a show of supportive exasperation.

"-and that guy in the coat was there at like six this morning," Sofia concluded.

"And he was still there just now?"

"Yeah. And he was standing in the exact same spot. It's like he hadn't moved at all."

"Ewww. Creepy," said the second woman, drawing the words out for emphasis.

The elevator arrived at their floor, and the two women laughed and apologized to Kevin for their conversation.

"Sounds creepy, all right. Maybe I should start carrying pepper spray," Kevin replied with a smile.

The women headed toward their offices, and Kevin spent the rest of the day lost in his work, feeling lightheaded but otherwise unfazed. His dreams that night were undisturbed.

He woke up Tuesday morning feeling lucid, the haze from the prior three days having vanished. When he tried to talk, however, he found that his throat was dry and his voice rough and hoarse.

Kevin was not sure if he had caught a chill or if this might somehow be another effect of the food he had eaten at that strange restaurant. After cursing his inability to catch a break after the prior week's success, he passed an uneventful day at the office, intermittently clearing his throat and startling a few co-workers.

In the evening, Kevin called a college friend, Bryce, to catch up. They talked about work (going well for both of them), family (alternately prosperous and struggling) and dating (not going so well for Bryce, while Kevin admitted that his schedule didn't allocate any time for romantic prospects).

Having exhausted the customary subjects, Kevin brought up the shady restaurant from Friday. Bryce agreed that the illness must have been brought on by the food-perhaps the meat was a little *too* fresh. After a few more minutes of chatting, Kevin and Bryce said goodbye and, with a smile, Kevin hung up and looked out the window-and froze. His smile faded.

Someone was standing on the sidewalk, staring. Staring up in Kevin's direction. Was he staring directly at Kevin?

Was it even a man? Kevin realized that he could not tell. He had assumed, based on the person's clothing, that it was a man, but the stranger's face was completely hidden from view between the brim of a fedora and a heavy scarf. A long, beige coat hid the person's physique.

Kevin remembered the conversation he had overheard between Sofia and the other co-worker in the elevator. A man standing in the lobby for hours, completely stationary, wearing a long coat, a hat and scarf.

Kevin frowned and moved away from the window.

Could this be the same man? There were millions of people in the city-he could not conclude that just because this person was wearing cold-weather clothes, it must be the man who was standing in the lobby of his office building. That was a different part of town. Maybe both people were homeless.

But how many homeless people were really walking around in the late spring's warm weather bundled in heavy coats and scarves? And what about the standing and staring? And if it was the man from the office building (had Sofia even been sure it was a man?), why was he now outside

154

Kevin's apartment?

These questions hung over Kevin as he fell asleep and remained with him when he woke up Wednesday morning and during his commute. He saw no sign of the stranger-he assumed this could not be someone he knew. None of Kevin's co-workers mentioned a new sighting. Kevin mused, despite himself, about the possibility of being followed by a private investigator (but why would one be interested in his activities or whereabouts?) or, worse yet, being stalked (who on earth would be stalking Kevin?).

The possibility of having a stalker struck Kevin as more disturbing than scary. He was no warrior, but he could handle himself, and the stranger, while stout-or perhaps only bundled in multiple layers of clothing-was short and failed to intimidate. At worst, Kevin initially pictured a scenario in which he would have to tackle the stranger and call the police, or ask someone nearby to make the call for him, and that would be the end of it. But then Kevin thought of killers hiding guns and knives under their clothing-and recent reports of violent crime in the city, while generally isolated to parts of town that Kevin did not frequent, did little to assuage Kevin's fears. And then Kevin remembered the recent spate of news stories about drug addicts attacking people-for money, or because of heightened aggression, or for some other reason, Kevin did not know, as he had generally ignored the reports.

Kevin began to worry. As he fell asleep that night, he resolved to go to the police if he saw the stranger again. He hoped that he would not, that it would turn out to have been a coincidence. Someone wandering through town. Perhaps a couple of different people.

Kevin drifted off and awoke in the middle of the night with a sore throat.

He shuffled groggily toward the bathroom and turned on the light. It shone harshly and hurt his eyes, and he winced as he moved toward the sink, trying to ignore the glare. He raised his head to look in the mirror-and let out a cry of fright.

Black orbs stared at him vacantly, nestled in skin a grayish-beige like tree bark, bordered by stiff, bristly hair. Sharp teeth jutted out from a protruding jaw in the beastly face in front of him.

Kevin stumbled back and shouted again, and came to in total darkness. He was sitting in his bed, drenched in a cold sweat.

Kevin stayed in his bed, trembling, breathing heavily, until his heart calmed down and the sweat began to dry. He was afraid to look down at his body, or to raise his hands up to the level of his eyes. The memory of the face in the mirror was vivid: leathery, lined skin, the forest of fur covering the head and shoulders, pointed ears, and two wide nostrils set directly in the face, rather than in a nose. The wide mouth, lipless and downturned with curved teeth like fangs. And those eyes...two jet spheres with slivers of dull gold set in a ring, staring forlornly back at Kevin.

Kevin almost felt pity for the sadness in the face-almost, but the fear was still too great.

Tremulously, Kevin climbed out of his bed and

made his way, slowly, to the bathroom. He stood in the doorway for several minutes, afraid to turn on the light. Eventually he flipped it on and, refusing to look down at his body, approached the mirror. He braced himself, took a deep breath, and stepped in front of the sink.

His reflection, quite human, in need of a shave but still perfectly normal, looked back at him.

Kevin sighed and closed his eyes. He splashed some water on his head and buried his face in a towel. He remained in front of the sink for several minutes. He was nervous about looking in the mirror, wondering if something he did not want to see might appear, but equally apprehensive about looking away and letting the soothing normalcy of his reflection out of his sight.

Kevin turned off the bathroom light and made his way to the kitchen.

He turned on the light and got himself a juice from the fridge. He stood in the kitchen for a while, sipping and thinking about the dream he had just had, the restaurant and the stranger in the coat. He could not shake the feeling that all three were somehow connected.

Kevin tried to dispel from his memory the face he had seen in his dream, but turning his thoughts away from the dream kept leading him back to the restaurant and the stranger. He mulled over the strange sequence of events, his mind lost in uncomfortable thoughts.

And then something did capture his attention. Something strange about the floor in front of the apartment door, just beyond the kitchen. No, not the floor-something strange about the light on the floor.

Kevin frowned, walked closer to the door, and felt a chill.

Two thin shadows blocked the light that streamed from the hallway through the sliver of space between the bottom of the door and the doorframe. The shadows were about shoulder-width apart, like legs. Someone was standing on the other side of the door.

Kevin's breath caught in his throat. He stood frozen in place.

The person was not making a sound, but Kevin knew that there was someone there.

Why was someone standing outside his door? How long had the person been there? Whoever it was must have heard Kevin moving around inside the apartment.

Kevin stood for what seemed like hours, unwilling to move and alert the person on the other side to his presence, but at a loss as to what to do. Whoever it was had been there for who knew how long-maybe even while Kevin was asleep. What difference would it make if the person stayed outside the apartment? But maybe the person on the other side was waiting for an opportunity to break in.

Kevin wondered if it was the stranger in the coat. Who else could it be? First at his office building, then on the sidewalk outside his apartment, and now outside his door. It couldn't be three different people. He was being stalked.

He began to feel faint. He told himself to calm down and think of what to do.

He had never had to deal with this type of situation before. Should he call the police? Should he signal the doorman downstairs? Would the doorman even come up?

Kevin started to doubt whether the shadows were truly cast by a person. They were so still, and the hallway was so silent-could there really be anyone out there? Maybe the superintendent had left some tools in the hallway, and they were casting a shadow. Even so, Kevin thought, what harm could it do to ask the doorman to check?

But then, as badly as Kevin wanted to call someone for help, he was afraid to let the stranger-if it was the stranger, or a person at all-hear his voice. If someone was following him, he did not want to confirm that the stalker had found his home. Kevin's thoughts began to blur together, swirling incessantly in his head.

Kevin woke up on his feet. He blinked and squinted in the morning sunlight.

The light was on. He was in the kitchen. Kevin rubbed his eyes and felt a headache coming.

Why was he in the kitchen? With a jolt, he remembered and looked at the door.

No shadows. There was nothing there. Kevin jerked his head around and scanned his apartment warily. Nothing was out of place. He was alone. Had it been a dream? First the mirror, then the shadows under the door-could that have happened? But he would not have woken up in the kitchen if it had not happened, would he?

Maybe he had fallen asleep in the kitchen after getting something to drink and then dreamed about

159

the shadows under the door. One bad dream after another. Kevin decided to ask the morning shift doorman, Frankie, if the doorman working the night shift had seen anyone.

"Last night? No, there's no note about anyone coming to visit you. Or anyone else, actually."

"Huh," Kevin replied. "I thought there might have been someone outside my door last night, but I couldn't tell. Thought I'd check."

"Yeah, like I said," Frankie replied, "nobody had any visitors last night. If anyone was walking around, it was probably someone from another apartment. You know it's our policy not to let visitors past the front desk unless we get an okay from whoever they're visiting."

"Yeah, I know," Kevin replied. "Just wanted to be sure. Thanks."

Kevin went to work. He wondered if he would see the stranger on the way there or if he was letting his imagination get the better of him. Perhaps there was no "stranger" at all. He decided to go back to the restaurant during his lunch break.

He did not know what he expected to find. Perhaps the stranger in the coat would be sitting inside, shrouded in the heavy haze that filled the place. What would happen if he actually found the stranger there?

A possibility he did not expect, however, was finding nothing whatsoever.

Kevin arrived at the place where the restaurant had been only six days earlier and found nothing at all. The man in the apron was gone, as were the waiter and the shadowy figures within. There was no restaurant. Just an empty space available for lease.

Kevin was now sure that something was quite wrong. He had definitely eaten a meal here just the week before.

He remembered the faces of the servers perfectly. He could still smell the smoky air that had sifted out to the sidewalk from the now-vacant space. Kevin decided to talk to the police.

That evening, he called Bryce and told him about everything.

"And the police wouldn't let you file a report?" Bryce asked.

"No," Kevin said. "Since nothing's actually happened, aside from the food poisoning, they told me to keep an eye out and let them know if I see any of those people again-the one in the coat, the guy in the apron, the waiter. They agreed that it's all suspicious, but without any ID of the guys at the restaurant or the one in the coat, they can't really go after anyone. There are no witnesses who saw someone at my apartment building, and they couldn't find any recent record of someone having been at the address where the restaurant was last week. They figure the people I ran into were just squatting and trying to make some cash by selling a hot meal to passersby. I guess the worst crime they've really committed is selling food without a permit, and the police can't do anything about that if they don't know where they are."

"Man," Bryce replied. "Well, I hope those losers packed up and left town. Did you tell your family about all this?"

161

"No," Kevin responded. "My mom worries about me too much as it is."

"I can't blame her," Bryce laughed. "Well, you stay safe, man. Let me know if I need to come over there and rough someone up."

Kevin laughed and thanked Bryce, and the two wished each other a good night.

Kevin awoke slowly on Friday. His body felt limp and heavy. He struggled to open his eyes, and even when he managed to open them, his vision was so blurry that he couldn't see. There seemed to be an odd shape in front of him, but he could not tell what it was. He lay on his bed for a while, waiting for his vision to clear. When it finally did, he stiffened in terror.

A face stared down at him. Kevin wanted to scream and jump up, to push the intruder away, but he could not move and he could not make a sound. His arms and legs lay flat against the bed, heavy and useless. His throat felt tight and sore. Try as he might, Kevin could not sit up, could not roll over, could not even look away.

And then he realized whose face he was looking at. Kevin's own face was staring down at him, placid, unflinching. Unblinking.

Kevin felt his heart skip a beat. His breaths became short and raspy. The jolt of seeing his own face above him gave him enough strength to lift his head, and he looked down at his body to see why he could not move.

The sight gave Kevin another shock. Kevin saw a short, stout torso with leathery skin and bristly fur, long arms, and short legs with apelike

162

hands for feet.

Kevin let out a guttural moan. The sound was inhuman.

The stranger with Kevin's face smiled, his eyes cold and empty. He straightened up and walked toward the front door of the apartment.

The stranger was wearing a suit. Kevin's suit. He straightened his tie-Kevin's tie-and walked out of the apartment, locking the door behind him.

The End

Ceschino's (an Italian nickname pronounced "Chess-Kino") first published short story, "The Argument," appears in the anthology *Love and Darker Passions* by Double Dragon/Blood Moon Publishing.

MERCY AND THE MERMAID

by Alexandra Dairo-Brown

It was a hot summer day when Mercy was born. The sky remained cloudless while the sun beat down on the pale blue Florida water where Jolene gave birth.

She had decided to go down to the beach with her friends in an attempt to cool off from the sun's assault. Jolene walked toward the water and was relieved at its cooling touch. She waded deeper into the welcoming arms of the ocean and stopped right before her feet could no longer touch the bottom. Jolene leaned her head back and allowed her body to follow, floating on top of the water. The lemon yellow dress Jolene wore became one with the water and cascaded outward, making her seem ethereal.

Suddenly Jolene raised her head out of the water, causing her body to jerk upright. She began to have shooting pains. Jolene attempted to walk toward the shore, but her legs were barely holding her up. She called to her friends between screams while she stumbled closer to them. As Jolene's friends started rushing to her, it seemed as if the baby began to rush as well and forced Jolene to push her out.

Jolene reached down as her child emerged into the watery world and, grabbing her tiny arms, lifted her up to the sky. All Jolene could remember before she fainted were her daughter's big, beautiful eyes and her friends' voices saying in amazement, "Lord have mercy," which is how Mercy got her name.

As the years passed, Mercy grew into a beautiful little girl. She was an upbeat child who was pleasant to everyone she came in contact with, even her stepfather, Obie, who gave her nothing but sour looks. Mercy never knew her father and had grown up with her mother and Obie since she could remember. Obie never showed anything but meanness and was known around their town by exactly that reputation.

Mercy was forced to work on the family farm when she turned five. Obie believed Mercy's duties were simple: she was responsible for the chickens and everything that had to do with them. As Mercy got older, her responsibilities tripled. She had to take care of all the animals, which included the chickens, horses, cows, and pigs along with household chores. At twelve years old, Mercy had become hopeless because of the treatment she received from her stepfather. Obie blamed Mercy and Jolene for anything that went wrong in their lives. Jolene never said a word in defense of herself or her daughter because Obie had instilled fear in her, and Jolene was afraid that he would leave her if she ever opposed him.

***

On the fifth day of spring, the sun came out and warmed everything it touched. Mercy woke up to a warm house, which made her feel like jumping out of bed and running towards the ocean, which is exactly what she did. Ever since her birth, Mercy seemed to have an affinity with water. She had learned to swim on her own and went down to the

165

beach any chance she got.

Mercy was not afraid of the elders' tales of what lurked in the ocean at night. If anything, those tales of people disappearing in the depths of the water intrigued Mercy. When Mercy got to the beach that day, she was out of breath from running all the way there, but she kicked off her shoes and jumped straight into the water. Mercy let herself float on top of the waves while she stared at the sky and hummed a song she had learned from her mother.

As the minutes changed to hours and other children from town began to migrate to the beach, Mercy knew she had to get back to her house and start her daily work before her stepfather came looking for her. Reluctantly, she swam back to the shore, picked up her shoes, and prepared for what awaited her when she got home.

***

Mercy took her time getting home, since she knew she was already in trouble. As she walked along the trail that led to her house, Mercy heard the sound of a horse trotting toward her. She quickly put her shoes on and climbed the nearest tree, which overlooked the path she had taken. Mercy knew that it could only be one person coming from that direction, and she did not want to run into him.

Minutes later, she heard old Obie yelling at the horse to hurry up. When he neared the tree Mercy had taken refuge in, she distinctly heard him say, "When I get my hands on that gal, I'll barely leave her breathing!" This terrified Mercy because, if her stepfather decided to live up to his threats, she knew her mother would not intervene and save her. Mercy stayed in the tree all day, and as nightfall approached, she was forced to come down only because she almost fell out of the tree when sleep overtook her.

Mercy tried to assure herself that everything would be fine, but she knew better. As she opened the front door of the small house, she peeped inside and quickly scanned the room. Out of nowhere, her mother came from behind her on the porch and hurried her inside.

"Where have you been?" Jolene half-screamed, half-whispered. "Don't even answer that. I can tell by your wet clothes where you been. Do you know that Obie been looking for you everywhere? He thinks you're being lazy and don't wanna work, which means you can't stay here. I just don't know why you want to go an upset him like that. I do what I can to keep him from getting on you, but I don't know what more I can do. He said if I don't find you he's gonna leave us. I've been looking all over for you all day. I just can't... "

Jolene stopped in mid-sentence. She finally looked at her shivering daughter and saw the terror in her eyes. "Awww Mercy," she said and hugged her daughter. "Don't worry, baby. Everything will be okay."

Jolene led Mercy to the kitchen and fixed her a bowl of hot stew. She grabbed a blanket from her room and draped it around her daughter while singing, "Oh Mama Kay just bring me up. Up from my burdens of this world. I just can't take this. I've had enough. Enough of the pain that spins and twirls." Jolene continued to hum the song over and over until Mercy finished her food and went to bed.

***

The next morning, Obie burst into Mercy's room, ranting. He yelled and threw things around the room, but Mercy did not move. The thought of being ignored drove Obie into a furious rage. He charged toward the bed and shook Mercy, but she only made a whimpering noise.

Jolene rushed into the room and felt Mercy's body. She was met with damp, cold skin and went to the kitchen to get some hot water from the kettle on the stove. When Jolene came back, she saw that Obie had taken Mercy out of bed and was trying to force her to walk. "I know you just being lazy! Stop all this carrying on and get up before I beat you," Obie yelled.

Mercy collapsed to the floor, and as Obie raised his foot to kick her, Jolene threw the pot's hot water at him. Obie stumbled backwards, screaming in pain.

"Can't you see she's sick?" Jolene yelled.

Obie lurched toward his wife but landed against the door frame, instead. Jolene jumped to avoid Obie and raised the pot in self-defense.

"I should kill you and your daughter," Obie screeched. "I know what hurts you worse, though. I'm leaving." Obie walked out and put his clothes in a dingy cloth duffel bag while yelling the entire time that he never should have married a woman nobody wanted. "Your own child's father didn't want you. I must have been crazy to take you as my

168

wife," he thundered.

Jolene gathered Mercy off of the floor and put her back in the bed. She was afraid of Obie leaving her, but the fear of losing her daughter outweighed anything else.

Obie walked toward the front door while wiping his face and looked straight back at Jolene. The two stared at each other in silence for a moment, and then Obie said, "Ya'll both are ungrateful and lazy. I'm leaving now, but I'll be back for what's owed to me." And with that, he left.

Jolene stared at the open front door while she held Mercy. She pulled herself off of the floor and went to get some herbs to help her daughter. While Jolene stood in the kitchen soaking the herbs in hot water, she thought about Obie's last words and cried. Through the tears, laughter emerged, and Jolene realized that she still had the most important thing in her life: Mercy.

As Mercy recovered from her illness, Jolene worked to regain her independence, but it seemed as though nothing was in her favor. Mercy resumed her part of the work on the farm when she was able to, but the family was just scraping by. One evening, Mercy went to the beach when all of her work was done. She was exhausted from the day and felt overwhelmed by the life that was given to her.

Everyone had left, since nightfall was approaching, so Mercy had the water all to herself. She waded out a little way and looked up at the moonlit sky. She closed her eyes and began singing, "Oh Mama Kay just bring me up. Up from my

169

burdens of this world. I just can't take this. I've had enough. Enough of the pain that spins and twirls." Mercy felt the waves push her further from shore but paid no attention. She continued singing until something brushed against her leg.

Mercy opened her eyes and looked around. She realized how far out in the water she was when her toes were barely touching the sand, so she turned around to start heading back to shore. Mercy had taken three steps before she was able to stand up straight, and she stopped dead in her tracks. Directly in front of her was the most beautiful woman she had ever seen.

Her hair flowed downward in curly pink spirals that seemed endless. Her honey-brown skin glowed against the moonlight with flecks of sparkles that bounced joyously off the water. She wore hundreds of pearls that were daintily placed on black strings that created dozens of necklaces and bracelets, and her purple halter top was embellished with diamonds. She was flawless.

Mercy could not take her eyes off of this woman who smiled at her with such kindness. She blinked and finally spoke to the woman. "Who are you?"

The woman's smile grew wider as she answered. "You know who I am. You called me to you in your song."

Mercy looked around and remembered that she was the only one at the beach.

"Don't worry; no one else is here," the woman said as she circled Mercy.

At that moment, Mercy realized that this

170

woman was not standing up on legs because she moved too swiftly around her. She panicked and attempted to swim toward the shore.

The woman grabbed Mercy's hand and asked her, "Don't you remember me?" Mercy continued to back away. This woman was who the town elders always talked about. The thing that took people and made them disappear. This woman was not a human woman; she was a mermaid.

***

Mercy could not move fast enough away from the mermaid, who now had a sorrowful look on her face. The hurt in her eyes made Mercy stop because this look reminded her of her mother whenever she cried. "You're a... you're a mermaid?" Mercy stuttered.

"Of course I am," the mermaid answered back.

"But I thought the stories about you weren't real?"

"Of course I'm real. Don't you remember me?"

"No. I've never seen a mermaid before."

"I saw you when you were born and helped you to your mother" she explained. "The waves were going to carry you away, so I lifted you towards your mother's arms. I've been waiting for you to call me for many years."

Mercy looked at the mermaid in amazement and felt a sense of familiarity. "Mama Kay?" she asked.

"Yes, that's me. You remember me now."

Mercy smiled because she recalled a faint memory. Jolene had always told her the story of how she was born. Mercy asked every time about

171

the pink sparkles in the water, and her mother always laughed and said, "Pink sparkles? There weren't any pink sparkles in that water. You don't remember nothing from that day anyway. You was just a little baby trying to go along with the waves. That's why you so fond of water."

Mercy let the pink sparkle memory go, looked directly at the real thing and said, "That was you."

Mama Kay continued to smile and twist her pretty pink curls.

In the midst of Mercy's amazement, she realized how late it had gotten. "I really don't want to go, but I have to be getting back now," she explained.

"Yes, I know. Someone is coming down the beach as we speak to look for you."

Mercy looked toward the shore and saw no one.

Mama Kay spoke again. "Please come back to me soon. Just sing my song, and I will come to you. But make sure you are alone."

Mercy nodded her head in agreement and watched as Mama Kay quickly disappeared beneath the black waves. Before Mercy could blink three times, Mama Kay had resurfaced with a gift. "Here; take this. It is my gift to you so you won't forget me again," she said with a smile.

Mercy opened her hand to receive a beautiful coral pink pearl. She clutched it to her chest and thanked Mama Kay profusely. "I'll never forget you again, Mama Kay, I promise. And I'll come see you again as soon as I can."

Mama Kay nodded and let the sea engulf her

majestic body.

Mercy walked hurriedly through the water, still holding her gift tightly in her hand. When she reached the sandy beach, her mother greeted her. "I thought you would be here," she said, hugging her daughter.

"I was just on my way home, Mama."

Jolene looked at Mercy's wide smile that made her smile, herself. "Let's get you to the house before you get sick again." As the two headed home, Mercy kept her fist tight around the pearl and quickly glanced back at the calm water.

A few days had passed, and Mercy was looking for an opportunity to see Mama Kay again. As Mercy and her mother headed into the house for dinner, and daylight faded into shades of midnight blue, Mercy noticed the worried expression on her mother's face. "What's wrong, Mama? Didn't we get enough work done today?" she asked.

Jolene shook her head from side to side. "No matter how much work we do, it's never enough with only two people doing it." There was silence for a moment, and then Jolene continued. "Don't worry, baby. We won't have to live like this forever."

Mercy wanted their lives to be better, and she also wanted her mother to be happy. She thought about the gift Mama Kay had given her and decided to share it with her mother. Mercy got up from the table and walked quickly to her room. She kneeled beside her bed and reached deep into a hole she had cut in her mattress.

Mercy felt around for a minute, and then her

hand touched something smooth and round. She clutched it in her palm and snatched her hand away. There in the center of Mercy's mahogany hand was the coral pink pearl.

Jolene walked into the room and stared at her daughter sitting on the floor. "Mercy, don't let me put my burdens on you." Jolene knelt beside her daughter. "I promise we will live like queens one day."

Mercy looked at her mother and smiled. "Well, maybe it will be sooner than you think, Mama," and she opened her hand to show the pearl.

"Oh my lord! Where did you get this?"

Mercy knew she could not tell her mother the truth, so she explained that she found it beneath the sand on the beach. Jolene stood up and yelled with joy. "Do you know how much this will help us? I'm going straight to town tomorrow and pay off Joe, the landowner, and maybe buy us a few things, too."

Mercy was filled with happiness, knowing that she could make her mother so happy. Jolene hugged her daughter and walked toward the kitchen. She stopped abruptly and turned around to ask, "Is this the only pearl you found?"

"Yes," Mercy answered.

Jolene thought for a moment and said to herself, "Well, maybe there are more; then we would really be able to do some things." She looked at Mercy and asked, "Do you remember where you found it?"

Mercy answered quietly, "No, ma'am."

"Well, we'll just count this as a blessing, and if

174

we do right, we'll be blessed some more," Jolene said.

As soon as the sky turned a hazy orange, Jolene set out for town. When she arrived, she was able to trade the pearl for a nice sum of money. She went to Joe's house to pay her past-due rent. It took Jolene about ten hard knocks to get Joe to answer.

Joe opened his door and immediately began yelling, "Don't you know what time it is? If you come here to ask for more time to pay, just get away from my door right now."

Jolene took a step back and smiled. "Well, no, Joe. I come to pay you what I owe and a little extra for the coming months."

He looked Jolene over as if she was trying to play a trick on him. Jolene extended her hand and held out a small black pouch.

Joe took the pouch and glanced inside. He leaned against his door frame in shock. "Well, where did you get this money from, gal? Did you marry you a rich man while we was all sleeping?" he asked.

"No, Joe, I didn't marry no man. I'll be on my way. You take care, now," Jolene answered and turned around to head home.

Joe stayed where he was and looked in the pouch again before yelling after Jolene, "Well if you did get this from some man, you did better than when you was with Obie!"

Jolene kept walking with her head held high and prayed that she would never hear Obie's name again.

Later that evening, Mercy decided to head to

175

the beach. Jolene was busy setting up the new curtains she had bought. "I'll be back soon, Mama," Mercy said before closing the door.

"All right, baby. I'm cooking us a big meal tonight," Jolene answered.

Mercy smiled and closed the door. When she arrived at the beach, she looked around carefully to make sure no one was there.

Mercy walked into the cool water and smiled because she felt at peace with the sound of the waves washing up against the shore. The soft sand spread beneath her feet as she stepped lightly upon it. When Mercy was waist deep in the ocean, she began singing, "Oh Mama Kay just bring me up. Up from my burdens of this world. I just can't take this. I've had enough. Enough of the pain that spins and twirls." She closed her eyes and waited until the waves carried her further from shore.

She heard a familiar hum come from beneath her feet that sounded like the song she had just sung. Mercy opened her eyes and watched as Mama Kay surfaced. She was just as elegant as the first time Mercy saw her and even more beautiful.

"I'm so glad you came," Mama Kay exclaimed.

Mercy smiled and said, "I'm so happy to see you." Mercy told the mermaid what had happened since they last met and why she gave the pearl to her mother. "I really wanted to make her happy, and I knew that your gift would do just that," Mercy explained.

"Well, I'm glad that you were able to do that for your mother. You know there are many treasures that lie beneath these waters. I can show them to you, if you come with me to my home," Mama Kay said.

Mercy thought about all the beautiful pearls and diamonds that could possibly await her if she went with Mama Kay. She knew that she would see things she never imagined and meet other mermaids who had lots of stories to tell. At the same time, Mercy remembered the stories she had been told about people disappearing and was afraid.

Mama Kay sensed her hesitance and said, "I know what you have heard, but we have only taken people from this world to our own who wanted to go. If you don't wish to go with me now, that is fine. I just enjoy your company, and I had hoped to show you my world."

Mercy smiled and answered, "I would love to come with you, but I can't leave my mother all alone."

Mama Kay understood and said, "Well, let's talk for awhile, then."

Mercy was relieved that Mama Kay was not upset and began to tell her all about her life with her mother and Obie. Mama Kay listened attentively and was shocked to hear how badly Obie had treated Mercy.

When the moon rose high above the water, Mercy decided to head back home before her mother came looking for her. Mama Kay asked her to wait while she dove beneath the sea-green waves. When she returned, she handed Mercy an oyster shell with five gorgeous pearls of different colors.

"Oh, Mama Kay, thank you so much! You

don't know how much this means to me," Mercy said.

"I know, child. That is why I am giving you these gifts. You are honest and loyal which are traits that are hard to find these days. Take these pearls to your mother, but remember never to mention where you got them from."

Mercy hugged Mama Kay. "All right. I'll see you soon." She swam back to shore. Mama Kay watched as Mercy hurried from the beach and then allowed the water to carry her beneath its folds.

As Mama Kay and Mercy disappeared into the night, someone had been watching behind the two big stonewashed rocks that led to the beach. Obie had been lurking around town when he heard about Jolene's newfound riches. He followed Mercy to the beach, where he heard the song she sang that summoned the mermaid. He also watched them together and saw the treasure that Mercy took away with her. Obie's greed consumed him, and he plotted a way to get all of the treasure Mama Kay had in her possession.

Jolene and Mercy had an extravagant meal that night. After the two finished eating mashed potatoes, baked ham, pot roast, collard greens, sweet potatoes, cornbread, and a rich chocolate cake, they sat back in their chairs and laughed. "Did you ever think we would eat this good?" Jolene asked her daughter.

"Naw, I thought we would be eating vegetable stew and baked potatoes the rest of our lives!"

The two chuckled some more and thought about their lives over the years. Suddenly a loud knock on the door interrupted them.

"Who could this be so late at night?" Jolene inquired as she walked to the front door. Mercy followed close behind her mother and waited in the hallway. When Jolene cracked the door open, she stumbled away in fear of what she saw.

Obie pushed the door with his big hands and let it slam against the wall. His menacing frame created a shadow that covered Mercy's cowering body. "What ya'll looking all scared for? I told you I would be back for what ya'll owe me." Obie walked past Jolene and Mercy and went straight to the kitchen, dropped his dirty cloth duffel bag, kicked off his boots, and began eating from the various dishes on the table. "Oh, ya'll must have known I was coming, since you cooked all this fancy food," he said between mouthfuls. "Come on and sit down here. I got to let you know something."

Jolene and Mercy moved slowly toward Obie and slid into the chairs furthest from him.

"Well, I heard about all the money you done got you, Jolene. Yeah, the townspeople been talking like they always do. So I want to know exactly how much money you been hiding from me while I worked so hard to take care of you and your child."

Jolene looked at him to speak, but before she could open her mouth, Obie continued. "Well, I know it's a lot, since you can afford to pay off Joe and fix all this food. I seen Mercy coming from the beach tonight." He paused to reach for some cornbread. Mercy looked panicked as he continued. "Yeah, I seen your friend, too. I didn't believe my own eyes at first, but when I watched you leave with that treasure, I just knew I was seeing right, and all those stories was true." He chortled.

Jolene looked at Mercy, confused, and said, "Now look, Obie, I don't know what you want, but we ain't got nothing for you here. Whatever you seen wasn't really what you saw, so you can just get on up and... ."

Obie cut her off. "I knows what I seen, and don't you try to tell me different. I know you in on it, too, so just get on up and get me what that mermaid gave you."

No one moved. It was as if they were at a stand-off. Obie was convinced that he was about to become a rich man. Jolene was unsure of what Obie was talking about, and Mercy was extremely frightened. She knew that Obie was telling the truth, and her secrets were exposed. She was afraid of what would happen to Mama Kay.

Since no one was moving, Obie got up and grabbed Mercy's arm, stood her up and pushed her away from the table. "I said go gets me what I came for."

Jolene stood up and said, "Get your hands off of her and get out of here! We ain't got nothing for you. You done gone crazy with all this talk of mermaids and such. Just go ahead and leave, Obie!"

Obie looked at Jolene and laughed. "Well, since you say I'm crazy, I might as well show you how crazy I am." He walked hurriedly to the living room and began knocking things down and ripping off the new curtains. He continued his rant all the way to Mercy's bedroom, where he tossed her clothes drawers to the floor and scrambled through them. Unsatisfied, he flipped over her bed and continued his search. "I know it's in here!" he yelled, out of breath.

Obie crawled on the floor looking for the slightest glimmer of the treasure he saw at the beach earlier. Jolene held Mercy while they stared at the hurricane in their house. Obie was on his hands and knees, searching along the floor. He leaned against the overturned mattress and was just about to go tear up the rest of the house when he saw a wide slit in the side of the bed.

Obie looked at Mercy, who now had a look of terror in her eyes. Obie smirked and shoved his hand inside the mattress. He felt around frantically until his hand touched something hard and small. He grasped it and pulled it out to see what he had found. Inside Obie's hand was a wooden box. He opened it and saw the tiny round pearls. Mercy began crying, and Jolene was in shock.

"I knew what I seen! Ya'll tried to make me look crazy, but here it is right before your own eyes," Obie said. "Don't act surprised, Jolene. You had a plan the whole time I was with you. Now I'm going to be the richest man on this earth." Obie closed the box and put it in his pocket.

Mercy looked up to her mother and whispered, "Mama I was gonna tell you about the pearls, I swear."

Jolene comforted her daughter and stared at Obie menacingly. "All right. You got what you wanted. Now leave."

Obie looked right past her and retorted, "I'm

not leaving till I'm good and ready. I'm gonna go back down to that beach and catch that mermaid right now. We'll see how much of that treasure she really has." Obie ran out of the house toward the beach and left Jolene and Mercy in tears.

The water at the beach had turned as black as the sky. The stars reflected on the ocean and danced across the slow-moving waves. Obie dragged a small fishing boat into the water and paddled a little ways out. His raspy voice barked out the song he had heard earlier, and he waited.

Mama Kay surfaced behind the boat and looked around for Mercy. Obie turned and saw the glistening pink hair of the mermaid. "I got you now," he murmured and cast his fishing net over Mama Kay's head.

She began to sink under the net. Obie had connected weights to it, but she was able to swim away before she was captured. Obie pulled the net up while the agile mermaid stared at him angrily from a distance away.

"Where did it go?" Obie asked. He looked all around him but saw no trace of Mama Kay.

The mermaid pushed an oncoming wave toward the boat in her fury, which caused it to fly across the water to shore. Obie's plan was thwarted, but he dared not go back into the water. He sulked during his walk back to Jolene's house and had no kind words for anyone along the way.

Obie kicked the front door open and stated that he would not be leaving until he captured the mermaid and her treasure. These words burned Mercy's ears as she watched her mother try to appeal to Obie.

Jolene wanted Obie out of the house for good, so she tried everything to get him to leave the next day, including kindness. Mercy could not imagine going back to the misery she had experienced when her stepfather was there. In the middle of the evening, she dropped everything and left home.

Mercy did not know where she would go, but she knew that she could not stay there. She waited for everyone to settle down to dinner, and then she rushed into the ocean and swam as far as she could. The song she sang to Mama Kay was filled with despair. Mercy waited but did not see her friend.

She sang the song again, and minutes later, Mama Kay appeared at the top of the water, about a mile away. She saw that Mercy was alone and swam toward her cautiously. "I am so sorry, Mama Kay. My stepfather saw us the last time and found the treasure you gave me," she explained.

Mama Kay listened to the whole story and made a suggestion. "Well, I told you before that you could come with me to my kingdom and live a joyful life. Why put yourself through all of this misery?"

Mercy thought about it. "Well, I can't leave my mother. I just don't know what to do." The young girl began to cry. Mercy's tears joined the ocean water that flowed toward Mama Kay, who felt her pain.

"This is the last time I will make you this offer. Come with me and be happy. There are hundreds of mermaids you will meet and thousands of things I can show you. Leave your sorrow and pain here and come with me to paradise."

Mercy let her inhibitions go and agreed. Mama Kay gently took her hand and wrapped her flowing pink hair around her as they took off beneath the waves.

Mama Kay showed Mercy all the treasure she could imagine. She introduced her to other mermaids who were just as beautiful and kind. Some had blue hair with green emeralds strewn about and all kinds of pearl jewelry. What interested Mercy the most were their long green tails and the way the mermaids were able to swim so elegantly.

Mama Kay took Mercy across the ocean to different countries where she saw many wonderful things and met other humans who were accompanied by mermaids. They told Mercy of all their adventures and how glad they were to be there instead of on land.

Even though Mercy thoroughly enjoyed every moment she spent with Mama Kay, she still missed her own mother. One day, after the two had traveled back from Asia, Mercy told Mama Kay that she wanted to return home. "Can't I just see my mother one more time?" she asked.

"If you leave my world to return to your own, you can never come back," Mama Kay stated.

Mercy tried to imagine a life without her mother forever and could not handle another moment away from her, despite the hardships of life. "I think I'll have to go then, Mama Kay. I appreciate everything you've done for me, but I need to be with my mother."

Mama Kay was hurt, but she knew that Mercy would become miserable if she stayed. "I will take you back, but you have to understand that time passes slowly down here. When you return to land, you will be much older than you are now." Mercy understood and let Mama Kay continue. "You are twenty-two years old now. Young men will be looking to marry you, but your family name has been tarnished. Take this," she said and handed Mercy a large yellow bag filled with hundreds of pearls. "This will attract plenty of young men, and you will be able to live a wonderful life. Be aware that your stepfather will do anything to get your riches. There will also be many young men trying to pursue you that are like him. Do not trust any of them except the man named Marcus. He will not take advantage of you and will love you eternally."

Mercy thanked her longtime friend and prepared for her journey home.

Mama Kay wrapped her lustrous pink hair around Mercy and brought her back to the Florida shore. Mercy gave Mama Kay a hug and said her last goodbye. As she emerged out of the water, she felt a strange sensation. Her body began to grow taller, and she matured into a young lady right before her very eyes. Mercy looked herself over and ran toward her house, tightly clutching the yellow bag of pearls.

Once Mercy arrived home, she was shocked to see how bad everything looked. The roof of the house was falling apart, the garden was full of weeds, and the animals looked sick. She stepped up on the porch and knocked on the door. Jolene answered and looked at her daughter strangely. "Can I help you?" she asked.

"Mama it's me, Mercy!"

Jolene looked harder, and her face lit up. "Oh the lord has kept me in his favor!" she screamed.

They embraced each other and shed tears of happiness.

"Come on in here before Obie gets back," Jolene said.

Mercy was saddened by the mention of his name and asked why he was still there.

"Well, once you disappeared, he thought you had gone to get treasure from the mermaid, but when you never came back, he just settled right here because he was so miserable. He decided to make my life as horrible as possible," Jolene answered.

"Well, times have changed, Mama. I'm gonna fix everything up for you, and we'll get rid of Obie," Mercy said.

The next day, Mercy went to town to exchange a few pearls for money. She bought plenty of things for her mother and got the house and farm fixed up. Mercy hid the bag Mama Kay had given her in the flower bed outside of her window, so Obie would not be able to find it.

He searched every day around various parts of the house but failed each time to find anything. The young men around town started coming to court Mercy, when they saw how well off she was. Mercy did not entertain any of them, since Mama Kay told her what they were after.

One winter afternoon, Mercy was walking

briskly through the market with a bag of groceries when a tall, copper-colored man with broad shoulders accidentally bumped into her. He apologized and helped her pick up the oranges that had begun to roll away. Mercy thanked him and started to walk off when he stopped to ask her name.

"My name is Mercy," she answered.

He introduced himself, saying, "It sure is nice to meet you, Mercy. My name is Marcus."

She finally looked up at his face and saw the light in his eyes. Mercy had met the man Mama Kay told her about.

She was beyond pleased and enjoyed his company over the cold winter days. Marcus was passing through the town in search of work and had found a good job on one of the big farms. He decided to stay on longer at that farm, since he met Mercy.

Months passed, and Marcus asked Mercy to marry him. She did not think twice before accepting his proposal. Mercy knew how kind and generous Marcus was. His handsome face made her blush whenever he entered the room. Marcus was taken by Mercy's beauty, as well. Her spirit allowed him to be himself around her.

Mercy and Marcus were married in May. They purchased a home right next to Jolene's house and began to live their lives happily together. Mercy had told Marcus the entire story of Mama Kay and her life growing up. No one associated with Obie, so it was a surprise to Marcus when Obie stopped by their new house with a gift.

187

As Marcus welcomed Obie into his home, Obie handed him the gift and waited for him to place it on the table behind them. Once Marcus turned his back, Obie hit him over the head with a hammer he had tucked in the waistband of his pants. Marcus dropped to the floor unconscious.

Obie then went on a rampage through the house, looking for any form of money. He searched through everything but found no trace of jewels, money, or gold. As Obie walked out of the house in a rage, he knocked over a blue and white vase that was handpainted with decorative ocean waves. As the vase broke against the floor, colored pearls spread across the wood.

Obie stopped in his tracks and stared at the floor. Marcus started moaning and made an attempt to get up. Obie panicked and hit him again with the hammer. This time, Marcus no longer moved.

Obie gathered all of the pearls, put them in the yellow bag and took off. An hour later, Mercy returned home from town. She called to Marcus from the porch but got no answer. The front door was wide open, so Mercy cautiously looked inside. Her house was torn apart, and her husband lay lifeless on the floor.

Mercy rushed to his side and tried to revive him, but it was too late. She held his head in her lap and screamed. Tears drenched the top of her dress, and she looked around frantically. Mercy saw the broken vase by the front door and knew that Obie had come to her house to steal her gifts from Mama Kay, the pearls and her husband Marcus.

Word about the murder spread through town

quickly, and everyone was on the lookout for Obie. Jolene helped her daughter make funeral arrangements and consoled her throughout the day. The night before the funeral, Mercy ran to the beach. She stumbled into the water and cried, "Oh, Mama Kay, just bring me up. Up from my burdens of this world. I just can't take this. I've had enough. Enough of the pain that spins and twirls." Her tears once again intertwined with the ocean water and struck the mermaid's heart with sadness.

Mama Kay appeared immediately and rushed toward Mercy, who blurted out what had happened to Marcus. Mama Kay cried with her, and her tears created a turquoise glow around them. She took off one of the rings on her finger and pulled out the white pearl the ring held as its centerpiece. "Take this pearl and place it on the lips of your husband. If we have not run out of time, he will come back to you," Mama Kay said.

Mercy took the pearl from her sparkling hand and thanked her. "Hurry before it is too late," Mama Kay responded. Mercy swam as fast as she could to shore and ran back to her home.

Marcus lay in the casket dressed in a black suit. The funeral was set to start the next morning, so no one was there except Jolene. Mercy burst through the front door of her house and went directly to the living room, where her husband was. Jolene came in from the kitchen and asked what was going on. Mercy did not respond. She hurriedly placed the white pearl on Marcus's lips and took a step back.

She clasped her hands together in front of her face and prayed while Jolene hugged her, thinking that her daughter had gone insane from grief. Mercy moved her hands and stared at the pearl. The white pearl that Mama Kay had given her slowly started to change its color to a deep blood red. Once it had completely turned, Mercy took her husband's hand in her own.

She removed the pearl from his lips and watched as he opened his eyes. Marcus blinked twice and sat up. He looked around his house and at his beautiful wife and finally said, "Don't worry, honey. I'm right here with you."

Mercy began crying tears of joy as she embraced her true love. Jolene was astounded that Marcus had come back to them, but she knew deep down that the enchanting mermaid named Mama Kay had helped her daughter once again. Jolene picked up the scarlet-colored pearl and went to bury it outside in the garden.

Before dawn approached, Obie scampered toward a boat that was left on the beach. He pushed it to the water and jumped in. Obie squeezed the yellow bag containing the pearls he had stolen between his feet.

As he paddled the small boat along, a strong wave rocked it hard, which made Obie fall backward and lose his grip on the bag. The pearls spilled out and scattered in the boat. Obie dropped the paddles and tried to gather all of the pearls. A single pearl was swept overboard and sank to the ocean floor.

Obie looked into the endless ocean for that one little pearl. Another wave hit the boat and caused it to overturn. Obie fell out of the boat, along with his stolen goods. He struggled to stay afloat while still trying to catch all of the pearls that were spiraling toward their birthplace.

Obie was hit by another wave and was forced beneath the current. He tried to resurface, but something was holding him down. Mama Kay had caused the waves to crash into the boat, and now she was pulling Obie to her.

He looked down at her with a frightened expression, and she smiled at him and asked, "Are you the one who brought so much grief to Mercy?"

Obie was too stunned to answer.

"Are you the one who tried to capture me with your fishing net?" she asked.

Again Obie did not answer, but the guilty look in his eyes told it all.

Mama Kay pulled Obie so close to her that she could hear his thoughts. "You wanted these little pearls so badly that you were willing to kill for them," she said as she fingered her pearl necklaces. "Well, now I'll leave you in the place where they were created." And, with that statement, Mama Kay pushed Obie toward the darkest part of the ocean floor and swam away.

Months later, Jolene moved in with her daughter and new son-in-law. Jolene began to live a carefree life and occupied her days with gardening and sewing. She had a very well-stocked garden and was proud of the fruits and vegetables that she tended. There was a part in the garden, however, where nothing ever grew. Not a flower, weed, or food ever blossomed in this area. Jolene and Mercy had tried planting things there, but nothing ever came from their efforts.

In that particular area of the garden, the pearl that took death from Marcus's lips was buried. That scarlet pearl had sealed death inside of it, where it remained. Jolene stayed away from that part of the garden now so she could avoid the curse that lay beneath the soil. As she finished picking a few tomatoes to include with that night's dinner, Mercy and Marcus were walking along the beach. They sat down to watch the sun set and let the water brush against their feet.

Mercy closed her eyes and snuggled close to her husband. Marcus saw something floating in the distance but paid no attention. He often looked for the mermaid who saved his life but never saw any definite sign of her. Before the couple got up to leave, a yellow bag washed up on the shore. Mercy recognized it immediately and went to pick it up. Inside were the remaining pearls Mama Kay had given her.

She showed Marcus and looked toward the middle of the ocean for her life-long friend. Mercy saw no one but smiled anyway and waved.

As they walked away with their treasure, Marcus turned around and saw what resembled pink sparkles on top of the water. He smiled, knowing deep down that the special mermaid was still there. He waved, and the couple left to enjoy the rest of their lives together.

Mama Kay smiled back at Mercy and Marcus, waved her hand high in the air and swam back to her water-world kingdom. No one ever saw Obie again, but they always suspected that the creatures of the deep made him disappear.

The End

Alexandra Dairo-Brown is an award-winning critical essayist on African and Diaspora Literature and a high school teacher in the Houston Independent School District. "Mercy and the Mermaid" is her first published short story.

MY BOGEYMAN
by Novella Serena

The screen door was unlocked.

Maybe there is no need to be concerned. After all, no one comes out this way. Not very often. There wasn't much out here at this time of year but a lake and the remains of summer vacations.

Her shaking hand pulled the door open. The hollow white aluminum frame squeaked as it swung, *like nails across a chalkboard*, frazzled heartbeats in its wake.

The paneled main room was dark, save for the late afternoon sun indirectly offering the room a gray-blue glow. Everything looked normal. *Some messes look the same no matter how many times someone has rifled through them.*

Papers sat stacked on the counter and a card table, more or less-it was hard to remember how things had looked when rushing out that morning-the way they had been left. The sink, unfortunately, was still full of dirty dishes.

Would some disturbance be found in the bedroom? She pushed the half-closed door open into the compact whitewashed space. It looked green, perhaps because she was queasy with anxiety. *Nothing.* The abandoned bed looked just as it had, its covers waiting, open like a dejected lover's empty arms.

Pajamas and used under-things sat in their makeshift laundry pile in front of an out-of-commission hamper. Folded sheets and towels tucked neatly in the remaining three walls of a formerly four-walled container looked and smelled as fresh as when they'd been placed there a few days ago. The bathroom, ever the stoic cramped sanctuary of the clapboard house, looked-and smelled-the same. *Old plumbing has a way of keeping clean spaces from putting their best self forward.* The room didn't quite stink, but the mustiness of the poorly vented space was an annoyance.

All is safe. All is well. Nothing could be found to prove that the outer door was more than the oversight of a rushed woman. *What a silly mistake.* How fortunate that it was made in this lakeside valley of retirees and absent timeshare-holders.

Dinner was nothing special. *One of the nice things about seclusion is that there is no one to question the quality of one's meals, habits or practices.* The food was plain, the water with it blessedly plainer, but gourmet food was waiting in the city. *Why complain about the few downgrades this space offers?* It was pleasant.

The sun went down. A big Texas moon was going to rise soon. It would be nice to put work aside for a while and go sit under it. *A log in the fireplace.* No snow out here, but the autumn chills were starting. It would be nice to have warmth waiting after watching the moon rise.

The best way to pass the time after the sun went down until the sky was dark enough to catch not only the moon but also the stars was to piece together a puzzle. An intricate one sat on a small rug under the coffee table. In half an hour, it would not be whole, but it would look a lot more complete than it did at the moment.

Working the puzzle was fun. Her feeble fire burned valiantly and the shadows of the puzzle pieces danced wildly in its glow as they were picked and placed on the mat.

There was no sound. Maybe the lack of any sound should have alerted her.

She lifted her head from the puzzle to the porch door. She froze, mid-reach for another puzzle piece.

He stood there. Just stood there.

No movement. No sound of breathing. Just this silent mass of blankness, watching.

The speed with which the blood drained from her cheeks throttled her and threw the lead blanket of a migraine over her skull. *Move? Scream? Run? Which way?*

She wasn't sure she was breathing. Her torso and arm were suspended midair as if she'd become stuck in some advanced yoga pose. The sheer power that comes with absolute fear clenched her muscles and kept her from making another move.

Like a lizard sensing imminent danger, she stayed still as stone.

So did he.

The porch light was behind his head, so she could see nothing past the golden glow it cast through his mousy hair. He was wrapped in an ultimately forgettable flannel jacket over overalls and a shirt so blah she forgot what it looked like the moment she saw it.

Now she couldn't blink. This nondescript horror on the other side of the screen door was so unmemorable that she feared she might forget he was there if she stopped looking.

His broad shoulders filled the screen window. The shadow he cast against it was like a shroud. She couldn't let it reach her. She would be done for.

They both remained, motionless, on either side of the door. She knew he was watching her as closely as she watched him-*No, more so.* One of them had to give way, eventually.

A puff of breeze ruffled strands of his hair.

She sprang from the floor and threw herself at the wooden door that had been propped open all day. She wrenched at it, looking down-and away from him-long enough to see and kick away a pile of books that had kept the door from drifting shut. *Uh oh.*

She had the gut feeling that he moved when she looked away, though what she could see through the storm door's window never shifted. *His hand, maybe? Something?*

She felt he was getting closer to the door, though he probably could not get closer without actually walking into the screen. She couldn't see his face. Or she could, but she felt such an overwhelming lack of being struck by it that she really couldn't remember what it looked like.

She felt his eyes flicker down her arms to her hands. Her eyes shot to where his eyes would be if she could see them.

They stared at each other.

The door wasn't moving quickly enough.

It could have been a fraction of a second. It could have been many minutes that they gazed at each other. She put all her strength into moving the door, but the door gave them a while longer, like first-daters working up to a first kiss, before calling curfew and sliding free.

The moment she felt it give in her hands, he took a breath. The expansion of his chest and shoulders blocking the useless porch light definitively shifted. She threw herself behind the door and slammed it shut, locking the deadbolt.

***

For most of the day, she sheltered inside. Every door and window was checked. Nothing had been tampered with. She peered over each sill. No trampled plants, scraped frames, tried hinges. No footprints. No signs of any effort to break in. No shadows skulked in the distance.

She scrutinized the slender trunks of each tree, to make sure that no hulking figure hid behind them.

She didn't see him. She wasn't sure she felt him. Maybe all she felt was the dread of the night before.

Eventually, a car pulled into the rough driveway. From it stepped a colleague with some more work and a care basket. Tentatively, she crept through the front door and into the fresh air outside. Her colleague smiled, laughed, chatted. Together, they walked around the house, admiring the lake and soaking up the sun.

There was no sign of him. He was not there. By the looks of it, he had never been there. Reassured, she sent her colleague off with a hug and a wave, promising to call as soon as she needed anything. "Call anytime. For any reason." As relaxing as this time away had been for her, she should rest assured she was always welcome to reach out.

She stayed outside to tend the property and continue to allay her fears. If she didn't go back in, didn't turn her back, there would be no way he could sneak up on her.

Sunlight warmed the piles of fallen foliage around the yard. Thin trees framed the property, growing increasingly dense as the yard transitioned into the forest beyond. Behind the trees was the gentle lapping of the lake, licking the pebbled and muddy shore by the cottage. Wild birds and small chirping, clicking animals enjoyed the pleasant weather. They sang along to the rhythmic shushing of her rake on grass and leaves.

The air changed.

The birds kept singing. The breeze kept blowing. But now it carried ... *him*.

She clutched the rake and looked toward the trees. *Nothing*. At no time had any shape disturbed the afternoon sun streaming through the pines.

The light play of air against the back of her collar was heavy and warm. He breathed against her neck.

She dropped, straight into the large pile of orange leaves at her feet, and rolled forward, clutching the rake. Even with him towering over her, she felt with distinct unease that she would not be able to recall his appearance to police or, worse, might forget he was there as soon as she turned her head. His mousy hair matched the dull eyes that followed hers as she fell. He leaned forward into a body that no longer stood before him. As she turned, she saw his thick arms close around thin air. He stumbled.

She slammed his knees with the rake. He fell forward into the leaves.

Still turning, still moving, she sprang to her feet and swung the rake at his head with the force of her whole body. Before his face hit the ground, she turned and ran.

***

Why here?

The endless aisles of the factory warehouse led her to another long stretch of subterranean hallway. Artificial light against artificial structures made every turn look the same. Was there a way out?

She knew he was there.

She could feel him in the distance. He was far enough behind her that she still clung to the hope she would find an unlocked door or an open vent through which to pass before he could spot her. He was moving. She had to keep going.

An alarm sounded. Something felt wrong. Smelled wrong.

A door.

Further down the hallway, she could hear the clank of emergency locks. Whatever was going on, escape was probably not in that direction.

The door.

She tried the heavy handle. It was so hard to move. She leaned into it, pushing with her shoulder, then her thigh, until it gave and nudged open. She leaned against it until there was just room to squeeze through. On the other side, she struggled to push the slow monster shut again before he got there. Her fear pounded in her throat. There was no lock.

She peered around. The low lights in the windowless room showed a series of pipes, valves and switches. She crawled toward them. Against the far wall were the maintenance entries to the sewer and venting lines of the factory. One direction or another, they all led out. She pried at their covers.

They seemed not to budge. Her fingernails cracked into their beds as she struggled to drag the covers open. She kicked at the covers and at every button, latch or switch near them until one dropped open with an alarmingly loud crash.

So what if he heard? This was her only way out.

She ducked into the black hole in front of her and did not look back.

She crawled out of the pipe gasping for breath. She was out.

She turned and looked back at the factory. Its flat, wide, endless structure seemed so far away. She was surrounded by green grass. There would be people further ahead.

The bright sky and clear air were such a change from her ordeal, she felt almost convinced it was a dream.

But there was no time to think. Her pounding heart pushed her on. She turned to run.

As she did, heavy hands closed on her.

***

He shivered, drenched in his own sweat and urine.

"Please see to it that the prisoner is fitted with a catheter before his next session."

Session? How many more of these could he face? How many women had he killed? He had lost count. How many more times would he die with each of his victims?

There was no comfort in knowing he was alive, and he himself was the monster he fled.

A voice spoke to him. "You will be back in a week to experience your next murder."

A week? Every moment he closed his eyes, he could feel the women's terror as his own. There was no escape from their memories.

The End

Novella Serena is the pen name of an award-winning critical essayist whose publications on spirit children and African/Diaspora literature of the supernatural are referenced in doctoral dissertations and master's theses. She is an English instructor at Houston Community College and the author of "Cacie's Prism," published in *Love and Darker Passions* by Double Dragon/Blood Moon.

SANS LAKE
by montage

November 25th Sunset:

Her vision had become somewhat doubtful. The sky flowed into her aged eyes as the liquid horizon began to collapse. The water within them was drying out from the warmth of the golden sun. Everything she saw, everything she imagined, each different face, each image of life, came with imprecision. That is what she told me, even before it happened...

November 15th:

9:33 a.m.

She had just returned from a seven-month frequent at SouthPoint. Time and change produced few results. We sat on the back porch near the marigolds; they used to bring her happiness right after Linda ran away. The pecan trees grew in the front, leaving the backyard exposed to the blue universe. The golden sun did not do as intended; her skin remained cold throughout the morning.

I asked if she wanted to go for a walk down the path near *Sans* Lake. "The country air might do you some good, Marsha."

She turned her head, signifying her disapproval, but I insisted: "This is the time of year the water is said to give off... ."

She cut me off by making a sound with her mouth, sort of like "Bah!" but hers came out a bit more vindictive. She did not want to hear the story of *Sans* Lake, of what the old folks believed, of any possible help outside of what doctors could achieve.

She believed in science, and when it let her down, she gave up her fight.

I suggested the walk would help her health, not concentrating on her face, the frown that somehow looked like happiness, until later that night. She closed her eyes for rest.

4:46 p.m.

She reminded me of dying marigolds, yellow wilting stem, petals falling. Her face seemed so pale, the wrinkles were devastatingly vague. Her eyes were ripples that danced beneath the sunlight. I wanted to touch her but was afraid I might startle her. I could see her body shivering. I hid my fear as best I could, my fear of her shaking herself right into death's lap. There is this incredible sense of guilt that I feel when I'm near her. The way she looks at me without speaking intensifies my guilt.

6:17 p.m.

It is now dusk. The night critters have begun their beguiling songs. Marsha remains disinclined to speak. I offered to make her a dinner plate, but she turned it down as she had done previously with breakfast. "I'm no doctor, but I do know that if you engage in a cycle of not eating, you will not be healthy."

"I'm not hungry."

"Try. For me, Marsha."

She forced a few spoonfuls of potato soup through her mouth. Within seconds, it came back up.

November 16th:

She spoke for the first time today. The ripples in her eyes stilled themselves deep within her pleasant, calm face. "I long to eradicate it, to wipe it out completely, but its mystique makes it difficult to detect." Her eyes rolled to the back of her head for a while.

The ripples were gone. I saw the yellowness in her eyes, rings of insanity trying to claim her spirit. I mentioned *Sans* Lake again in hopes that she would reconsider the possibility. She looked at me with those pained eyes, suggesting my inconsiderateness to her position. I turned away, looked off into the yard and commented on the marigolds. The next ten minutes of silence were utterly dreadful. The sun changed positions in the sky, and those night critters returned with their songs.

"Where's my daughter?" Marsha finally said.

"Her flight was delayed." I had to lie. Lies aren't always awful. If spoken right, they can become calming spirits.

Marsha responded with, "Can you give me a pen?"

I handed her one and cut the big porch light on. She took a small, travel-size notepad from her brassiere. She began to write.

Dear daughter:

Although you may never read this letter I write it in hopes that it will someday shed light on what I passed to you when you were a child. I don't understand the essence of it, this unseen disease, this invisible death, and I protect your hatred of me. Shame has driven me into a desolate dwelling. I'm living inside of my mind, in the past, living with faded hope. I am constantly overcome with despair,

205

and sometimes, selfishly maybe, I have prayed for your death. My prayers for safety and peacefulness died out when I allowed you to pass into this life, knowing what you would become on your journey. I thought the powers of that lake were a myth. I heard the stories. I ignored them. We were just kids. That's all. Reckless kids looking to escape summer boredom. I'm still at odds with those tales. The worst thing you can do would be to fight it. It's too powerful, this myth that we have contracted. We should be together. Just let yourself be free, relax, and you will no longer feel sick. We will defeat the lake on the other side.

Sincerely,

Your Mother

The pen dropped from her hand and her breathing became abnormal, but only for a second. I had become immersed in the songs. Before I could get out of my chair, she seemed relaxed again. Her eyes looked somewhat peaceful against the waning day-the moon that just started to peak, really a white intimation with shape and purpose, and the brightness of the porch light. I did not cry when I read that letter.

November 18th:

Her voice was the weakest and lowest since her return from SouthPoint. Yesterday she slept. Today was reserved for chitchatting.

"It was hereditary and I didn't even know it. Had I known I swear on my life that I wouldn't have let her come here."

"Marsha, don't talk like that. Linda doesn't blame you for anything. It's not your fault. It's no one's fault."

"Yes it is, Sam. Yes it is. You remember when we were kids? You remember how we used to play at that lake? Even against our parents' wishes. You remember that?"

"Of course I do. Don't be silly now, it's getting late. It's time for your bath."

"Can't remember if it was me who took you there first or you who took me there. Well, that doesn't matter now does it? That was so long ago. You remember the games we used to play at that lake? The times we used to have."

She paused and took a sip of water. The liquid settled in her eyes.

"My mind sometimes travels back to that day at the lake. If I could take my body instead of my memory, I would do things differently. I wouldn't have gone in." She looked at me but her eyes saw something else. "Something in that lake got inside me, put me in the family way. My belly only grew after Jake began courting me some years later. We never made it. He died in a hunting accident the day we were to become adults. It was me who created this tragedy. I never meant for it to meddle with my daughter's happiness." She turned away from me again. "Before I went into labor, I felt a pang in my heart that reached to my lower back that caused me to cower from the mirth of motherhood, to shrink away from myself, away from what I had done to her. That pang was my time to choose between death and life. I hesitated. I chose wrong." A streak of tears marked the sides of her face. She took another sip of water. "I used to sit up in my room late at night with my ears pressed to the wall and hear her praying to the Lord: 'Come kill me, please!' and I would think: 'Hold on, Linda. Just hold on.' She wasn't born yet and I could hear her, inside my belly begging not to become this disaster."

Her eyes rolled back, something they'd been doing a lot lately. She continued. I listened, her voice barely audible. "I had her despite my inner protests. I knew I could never protect her. Yet, I had her. She was only a naive child. The disease came and went; summer flu, doctors said. It will pass. In time, it will pass. In her mind, she sensed it, and when she stared at her own arm, this terrible image of decay glanced back at her. Her skin would sometimes be pale; her beautiful skin started losing its texture. I told her it was the flu, like the doctors. 'It will pass soon.' And she believed me."

She stared at something in the sky. It wasn't the birds that flew above; it was something more divine than that, something only she could see.

"Your mother is sorry, Linda."

November 19:

Dear Marsha:

I sent your daughter to the hospital this morning for another check-up. She was complaining of severe headaches and nausea-a lethal combination. She screamed at the doctors when they said it must be the flu again. I managed to get her out before the back pain started.

Back at home, she was saying something about before she was born you did something to her. This isn't the first time that she has come to me with these laments, as you very well know, but I never really paid much attention. But today was different. Maybe it was the ripple sound that seemed to hold back her voice. Maybe it was the water she threw up. She couldn't walk very far because the pain in her back had gotten worse, and that is what worried me the most. Maybe I'm just overreacting, and I shouldn't. I suppose she will be all right. I don't see the slightest thing wrong with her except fatigue. Her head is normal, and her eyes are bright as ever. I advised her to get plenty of rest and lots of fluids and in a day or two she will be fine, like always. She keeps mumbling something about this lake again. I think it's called Sands Lake. She pronounces it funny, I guess because of her condition, like Suns. She said I need to take her there.

Your son-in-law,

Timothy

November 20:

When I last saw her she was staring at the sky and talking in circles. She told me that she could see the sky falling, and she thought that it would be better if we hid in the basement. I took it for some more of her silliness at first, but then I realized the reality of her softly spoken words. I saw it in her eyes. She was looking at me terrifyingly. Her voice fierce, empty of color, distraught, sounded like wind rushing over water. It was hard for me to look at her and tell her what I thought, so I didn't.

It stung to see her under such conditions. How can I tell anyone that the child I used to care for is losing her mother to obstinacy? All I could say is:

"We don't have a basement, Marsha."

November 21 (In a dream):

I stood by my wife's side and held her while she told me the following:

I closed my eyes and when I opened them again, mother appeared. It was dark. I couldn't see her but I could hear the ripples.

"Mama, come and speak to me." There was no answer, only the sound of wind colliding against the trees, ululating. A lake between mother and me kept us separated, unwilling to let either pass, unwilling to let us meet, unwilling to let us be as one. I could smell the dark, blue water as it rose.

Mother's image appeared on the opposite bank. I couldn't see the ripples. Her empty, translucent sockets carried a sense of urgency about them, full of fright, terror, and hate. Her eyes were a tyrannical reflection within the dark, blue lake. I wanted to know why mother was there, why she wasn't speaking to me, if she could help me in any way, and why, like her, I wasn't dead.

Mother was dead. I could smell her death in the lake.

"Did you come to save me, mother?" I stood on the opposite bank, reaching my arms out to mother. My voice cracked like dried ice as it found its way through the wind and over the lake. I waited for her spirit to come near.

The wind picked up. Guiltless pain escaped mother's lips when she spoke. Her voice seemed curiously cheerful as the wind carried it over the lake, a voice that rose above the noise of the wind. "Put your arms down." I did as told. "You mustn't reflect on the pain. When I was wrapped up in its net, my mind felt renewed. It was the greatest experience of my life because I knew that I would be leaving this hell and entering a new world. You have been given the opportunity to do the same. Will you follow me, Linda? All you have to do is step into the lake."

I saw a bridge but did not move. Then the wind became still. Mother's tone changed as she waited for me to put my foot into the water. Her voice stuttered and trembled and shook like angry waves as she searched for the right words. "I've always dreaded this day. I hope yours is an easy passage, like mine. I cannot bear to see you suffer any longer. Once it grabs you, I want you to relax. I will be right by your side to guide you through it." She paused to stare into the water at her reflection. I did the same but was unable to see myself. It didn't frighten me. "I'm glad you had no children," she continued. "There isn't any logic in bringing another child into this terror. You were smarter than I was. I always admired that about you. The past never dies; I still cannot erase that part of life. I've learned to live with my mistakes. I hope you can forgive me, and I will see you soon." She touched the water with her index then placed her finger to her nose and vanished.

It began to rain. My skin was warm and dry. I was at ease. My pains increased. I knew I would be joining mother soon.

"Honey, why do you think mother dipped her finger in the lake and was talking as if she was already dead?"

A Confused,
Timothy
November 22:

The entire outside world remained idle and pretty just like it did when we were young and playing in the bosom of a meridian sunshine near *Sans* Lake that embraced us by shedding warmth and washing away cold and drying tears...

Her eyes fought off sleep like a wounded bird falling and fluttering on one wing, trying to reach its nest. But every time she blinked, intervals between reopening grew longer. *Fight it, Marsha.* But she didn't. If only the world could see the pain in her face, how all sufferance was drawn into it, how the sadness swelled there, how confusion mocked her. If only they knew. And I asked myself, *Who killed her?*

I knew the answer to that question. I was the one who brought her into this rippled abyss. I wanted to blame that lake, the people who polluted it, and the people who lied about it, but I knew it was just as much my fault as it was theirs. I am the one who ruined Marsha's universe.

November 23:

To whomever it may concern:

I no longer fear hell for I have finally realized that I've been living in hell all my life. I've been punished for abominations that I have neither committed nor understood their meaning, crimes that were passed down to me from what mother did as a child. I'm lost. It has been over five years since I've spoken to her. She used to speak to me every month. In my dreams. She no longer answers the letters I send in my dreams. There is no use, and I need to preserve the rest of my energy. Spiritually, I'll still care for her; she is my mother.

The days have slowly disappeared when I used to sit in this same chair and stare into nothingness, shedding tears, body shaking from pain, praying perpetually for this woman who obviously doesn't care enough about the pain in my back to help me. By the time you (whoever you may be) read this letter, I hope that I will be at peace with myself.

October 24:

Dear Marsha:

Forgive me for taking you to Sans *Lake that day. I've hurt you and made you suffer and kept you from enjoying life. I swear, after this I will never appropriate something that does not belong to me again. I am truly sorry and I hope that you can understand why I must do this. I also hope that you will someday find it in your heart to forgive me. Ultimately, you will thank me for this because I am savingyou from a greater tragedy.*

Cordially yours

Samantha

November 1 (Early Morning):

It remained a hidden lake up until 1631 when a group of recalcitrant slaves escaped a plantation under Spanish rule. They traveled in one large pack through the thick forest searching for salvation until they stumbled across what no world map knew existed. The partially cratered lake with its glittering contents appeased the abject runaways. The lake was nearly perfectly rounded and vast, at least 14,000 kilometers on each side, and running east to west was a grand viaduct leading to the other side. They traversed it, man carrying child, woman big with child, wife and husband holding hands, teenage boy with teenage girl, strangers to sovereignty. Once they made it to the middle of the lake, the bridge collapsed from the outside in. Before they fell in, a silver rainbow appeared in the sky on the other side of the lake. Freedom; they knew the vision. The rainbow grew with each splashing body, but the freedom it represented slowly disappeared. The first wave perished. The hounds failed to sniff them out in the dark once their scent belonged to the unknown. The unknown is a divine place that exists without human intervention. Their bodies, unfound and unseen, float atop the water, still searching out their freedom.

But one scared little child did not cross that lake. He crouched behind a boulder until the tragedy ended, body after body consumed by that great lake, even his parents. It is said that he lived there in solitude until he became a man, blending with nature, learning the secrets of the lake. When he could no more see his reflection in the lake, he was given instructions, whispered to him from the wind that brushed across the water. The ones who can no longer see their reflection in the ripples of the lake are the ones who possess the secrets of living. This child-his anonymity preserved-led the second wave of runaways and showed them how to survive. Because this group went without their captivity or their freedom in mind, they were able to find liberty. They fled bondage and found bliss within their new home, *Sans* Lake.

The history of *Sans*Lake is great. Some of it has fallen victim to conspiracy, but oral tradition never dies if you can find one unafraid of the history. I tried to forget as much of it as I could. It is not something the memory can discard. After 1884, the lake was 'discovered' by some French-Canadian adventurers. Their discovery was no accident. *Sans* Lake needed to revive itself. Surprised by the beauty of their discovery and the wondrous sound of the ripples, they sought to claim the place as their own. But *Sans* Lake belonged to no man. They entered the lake without restraint and suffered a long-term illness coupled with back boils before they perished. It was the microscopic crystals in the water.

In 1901 the lake was closed only to be reopened the following year for economic purposes. The new construction around the lake attracted foreign tourists. Campsites were identified and boundaries were set. They were given specific orders. Respect the lake; but they were never told why. They broke the rules-skinny-dipping, polluting the water with the friction of their bodies, photographs, and water polo. They became a part of *Sans* Lake. And thirty years ago, in 1952, I took your mother there and dared her to get in.

The government tried to hide the story of *Sans* Lake. The lake regenerated itself back to its original form, so they lied about the transpiration of the 1901 construction. Then it shrank in size. They lied about its condemnation in 1959. It wasn't because of anacondas. No creatures live within that lake. It

215

is because of what I have just told you.

November 25:

The sunlight continued to creep through her shades, but it became weaker every second. Her eyelids were drooping, drowning out the sounds. Small clouds covered small sections of the sun. A draping shadow began to touch the earth's surface. Rural darkness came like an eclipse. The marigolds seemed but a dream. Shadows were beginning to be covered by darker shades of shadows, as if the sun's rays were being reflected off the ground directly back into the sun. All around, light grew faint.

When she tried to speak, the lake took away her voice. Her chin touched her chest. She had already succumbed to death.

I just kept staring at her from behind the curtains of heaven. They were white with yellow flowers. Dandelions, I believe. I wished I could give her one. They blew over the marigolds. My eyes zoomed her into focus like a microscope. Zooming in my love. She is my heart, my best friend. I can see it now. She was blurry at first but slowly the picture became sharp. She wore a pink dress. It was nice. I wanted to be next to her. She seemed a million miles away. I can't love her too much. I continued to look, barely peeping, not wanting to be seen for fear that I might frighten her away. She takes off her pink dress and dives into that lake. She is mine alone. Her face looks sad. She is not crying. Her tears are concealed. I can see them in the night. They look like clear rain, crystal and pure. I want to touch her, to wipe away her tears before they fall, to feel her one last time, to fill this empty

216

void within me. I want to put my fingers on her lips and stop them from trembling. Go inside of her and intercept her pains. Interpose myself between her ears so that nothing bad will enter her mind. Be preventive of her lamentations. I belong to her, and she to me.

I am sad, like someone else is in my place. I can't feel myself but I do feel a pang in my stomach, like from hunger, choking me up, bending me over. It is now in my back. I want to talk to her. Tell her how sorry I am. I need her to tell me how I can make it better. Will she ever hear my plea? Linda, I love you. I apologize. Will you forgive me? We have a chance to start all over. Just follow me to Sans Lake. *I'm sorry for all the pain that I've brought you.*

November 25 Nightfall:

Mama, I have an ailing disease. I am dying. Do not mourn me. It is my time. I am prepared. I have been for quite some time. I am at peace. It is not your fault. You have done all that you can to protect me from evil. Myth has a mind of its own. No human being can control it. Its powers are protected by human fallacy. Do not worry about me any longer. My pains are gentle. I love you. I am yours alone.

Linda

She took me to *Sans* Lake. She told me the story, the story she said you never told her, the story you thought she didn't know. Samantha told it to her. She didn't believe until her dream. Samantha said Linda's dream meant that she had to go to *Sans* Lake without her mother. That was the missing

217

reflection.

She waited under a pale moon for death to set in. She stared into the sky, into the stars. She waited. And waited. She called upon her mother. The ripples were quiet. She waited to see the spirits from the first wave and for the bridge to collapse. She waited for the rainbow to grow with each splash. She waited for death. It never came.

Timothy and Linda
In life we grow.

The End

montage is the pen name of a creative writer and essayist who is a member of several scholarly, artistic and honor societies. montage is an Adjunct Professor of English at Prairie View A & M University and the author of *Duggan* and *The Women of Sugar Hill.*

THE NANO-FISHERMAN'S WIFE
by A.J. Maguire

"You mustn't panic," I told myself.

My voice echoed back to me through my earpiece, sounding strangely filtered. I knew the others could hear me - if there was one thing that worked on this dusty satellite it was the communications systems. That probably had a lot to do with the fact that our earpieces were never exposed to the moon dust; they remained safely tucked away in our helmets.

"Panic? Ellie, what's wrong?"

George's voice. He was manning the main console back at Moon Base V. Although it was his job to monitor all communications and life support functions, I couldn't help the bitter resentment that swelled in me. George responded first, not David; not my own damned husband.

Still, the resentment paled when compared to the alarmingly large tear in the elbow of my space suit. So far it appeared to be in the outer layer only, stretching out past the hinged joint that allowed me to freely move. I checked the computer mounted to my left forearm to make certain I still had the right pressurization within the suit: 0.29 atm.

"I have a two-inch tear in the outer layer of my suit."

"Of all the clutzy, dumbass ... ." David's voice now.

"Air pressure?" George asked.

"Normal," I said.

"How did you do that?" David asked.

219

I counted to five before I answered, throttling down several expletives of my own. "Well, you see, there's this gray stuff called moon dust all over me. I don't know if you've noticed, but the material is abrasive. I imagine that - since I had to stay out an extra hour while you took an early lunch - it scrubbed its way into the crevasse of my suit and *voila*! Instant tear."

"You're blaming this on me?"

George's voice overrode him. "You're five kilometers out. I don't want you moving that far; you'll risk tearing into something important. I'm coming out with Dobber."

"Dobber?" David said. "Oh yes, she'll love that. It'll feed her sense of the dramatic."

I closed my eyes and counted to ten.

"Quit being an asshole," George said. "Sit tight, Ellie. I'm on my way."

Opening my eyes, I stared at the tear for a moment and wished with all my might that David could love me again. It was a purely sentimental and girlish wish, born on the sense of pure loss. And now that I thought about it, I wouldn't know what to do with him if he actually did love me. I'd certainly lost most of my affection for him.

We hadn't always been this way. But then, nobody started a marriage based on hatred, and I couldn't say that I really hated David. I did, however, hate what we had become.

Everything had been fine back on Earth. We were students and poor, happily spending three *deutschemarks* to split a hamburger between us. I could clearly remember laughter back then. We could spend hours walking along the beach of Jade Bight. It wasn't far from our home in Varel, so we went there often.

I sighed and stared out at the vast gray expanse of the moon. I missed Germany. Germany had color. Vibrancy.

It was David's idea to take the lunar assignment. NASA International needed the nano-particles found in moon dust to help feed the ever-growing technology for space travel. It was used in everything, from the computer mounted to my arm to the mechanical system on board the Dobber rescue craft. It made smart machines, ships that could think quickly enough to negotiate meteor showers without getting hit, and holographic interfaces that looked real.

Above me, hovering in orbit, the Odyssey 9 Intergalactic Space Ship was still under construction. Beyond its massive steel-gray form I could see Earth shining blue-white at me. It felt so desperately far away that I sucked in a pained breath.

White lights rimmed my vision.

"Ellie?" George asked.

Something wasn't right. I could feel it. Light-headed and dizzy, I looked to the computer. My oxygen levels were far too low. But that didn't make any sense. The tear wasn't near any of the oxygen seals.

"You mustn't panic," I said again, coaching my heart into a slower pace.

I tried to think back to the beginning of my lunar walk. But even if I had grabbed the six-hour gear, I should have been fine for another hour. An hour, I realized, hearing again David's complaint that he needed a break early. And like the passive-aggressive idiot that I was, I had let him.

"Ellie?" George sounded worried.

"My oxygen is running low."

"How low?"

"Ten minutes and counting."

"I'll be there in eight," he said. "Stop talking. Stop moving. Think happy thoughts."

"Ellie?" David this time, and he actually sounded concerned.

"Not now, David."

Happy thoughts, I told myself. Bless you, George.

It was all David's fault that George was out here, too. We had all signed up together, planning on traveling with Odyssey 7 after spending our five years as nano-fishers. David was convinced that seeing the far side of the galaxy would be the ultimate adventure, and so we had been convinced with him.

But our five-year term as nano-fishers turned into seven, and then ten. What started out with hope and optimism slowly faded into distrust and anger. Time, I thought, was just like the moon dust we were sent to collect. It was fine and deceiving, with a coarseness that could jam gears, or rub skin raw.

Almost ten full years cooped up on Moon Base V had scoured our marriage to breaking point. David no longer looked at me as his life partner. All of the little things kept piling up between us. All of the big things, too. We had seven months left, and then we could catch a flight home or join Odyssey 9 in its maiden voyage.

I, for one, was going home.

It hadn't dawned on me until that moment, staring at the bulbous, magnetic nano-catcher beside me, but I was done with space. I was tired of recycled air, the hum of generators and the eerie silence that came when walking on the lunar surface. I wanted fresh air and sea waves and the call of gulls overhead.

David would go with the Odyssey.

He was, as I had come to understand him, the male version of the Fisherman's Wife. Mother used to read me the story when I was young. David fit the role of unhappy spouse perfectly. He was never satisfied with what he had, constantly searching for the magical fish that would grant his every wish.

Fish wish, I thought with a smile.

What would be my fish wish, if I could have one?

Lights peppered my vision again. I looked at my computer: four minutes of oxygen left. I had to lean against the sloped surface of the nano-catcher. My suit scraped the metal as I slid down into a sitting position. I reached out and switched off the magnetics that were hauling moon dust into the gaping mouth of the catcher. If I was going to die, I didn't want the rumble of the catcher to be the last thing I heard.

The gray expanse of the moon stretched out before me. Lumps and craters that had been so spectacular ten years ago seemed now like burial mounds and open graves. It doesn't matter what they tell you; nothing can hide the presence of death in space. You can play all the music you want, you can bring out a mood stabilizer and play sounds of creeks and waves and forests, but there is no escaping it. Underneath all the noise you make will always be the deafening quiet of death.

Happy thoughts, I ordered myself.

David and fish.

It was an effort, but I managed to ignore the strained sound of my own wheezing.

Fish wish, I thought again.

Screw David and all his striving. What did *I* want?

I could see the Dobber rolling toward me. It was a large, tank-like structure, all clunky angles and black material. Two minutes and George would be there. Two minutes and I could be safe in the cocoon of Dobber's belly, breathing normally.

I looked at my computer again: thirty seconds of air.

"Ellie, I'm almost there. Hang on," George said.

I could hear the strength in his voice, the determination he had. He loved me. He always had. We'd never spoken of it, though. By the time we met, David had already proposed to me. But it was there, just under the surface of our interactions, a gentle pull that kept us both sane during David's rants. And I suddenly realized what my fish wish would be.

I'd wish for George, not David. I'd wish for a crappy one-bedroom apartment, cheap hamburgers and a noisy cat that shed everywhere.

I held my breath for as long as I could. My

lungs strained, and darkness rimmed my vision. I didn't want to think about dying, so I thought about George, instead. I remembered breakfast three days prior, when David was still asleep and the last shift of nano-fishers had already gone off to bed. It was just George and me, sipping coffee and trying to pretend that the landscapes plastered to the dining facility walls were real.

He'd asked me then what I was going to do when the term was up.

"I don't know," I'd said. "David is going on the Odyssey."

He was quiet for a moment. It hadn't occurred to me then, but George hadn't been surprised that my decision might be different than David's. He must have known that I was done with David. He must have seen it.

It was disconcerting to think someone else could be as intimately acquainted with my marriage as I was. But then, this was George. George who braved ice-skating with me when David scoffed his way out of it. George who showed me sailing even when I was frightened to death of the deep sea. George who made certain I didn't work myself into the ground no matter what deadline we had, and who was rushing out with Dobber because I'd torn my suit.

George, I thought as my lungs burned, and my vision blurred.

"How is she?" David's voice filled the Dobber.

"Stable," George said. "But it was close."

I could feel the rumble of the Dobber underneath me and knew we were heading back to base. My eyes felt heavy, but I opened them anyway. George was at the controls, his helmet off and his hard features set at grim lines. Suddenly, I wanted a fish that could magically erase the last ten years, a fish that could break apart my marriage without all the emotional mess and legal hassle.

But then I thought how George had loved me through the mess.

"She should have headed back sooner," David said. "This isn't going to look good on the report."

"You should have stuck to your schedule." George glared at the console.

I could sense the frustration in him, the underlying fear of what he'd just been through. Strewn about the belly of Dobber was the evidence of his fight. Medical supplies surrounded me, one in particular catching my attention: the portable resuscitator. He'd had to shock my heart back into beating.

"Oh, now you're blaming me, too?"

"David," I said. My voice was surprisingly hoarse, and my whole body ached.

George started a little in his seat and glanced back at me. He smiled, and the relief on his face was evident. He wasn't as handsome as David was, but he was five times more of a man. I met his dark brown eyes and felt the security and warmth that flowed from him.

"Ellie, are you all right?" David asked.

Screw the magic fish, I thought. I can grant my own wish.

"David, I want a divorce."

The End

A.J. Maguire is the author of the *Sedition* series, the *Witch-Born* series, and the new single releases, *Deviation* and *Dead Magic,* published in August, 2014 by Double Dragon Publishing. Her first short story, "The Man Who Loved Medusa," was featured in the *Love and Darker Passions* anthology, available through Double Dragon/Blood Moon.

SEE THAT MY GRAVE IS KEPT CLEAN

by F. Brett Cox

I never understood what the fuss was about. It was just a job, and everyone needs a job. I needed a job. I had already decided that Billy was the one, but until we were married I was going to have to take care of myself. Not that Ma and Pa didn't take care of me, but you know what I mean. A girl always needs some money in her purse. You don't want to get caught unprepared.

And it's not like I had a lot of options. I could type, but I wasn't very fast, and I was really good at filing, but the offices weren't hiring for that right then. Waitressing was out of the question. I didn't want to serve anybody. I did think being a carhop at Renzo's Drive-In might be fun, but then my cousin Theresa got a job there and it turned out the place was a front for something else they needed girls for and uncle Mike went over Theresa's first night and hauled her back home, so that was out.

But then I heard Marberry Funeral Home was looking for someone, and when I found out all they wanted was someone to sit with the bodies when nobody else was there, I went right over, and they hired me on the spot. In fact, they seemed grateful. I think I was the only one who applied.

Ma didn't like it, and Pa said I couldn't do it, but when I told him I'd kick in part of what I made to the household budget, he hesitated, and I could tell by the look on Ma's face that I'd won. Pa was

228

doing OK at the plant, but they were saying there might be another round of layoffs, and that had Ma worried. If you ever saw the look on Pa's face when Ma acted worried or scared, and saw the look Ma had then, you'd know I'd won, too.

So I sat with the bodies. I never really understood why they needed someone to do that, but Mr. Marberry, who was the grandson of the man who had started the business in the first place, said that they had to guard against anyone disturbing the bodies. He said it was a matter of law. I didn't know how anyone could disturb a dead person, and I didn't know how I was supposed to stop anyone who did, but Mr. Marberry said they had hired girls before and never had any problems. He said again it was a matter of law, and even if there wasn't much chance of anything happening, they had to have someone there. My cousin Marcie used to say that Mr. Marberry was the ugliest man she'd ever seen, and he gave her the creeps. He was ugly all right, but he had a steady voice and talked to me like I was just someone who was working for him and not like I was a kid. He was very matter-of-fact about everything, and I liked that. He even shook my hand when I accepted the job.

The late hours were kind of a struggle at first, but Ma said it was OK for me to sleep in since I was working late, and once I started doing that it was fine. I knew there were a lot more bodies down in the basement where they got them ready to be buried, but I just had to be there in the main area where they kept the bodies after they'd been prepared but before the funerals. I got to sit behind

229

a desk in the main room, like I was running the place. From there I could see into the smaller rooms where they kept the individual caskets. The main room was fancy but very serious, with paintings that blended right into the walls. The smaller rooms were plain with maybe only some flowers on a table. Best of all, the whole place was air-conditioned, which wasn't common back then, but they needed to keep it all cool for obvious reasons.

And honestly, I didn't mind the bodies. The caskets were closed except when the families were viewing during regular hours, so from where I sat all you saw were these long polished boxes through the doors, and unless you went in and took a good look they could have been anything, really.

Of course, I did go into each room and check on things a couple times a night. That's what they were paying me for, after all. And for the first week or so that I was there, every once in a while I'd open up one of the caskets and take a look at the body inside. Maybe I shouldn't have, but nobody specifically told me not to, and I was supposed to be making sure the bodies weren't disturbed, right?

Sure enough there they all were in their caskets, but now they just looked like mannequins lying there with no expression. That was true even when every once in a while there was someone I had known, like Mrs. Nielsen, who had taught me and both my parents fourth grade, and Johnny Martin, who got killed in a wreck. Johnny was one of those kids who was mean to you until he decided to be mean to someone else, and I had never liked him. Of course that didn't mean I wanted him dead.

The mortician had sure done a good job. You couldn't tell that anything had happened.

But I have to admit that after the first week I seldom looked inside the coffins. I poked my head in the rooms once or twice each night, just to make sure. Otherwise I just sat there behind the desk in this great swivel chair and read, mostly my library copy of *Gone with the Wind*. My cousin Kathleen claimed to have read the whole thing in a single day, starting first thing that morning and finishing after midnight. I don't doubt she did, but I can't read that fast, and even if I did I couldn't very well take a whole day to do nothing but lie around and read a book. My father's not rich.

So I sat there guarding the bodies against being disturbed. I read my book, and when I wasn't reading I was planning the life that Billy and I were going to have together once he realized that Alice wasn't the one for him. Even my parents talked about how sensible and down-to-earth Alice was, and how that was the sort of girl Billy needed. Maybe they were right about what Billy needed, but not about who. It was quiet and cool there in the main room and, let's face it, I didn't have to do anything. Really, it was the best job I'd ever had.

And then one night right after I'd finished a chapter, when I was resting my eyes and thinking how basically I really liked Scarlett although I didn't see why she had to be so dramatic about everything, I heard a noise.

I opened my eyes and looked around. Nothing. Then I heard the noise again. Second room to the left.

I got up and went into the room, taking my copy of *Gone with the Wind* in case I needed a weapon-it was certainly heavy enough. It was quiet, and then I heard the noise again. A scratching sound, coming from inside the coffin.

When I'd first heard the noise, I have to admit that I was a little scared, but now that I was in the room with the noise coming from the casket, I was just numb. I didn't know what to think or do. I wasn't even aware of moving, but I found myself beside the casket, leaning down with my ear practically on the wood. Scratch, scratch, scratch.

I put my book down on the floor and opened up the top half of the casket. There was an old man inside I didn't know. The scratching had stopped, but now there was a different sound. It was coming from the man's head.

I looked down and realized his mouth was moving without opening. I guess they had to sew it shut, or glue it, or do something to keep it from falling open.

Then he sat up. The casket was still closed below his waist, but there was room for him to sit up and get his arms free. He reached up and pulled at his face with both hands, and there was a sound not much louder than pulling off a band-aid, and his mouth opened and he said, softly but perfectly clearly, "See that my grave is kept clean." And then he lay back down and didn't say anything else.

I stood there and waited. I don't know how much time passed, but he didn't sit back up, and he didn't say anything else. So I closed the casket, picked up my book, and went back to my desk.

I tried to read some more, but I couldn't concentrate. I just sat there the rest of the evening and tried to decide what to do. To be honest, I didn't worry so much about the body sitting up or even talking. I'd never taken a drink of liquor in my life-still haven't-and I knew what had happened had happened. And there was that summer when we all read *Frankenstein* and *Dracula* and went to see that other Bella Lugosi movie about the zombies, so it wasn't like this was something I'd never heard of.

What I couldn't figure out was why he said what he said. Like I'm supposed to tend to his grave? Maybe he thought I had a different job here. Or maybe he didn't realize I was there at all. Maybe he was just hoping someone was.

I didn't read any more that evening. I just sat there and waited for another noise.

But there wasn't one, and when my time was up I got up and went home and didn't say a word to anyone.

It never happened again, which was just as well. If there had been more bodies sitting up and talking, I might have had to tell someone, and if I didn't, I might have had to quit my job, and neither one of those was something I wanted to do. Once Ma and Pa were used to me being there with the bodies, they would have been disappointed if I'd quit a perfectly good job. And if anyone was going to get Billy away from sensible Alice, it probably wouldn't be a girl dead people talked to.

So I didn't tell anyone, and like I said, it never happened again. When the summer was over I went back to school, and by the end of senior year, sure enough Billy saw the light about old Alice and started going steady with me. We got married, and here we are. Everything's fine.

I don't think much about what happened, but sometimes I have these dreams, and when I wake up it's hard to get back to sleep. When that happens, I look over at Billy, and I'm so happy he's lying right there beside me. If Billy dies before I do, and he wants to sit up and pull his dead mouth open and start talking, he can just forget about it. He can just lie right back down.

The End

F. Brett Cox's fiction, poetry, essays, and reviews have appeared in numerous magazines and anthologies. Recent and forthcoming publications include stories in *Eclipse Online*, *New Haven Review*, and *Shadows and Tall Trees*, poetry in *Manifest West: Even Cowboys Carry Cell Phones*, and a monologue in *Geek Theater*. With Andy Duncan, he co-edited the anthology *Crossroads: Tales of the Southern Literary Fantastic* (Tor, 2004). A native of North Carolina, Brett is Associate Professor of English at Norwich University and lives in Vermont with his wife, playwright Jeanne Beckwith.

THE SAVANT

by Alexis Brooks de Vita

I used to tell people, "I am the idiot, and my sister is the *savant*," and they would laugh at me.

Because other people found Celestina strange, perhaps even frightening. Whenever *Maman* took us to the library with her in our little Great Lakes college town, we used to nestle in the darkest corner, hiding from the shrieks and taunts of the lucky ones who gathered for The Children's Hour. We read books to ourselves while our mother worked. Or, rather, Celestina read to herself while I looked at pictures, until Celestina's bubbling tears at being deprived of The Children's Hour drove me to learn to read aloud to her.

I was not quite sure why children screamed and said "ugh" when they caught sight of my twin sister until I went to primary school. Then it occurred to me that I never saw other children who looked anything like Tina, even then when she was small and soft all over, down to the spiny ridge of bones that jutted above her curving back. I still remember standing before my mother's mirror, dumbstruck with disappointment that even I, her twin sister, looked nothing like Celestina.

But, even so young, I knew that we were one whole person, and she was made up of the very best parts of the one person we were.

That's why I hated reading to her the "Two Sisters" stories she loved. I would push aside the old books *Maman* dragged out of the library's dustiest shelves or even from Special Collections, bearing "Negro folktales" like *Doctor to the Dead* or *Uncle Remus* stories, or a Jesse Wilcox Smith or Kate Greenaway-illustrated set of English fairytales, or a Walter Crane or Virginia Frances Sterrett-illustrated set of French tales. I would reach for familiar books I could find for myself and scramble through the pages, searching for the safer stories that I loved.

"Look, Celestina," I urged her, "'Sleeping Beauty' or 'Donkey Skin' or 'Beauty and the Beast,'" my favorite. Stories of love arisen from waste and despair.

But she would not cease to cry-a sound like mourning doves cooing. Or, with her legs like warm tentacles wrapped around her middle to prop her up like a snake waiting to be charmed, she would stare with huge un-lidded eyes shedding creeping tears until I chanted, fingers fumbling from one well-worn page to a detested other: "'Once upon a time, there were two sisters.'"

The "Two Sisters" could be African American or English or Scottish or from somewhere in India. It didn't matter to Celestina. *Maman* had told us that we ourselves were a hodgepodge of New Orleans Creole and English-speaking runaway mixed with Creek rebel. So, though "Sweetheart Roland" was Celestina's very favorite, in truth she loved them all and laughed with delight-pigeons crooning-each time an elder or otherwise unfortunate sister from anywhere in the world met her downfall. Thorns that tore a hateful sister's hands, an old woman who beat her savagely with a stick, seawater that filled her mouth to drowning, or even a knife in her own mother's hands that sliced her throat, all brought joy to Tina.

I read dutifully to stop her tears-her misery was mine-but sullenly, too. For I nursed a bitter suspicion that, as I was the elder by nearly half an hour between us, I was also the cruel ugly sister who needed to be taught a lesson. But wasn't I already trying my best? I reasoned with myself, *Ugly can be perfect too, someday. Please, Teenie. No more "Sisters."* But Tina's happiness soared beyond the reach of my pique.

Besides, talking with Celestina didn't work like that. She could not explain herself or tell you what she wanted. You either got it-like when she needed *Maman* to trundle her to an empty bathroom and lock the door against intruders as she braced Celestina in the sink to "tinkle"-or you didn't.

So, instead of talking to Celestina, I used to tell people about her. I explained, "We are one. My sister is the soul, and I am the body," or "My sister is the brain that thinks, and I am the mouth that speaks." Meaning, *My sister is Beauty, and I am Beast, and we are one and complete in each other.* And they would laugh because they didn't understand.

Or, at least, that is what I believed until *Maman* died. And then I was no longer sure. And I stopped talking about Celestina altogether.

Life became very hard for both of us in the year that followed *Maman*'s death. Of course, we thought life was hard before *Maman*'s death, as the young tend to think. Silly worries as well as serious ones: girls who did not like me and whispered and

237

passed notes saying unkind things about my sister who never came out of our house anymore, and boys who protected me but would not walk me quite all the way home, and the children's librarian who tried to get me fired from my clerking job at the library.

Those early worries were the reason I knew about Celestina's being the *savant,* between us. I was the idiot who didn't know why girls hated me and boys were afraid to carry my backpack all the way up onto our front porch, or what was wrong with borrowing library books for my sister shut away in our bedroom and not returning them until she was through. Which might take months. Or years. But she would always have done, eventually, and I always brought them back.

That was what I told the children's librarian when she tried to have me fired. "But I always bring back the books, Mrs. Hargreaves," miserably. Confused, as always. "As soon as"- *But what to say, if I didn't want her to blame Celestina?* - "I am done with them."

An unsmiling woman, Mrs. Hargreaves let a smirk twist down her mouth. "And is it your contention, Leticia, that our patrons should wait upon your leisure to return books you have not properly checked out, so that they must read them at your discretion and pleasure?" She enunciated carefully, nastily, as though I were stupid.

Which, truthfully, I was. But "No, ma'am," I avowed, for that was surely the best answer.

Mrs. Hargreaves tapped her foot in anticipation of an argument I had no intention of providing.

When my failure to dispute the wrongness of my actions disappointed her beyond anything I might have actually said or done, she pronounced acidly, "You understand, of course, that I will have to have you terminated."

I, of course, had understood no such thing. "Mrs. Hargreaves, you will have me fired?" I asked, to be certain.

"Of course, Leticia." A glimmer of interest returned to her stern face. I realized that the slackening of her set jaw indicated that she was-perhaps for the first time since I had met her when I was a child patron of the library in the reluctant company of my sister-probably grinning.

"But how will I-" and I bit off the unspoken questions: *How will I get enough books for my sister to stay in our bedroom waiting, watching at the window, so sure that I will come and she will find something in my arms, in my backpack, in my coat pockets to make her warble her contented sounds?*

But I did not ask. I knew better than to ask that question of someone as heartless as Mrs. Hargreaves. Even before *Maman* died.

Instead, I waited until my shift was done and rushed home to Celestina, who still shared our childhood bedroom with me.

"Mrs. Hargreaves will have me fired from the library," I sobbed beside Celestina on the window seat above the honeysuckle and almond blossoms in our front garden. "I'm so sorry, Tina. I won't be able to bring you so many books anymore. And we won't be able to keep them for so long." I buried my

239

face in my arms on the windowsill.

What would Tina-I still used my baby name for my twin sister-do for the long hours of the day that I was away from home? What would she feed her insatiable mind in preparation for the hours spent rocking on her haunches, staring from under transparent lids into the middle distance, responding to nothing around her, if I could not supply her with copious stacks of books?

Soon, I felt Celestina's hooked page-turning finger snag my thick black braid out of her way so she could scratch softly at my back, her way of petting and soothing me. She crooned to me her comforting sounds-whales calling to each other beneath vast Arctic waters.

I would have to stop crying, dry my eyes and think. What might I find, something that reeked of Mrs. Hargreaves, to put under Celestina's hand? Then Celestina would *know*.

Or, at least, before *Maman* died, this is what I told her. "*Maman,* Tina *knows* things. I only ask her to find out. So I will know, too. I am the stupid one. I don't understand anything. Oh, *Maman,* don't cry."

But *Maman* cried because she did not understand.

Scrubbing tears from my face with my palms until the cheeks burned, it came to me. *Just the thing!* A book Mrs. Hargreaves hounded me for, watched for like a hawk, like a vulture, every time I checked it out. Mrs. Hargreaves had even run to the district manager to demand a limit to the times I could check it out, she so much wanted to keep this book from me.

I didn't know why Celestina loved this particular book-I still don't. She had these phases: for books, for animal sounds to communicate her feelings, for a particular view from a window of a room where she hid herself away.

So I lay the luxuriously illustrated copy of *The Tale of Silver Nose* under Celestina's hooked page-turning finger and opened it to the return date stamped inside the front cover. "Mrs. Hargreaves," I whispered, perhaps unnecessarily, "is the one who makes me take this book back to her at the library every two weeks."

With the cry that startled and frightened me so that I never got used to it-the one like elephants trumpeting across a sun-seared savannah-Tina's hook raked the book from my hand to tumble down with her to her rag rug on the floor.

She slithered from the window seat to hulk over it, growling low in her throat.

And then it happened: Celestina's gift. What made her the *savant*.

Her clawed hand lifted, hovered over the roster of hated return dates. Her bulbous fetus-like head bowed, eyes slitted and sightlessly staring, as she rocked. Waiting for the power to gather. Waiting to *know*.

I drew up my legs onto the window seat, tucked the ankles against my bottom. Tried not to touch this rocketing, snarling *savant,* not to come to her attention at all as she built into the very atmosphere around us, like a hologram, the reality of our enemy's downfall.

When it happened, when it was done, when she

241

knew and nothing could stop the new reality from coming, Tina screamed her wild boar trumpet of rage and ripped her hook down the stamped page so that it tore from the book's inner binding. The damaged book flipped as it was unshackled from the ink chain that bound it to our enemy. And the book was un-tethered, ours forever.

Exhausted, Celestina began to mewl and raised her hook to me, piteously seeking my help to remove the punctured return date page. I uncurled my legs from out of her reach on the windowsill and stretched for her clawed hand, unsure how to slide the stabbed paper from it without touching her.

With her whale's cry returned, Tina nudged the finger against my hesitant hand, as if to show me that she would not harm me, if I would only help her.

So I laughed and scrambled down to the floor beside her and wiped her tears as well as my own that had somehow come again.

Tina whimpered and rocked herself on the floor into the stupor that passed for her way of sleeping. The sun sank, bathing our room in its bloody triumphant shades. When she still had not moved after I returned from dining with *Maman* downstairs, I undressed her curling spiny body and gowned it for bed, and wrapped her crocheted blanket around her there on her hooked rag rug, and plumped up her favorite tasseled pillow before her, in case she should topple forward in her sleep.

I woke several times that night to see Celestina still huddled and swaying gently back and forth, as if she were still a baby in *Maman*'s arms in a rocking chair. "Tina?" I called into the shadow-striped light thrown through our un-curtained window from the streetlamps outside. But she was far into another of her worlds and didn't answer.

Imagine my relief, the next day, upon discovering that Mrs. Hargreaves's efforts to get me fired by the district manager had, instead, resulted in the branch manager's moving me to our library's small Special Collections section.

"But Special Collections doesn't need a filing clerk," Mrs. Hargreaves screeched in the manager's office, so that we all heard at the front desk.

All of us, the filing clerks and the librarians, ducked our heads back to our tasks of checking books, audiotapes, CDs, and DVDs in and out of the library. We pretended not to hear.

The day I was transferred to Special Collections, I brought the damaged *The Tale of Silver Nose* back to the branch manager, my head bowed in a silent apology. "I'm sorry, Mrs. Willoughby," I assured her and could say no more, for I was unsure what more to say.

She took the book with a soft smile. "It is probably time for this book to be withdrawn, anyway, Leticia," she pointed out and dropped it on her desk.

That evening, at closing, she presented it to me with a gentle nod. "Tell your mother that we all miss her," she said mysteriously.

I rode home next to *Maman,* clutching *The Tale of Silver Nose* to my chest, for I was unsure how I'd ever get Celestina any more books. "Good news," I said quietly to *Maman*. "Tina can keep *The Tale of Silver Nose* now. And bad news. I don't see how I can take home Special Collections books for her. But Mrs. Willoughby says they all miss you."

Maman sighed. I knew how badly she missed working at the library even though I worked there, almost in her place. "Will you begin to go to college, Leticia," *Maman* asked suddenly, "now that you know your job is assured? Special Collections is an honor. Mrs. Willoughby is trying to make you a permanent employee, as I was."

I raised my head stubbornly. "Tina would miss me too much, away half the day at college and the other half at the library. Like she missed you too much."

Maman frowned her frustration.

Nor did she seem relieved to learn that Mrs. Hargreaves had fallen and broken her hip, a week later. "Did Mrs. Hargreaves do something to upset Tina?" *Maman* asked me suspiciously. Then, coaxingly, "Ticia," the baby name invented for me to match my sister's "Tina," "did Mrs. Hargreaves's fall have anything to do with Tina's getting *The Tale of Silver Nose* to keep?"

First I played the idiot, my particular talent. "How could Tina have anything to do with getting *The Tale of Silver Nose* withdrawn from the library, *Maman*? Tina never goes out of the house, since you stopped working at the library and can't take her there."

Maman said, "It's all I can do to get this wheelchair into the van to drive you to work and back, Leticia. How could I possibly help you carry

244

Celestina into the library, in my condition?"

"I'm not blaming you, *Maman*. I'm just explaining," I persisted. "Tina couldn't have had anything to do with what happened to Mrs. Hargreaves. Aren't you glad I can keep my job at the library?"

"Talk to Tina and see if you can get her to understand that you must be allowed to attend the university and get a Library Science degree, so you can keep your job in the future, Ticia," *Maman* insisted. "I can't live much longer, and Mrs. Willoughby may not always be there to protect you, after I'm gone."

I will always believe that *Maman* might have lived forever-or at least a while longer-if she had gone to Celestina to explain the degenerative disease wasting her away. But she died weeping alone in her bed, for neither of us knew how grave her deterioration was until Mrs. Willoughby gave me books to help me understand muscular dystrophy, after the funeral.

And Celestina crept whimpering through the little crawlspace in the upstairs bathroom into our attic full of wiring and would not come out beyond the bathroom door.

Celestina's crawlspace did not enter a real attic, *Maman* used to say. It was a dangerous crossroads of all the wiring in the house, and we had never been allowed to go in there and play because we could be killed. This enticing deadly space waited behind a small wooden door in the slope-ceilinged bathroom between our bedroom and *Maman*'s. Perhaps Celestina first worked open the lock and dragged herself into the forbidden space because she had always loved to find tight dark places where she could hide away.

Though I braved crawling through after her to set up a cozy cubby by the slatted attic window with her rag rug, crocheted blanket and tasseled pillow, I dreaded following her in each day, to bring her food and books. So I took my courage in both hands, as *Maman* used to say, and set up my beloved wooden dollhouse in Celestina's back-breaking space. I turned the dollhouse floors into cupboard shelves to hold Tina's prepackaged juices, snacks, and her very favorites of all her books. The familiar little dolls, staring from where they leaned against their perfect miniature furniture, should make Celestina feel less alone. For there was no room for me, alongside her in there.

I hated to think how hard Celestina worked to wedge her huge head through the crawlspace's narrow safe passageway back out through the attic door, to make use of the bathroom each day. But I could think of nothing I could do to alleviate that necessity.

She must have managed it. For I needed to replace the tissues and scented moist wipes in the little box by the open drain in the floor that was her toilet, and I needed to pull the plug out of the claw-footed bathtub each evening to change the few inches of wash water I'd left in it. I had to keep scrubbing clean my sister's damp washcloth and clothing and hanging them neatly on the edge of the tub to dry. And I had to find where she'd let skid the fragrant lavender soap she loved, to place it back in the bathtub's soap dish. Each day, the bathroom's trash can held a fresh wrapper or two of my sister's favorite snacks from what had become "our" dollhouse and emptied plastic bottles that had held juice or water. And if I left a tray of freshly cooked food at her attic threshold, I'd come back later with a new tray to find the previous day's dishes emptied.

So it was like this, sitting cross-legged on the bathroom floor at the open attic crawlspace door after *Maman*'s funeral, coaxing Tina to come to me and eat, that I was stunned by the thought: *Why is Tina so inconsolable? Even I, who rode to and from work in* Maman*'s van, who dined with* Maman *every night, who-for Heaven's sake!-wonder what we will do to live because* Maman *is dead and we must someday soon lose her disability check, even I have ceased to weep.*

I don't know why the unspeakable suspicion first crept up on me: *Did Tina know* Maman *dead? Is that why she won't stop crying?*

At first, I argued with myself: *Tina does not do the deed. She only* knows *it will happen. She would never have killed* Maman.

Yet, listening to my sister's sobs like baby wolves howling, I thought: *But* Maman *thought Tina knew Mrs. Hargreaves away. Is that why Tina knew Maman to death? To keep Mrs. Hargreaves's accident a secret?* I had no idea why this terrible train of thought seized me and would not be shaken off.

To stop the hateful thoughts, the terrifying suspicions, I would rush to read to Celestina at her attic door, sing to her until she fell asleep, pedal furiously on my bike to the store to buy her favorite snacks and canned soups-anything to keep from thinking: *Did Tina kill* Maman? *Will she kill me, too?*

I think the librarians were confused when they did not see Celestina at *Maman's* small memorial gathering. I said nothing to anyone about why Celestina was not at the funeral. So perhaps anyone who remembered *Maman's* keening creature bending its bulky pale head over piles of books in the library's darkest corner assumed that the odd child, too, had deteriorated to death, and I was now alone in the world.

The thought came to me: *I could easily be alone. Just turn the lock outside the attic door. Put a lock outside the bathroom door, for good measure. Live downstairs for a while. Who would know? Who would ask?*

Long after those rainy afternoons following *Maman's* death and the installing of Celestina in the attic crawlspace, I found it almost impossible to force myself across her new room's threshold.

For I now feared my *savant* sister. *May she not know,* I found myself hoping. But how could Celestina not know how I, her own twin sister, now felt about her?

She knew everything.

Out of the house, far from Celestina, such thoughts made me bury myself in the stacks of Special Collections and weep. But when one day Mrs. Willoughby found me crying there, I said absolutely nothing about Celestina. Thinking

248

quickly, lying by telling a different truth, I told Mrs. Willoughby not that I feared my sister, but that I didn't know how to enroll in classes at the university, as *Maman* had asked me to do so I could one day take care of myself.

"Your mother was right to try to get you enrolled at the university," Mrs. Willoughby counseled me gently. "Her disability pay is at an end, with her death, and soon you will lose her pension, as well. Can't you go to the university and talk with a counselor?"

"But I know no one there," I cried. "I wouldn't know where to start." *I am not the* savant, I almost said. *I am only the idiot sister.*

So Mrs. Willoughby sat me down with a catalog and explained to me how to apply for admission to the local public university. We discovered, however, that Library Science was no longer offered there. Mrs. Willoughby, shocked and saddened by how times had changed, shook her head and said she could not advise me about what courses to take-what major to undertake-instead.

So, as with all difficult questions, I determined to bring this one to Celestina, too. *Tina will know. Tina always* knows.

I sat at the opened attic door with a catalog, feeling horribly foolish and guilty, and called out. "Tina? Tina, will you come out to me?"

The whales cried, and I knew Celestina was, instead, inviting me in. *I must go to her.* I had no choice.

So I went down on my hands and knees and shoved the opened university catalog ahead of me through the dark with my fingertips. I crawled toward the slats of sunlight and the still figure, huddled in on itself, obstructing and refracting bright rays among the eddying swirls of dust.

I was deeply uncomfortable. "Tina? I haven't brought dinner up on your tray, yet. I will, in just a little while. But I need your help. It's this: I must go to study at the university, now that *Maman-*"

But the head lolled on the weak, struggling neck, and I thought, *No, don't start crying now, Teenie!* I bit off what I had been about to say and picked up the thread several thoughts later. "I can't major in Library Science, Tina. The university doesn't offer it anymore. So many libraries have been shut down."

Into my mind surged the thought, *Our library shall never be closed,* and Celestina's hook shot out and snagged the catalog by its inner binding and dragged it from me, toward her.

Suddenly energized, Celestina flipped pages like a whirlwind and stabbed her hooked page-turning claw down on a blurry object before her.

I hesitated to reach for the catalog, to see what she was so adamant about. Her animation, her conviction, scared me. *What will I see there? Something impossible. Computer Science. Something I cannot do. Astrophysics. Something that will make me give up and go mad. Organic Chemistry. I am not the smart one.*

Again, Celestina lifted her bird-like limb and dropped her hooked finger to the same spot on the opened page, more insistently this time. When still I hesitated, Celestina cooed softly, turtledoves in the morning outside my bedroom window. A sound I loved.

I relaxed but reached dispiritedly for the catalog.

Where Celestina had indicated, I found not a listing of majors nor even a listing of classes, but only the photo of a professor. I looked up to stare at Celestina. *What can I do with a professor's photograph?*

But Celestina had retreated into a rocking rhythm, the skin of her eyelids half lowered over the curve of her motionless eyes, and she said and did nothing more.

I crawled backward out of her lair but returned to the attic door within the quarter hour, having heated a can of Italian lentil soup for her. I thought, guiltily, that it was one of her favorite quick meals and might get her to answer my questions about my major and that photo of the professor, for I was too stupid to understand how they fit together.

Celestina was waiting at the attic door by the time I arrived with her soup. But she seemed, as always these days, exhausted from the effort. She whined feebly, like wolf puppies searching for their mother to suckle, as she struggled to grasp and lift the spoon.

If I did not feed her, I would soon be free of her, I thought wickedly and, shocked at myself, lifted the spoon for her to her beak-like lips. Ashamed now to ask my questions and confused by my uncharitable thoughts, I silently watched my sister struggle to slurp down the thick soup as I tilted the spoon again and again.

251

Finally, Celestina turned her head away and tiredly dragged her body back through the attic door. I waited, wanting to go after her but dreading the dark, the dust, the closeness. Afraid to trust her, as I had always done. Repulsed by my very love for her.

When I made myself get down on all fours and peer inside to the end of the trail through the attic, I saw that Celestina had resumed her sightless rocking, already fallen into the stupor that passed for her sleep.

So I carried the emptied soup bowl and sticky green spoon on the tray with the university catalog down to the dining table. There, I lit candles for my own dinner, as *Maman* used to do when she could still lift her arms. And over a slice of stale French bread dipped into a bowl of heated milk laced with sugared coffee, I read about the professor Celestina had pointed out to me.

He taught history and philosophy. Not knowing what else to do, I searched for the general education courses he would teach in the upcoming semester and enrolled myself in both of them. *Perhaps he will be able to suggest to me a major,* I thought resignedly.

But it took little time to realize that I would never work up the nerve to request a private conversation with this professor, let alone ask him to advise me.

I had never been particularly brave with boys and men, though they had always been kind and protective toward me. Nor had I ever figured out what I said or did to unnerve them. So, just as

Celestina had learned not to leave her room, lest she run into some relative who hadn't seen her since she was small or, worse yet, some absolute stranger such as a handyman and send him screaming out of the house, so I had learned not to interact with boys beyond the simplest greetings and shy smiles.

I couldn't have approached a grown man and begun a conversation to save my life.

Worse yet, the university campus intimidated me into near paralysis. The first day of classes, I stumbled from my bike and froze at the sight of its sprawling magnificence. Within seconds, I was reduced to shaking by my efforts to read the map I'd printed at the library to help me find my classrooms.

Even my accustomed sanctuary, the library, defeated me at the university. When I retreated into it, I was struck speechless by its soaring stacks of floors beneath a vaulted ceiling and its regimented rows of moveable bookshelves, rumbling as they shuffled like zombies in its basement far below.

All of my professors-at home in their impersonal wasteland-frightened me into incoherence. I said nothing to any of them, hoping to pass my classes by the worth of whatever I put in my written assignments, and escape.

Least of all could I open my mouth to address the professor Celestina had indicated.

He was tall, paler than Celestina, almost as pale as Mrs. Hargreaves, and as acutely angled as both of them put together. He leaned on a towering podium and thundered and snarled at the lecture halls jam-packed with people who had assembled just to hear him. Braver men than I could ever be quaked when they raised their hands to ask him questions, only to be shot down for their temerity, as soon as he acknowledged them.

I thought of the books I'd read to Celestina about voyagers and fools on a quest-which, surely, I was, every bit as much as Odysseus, Jason, Don Quixote, or the first card of Tarot's Major Arcana-and thought, *That man is a god. A tyrant. A demon. I will die, if I talk to him. He will ask me what such an idiot as I clearly am could possibly be doing at his university.*

I grew furious with Celestina all over again at the very sight of the man each day and fumed morosely at the back of his classrooms. My university career was doomed to failure. My predicament was all my sister's fault, and I hated her afresh.

And then came the day the professor I most feared called me to his podium as he dismissed the rest of my World History class. "If you don't mind, Leticia-may I call you that? You are Leticia, right?- I wonder how you got your hands on a copy of *Sears' Travels through Russia and Mongolia*."

My essay. He had actually sat down and set his eyes and his mind upon my essay. I trembled.

It had never occurred to me that he might care what I wrote in response to one of his assignments, let alone read it. *Oh, bliss. Oh, dread.* "Professor Aaronson, I assure you I did read a copy of *Sears' Travels through-*" I began.

But "Yes, I know you did. I can see by your exceptionally engaging essay that you did indeed read it. That wasn't my question, Leticia. What I asked you," and here he slowed down and bent forward to me over his podium, as if aware that he and his massive, impersonal institution must speak carefully to someone so slow to understand, "is how you secured yourself the perusal of a copy of the book." And he gazed with unflinching gray eyes into my terror.

Then he sighed and seemed to resolve to speak even more plainly. "I, too, would like very much to read that book, Leticia. But I-unlike you-am unable to find it. I appeal to your superior powers of research."

It took me a few moments. But then comprehension flooded through me and, with it, relief. I laughed in his face.

Professor Aaronson stared back at me as if dumbstruck.

Wiping tears of sheer joy from my eyes, I patted his hand with my free one, where he gripped the podium. When I could speak again I said, "You cannot find that book listed, Professor Aaronson. At least, not at my library," I explained carefully, as if our roles had been reversed, and now he just might be the stupid one. "I have withdrawn it from the available list and marked it as damaged or stolen. It is neither, of course. It is in perfectly fine condition. And just as soon as my sister is through reading it-" and then I gasped and slapped both hands over my mouth.

What have I done? I wailed to myself. For I never, absolutely never, for any reason whatsoever, allowed myself to publicly mention Celestina, anymore.

And here stood an outsider who now knew that she existed. *This never had to happen!* I chided myself. I waited for something terrible, some future catastrophe, to announce itself in Professor Aaronson's next words. Perhaps something such as, "You mean the sister you plan to lock in the attic and starve to death? Wait here while I call campus police to arrest and guillotine you."

I thought wildly, *I can do it tonight. She will be dead by this weekend. He can't prove I ever said I have a sister.*

But Professor Aaronson rallied himself and said with surprising gentleness, "Ah, you have a bibliophile sister, Ms. Beaulieu? Or is she an obscure histories enthusiast, as I assume you must be, as well, judging from your exceptional report on the quotidian habits of ethnic minority cultures scattered along the late nineteenth-century Russian/Mongolian steppes?"

What had he said? *Too many words. Most of them too big for me.* Best to exit while I was still at liberty.

I turned and stumbled, shoving my way through the knot of other students tangled at the threshold, still straggling, awestruck, out of his lecture hall.

All the way to the bike rack, I was sure I still felt the professor's stupefied gaze on my back. *I will leave the university*, I plotted as I made my getaway, churning the pedals on my bicycle. *No need to finish this semester. I'll never graduate, anyway. Better to end this now.*

256

For two weeks, I dutifully slipped my sister her tray but hid from her downstairs in *Maman*'s kitchen, by the fireplace in *Maman*'s reading room, or by candlelight at *Maman*'s dining table, except when it was time to pedal like a madwoman to my afternoon shift in Special Collections at the public library.

Only once did Celestina lie in wait for me at her attic door and hook my hand as I set down her dinner tray. Her head, as unwieldy as a water balloon, bobbled as she struggled to tilt it back on her thin neck to look up at me. She mewled her distress.

She knows, I thought, but, "It's all right, Tina," I chirped. "It wasn't going to work anyway. I don't know why *Maman* thought I should attend the university. I can't graduate." *Nor do I know why you thought I should have anything to do with that professor,* I fumed bitterly, wordlessly, and smiled at her.

Celestina soundlessly released my hand and withdrew into her darkness.

It was in the third week of my escape from the university campus that Professor Aaronson appeared at the Special Collections desk of my library.

With no sense of foreboding, I'd practically skipped up to the desk when summoned. For I loved to help people find books in Special Collections. Searching for their books, I always found something new to offer to Celestina, too, pacifying her, allaying her fears, putting off the awful day when I must finally work up my nerve to do something to protect myself from her powers and her from our inevitable descent into fatal poverty.

But I stopped with a reverberating jerk, like a cartoon character, when I realized why the towering man in the tattered tweed jacket with leather elbows and gray strands in his long blond ponytail looked so familiar.

"Professor Aaronson," I gasped.

He smiled, as if to show that he was harmless. "Ms. Beaulieu," he gushed. "I hope you don't mind that I took it upon myself to come to your place of employment. Has something happened? I thought perhaps you might be ill. Or your sis-"

"No," I practically shrieked and looked furtively about me from side to side. "Please. Did you come for a book? May I help you?"

Professor Aaronson looked puzzled but quickly rallied. "Well, yes, actually," he said, "I came to ask why you haven't been in my classes, as I would hate to drop you from them, and also to ask after that book, *Sears' Travels.* Do you remember?"

I sped around the circular Special Collections desk that acted as a barricade to keep plebeians from fingering the delicate books and slipped my hand into the crook of Professor Aaronson's arm. He reflexively bent the elbow as if to trap my hand there, even as he gazed down on me in astonishment.

"Please come with me, Professor," I intoned with the authority of an arresting officer, "so we can talk."

I tugged him into the Special Collections

circular office in the center of the second floor of the library and got him into a chair in front of an empty table.

"Look, Professor Aaronson." I glanced back over my shoulder at him as I got out a pillow and gloves from the cabinet, as if he'd ordered a Special Collections book. "I can't come back to your classes. Or any other professor's classes, as a matter of fact. The university scares me. I'm giving up."

I plumped up a dark red velvet pillow in front of him and helped him slide on a pair of white cotton gloves. "What book will you bring me?" he asked with curiosity.

"Not the book you wanted to see. Something as good. You'll like it." And I hurriedly found for him an original limited edition publication of Dante's *Inferno* with illustrations by Gustave Dore.

"How amazing," Professor Aaronson commented and then grabbed my wrist with his gloved hand before I could leave the room. "I want to speak with you about your education, Ms. Beaulieu," he said. "Please give me permission to use your contact information before you go."

I tried to twist my wrist from his grasp. "I'm coming back with a William Blake-illustrated limited edition of Milton's *Paradise Lost* that I think you will also enjoy and my answer to your question, Professor Aaronson."

He hadn't quite let go. "It isn't a question, Ms. Beaulieu. Leticia. It's a request."

"All right, Professor Aaronson. An answer to your request will come with me when I return."

And that is how Professor Aaronson ended up

strapping my bike to the rack on the back of his Jeep-("See? I knew we were meant to be friends!")-so he could take me to his favorite coffee shop before he dropped me at my house.

By the time we had finished our coffees-an espresso for him and a Pumpkin Spice latte with whipped cream for me-and he had set my bike down in front of my dark house, Professor Aaronson was my most trusted confidant. I took the handlebars of my bike from his grasp and wheeled it up to our wide front porch, relieved that Celestina was no longer ensconced in the window of my bedroom and could not see me come home in the company of a stranger.

But she was the *savant*. Would she not *know* that something about me had changed?

I locked my bike and went straight to the kitchen to check for a can of one of Celestina's favorite soups. I was in luck. I still had Italian wedding soup, one of her very most favorites.

Soon, I made my way up the dark stairs with the steaming bowl of soup and a whisper-thin slice of my own day-old French bread-buttered and heated for her, to freshen it-and an unlit candle in a candlestick on a tray, as a special offering.

I had to flick the lights on with my elbows and wrists, as I went. Even the bathroom light had not been turned on, as I hadn't known when I left that I'd be out so late. Couldn't have known. But I'd leave it on in future, as Celestina could not possibly reach that high.

I bent hesitantly to her attic door and called softly inside, "Tina?"

260

No sound.

Though I'd already turned the bathroom light on, I struck a match from the box on the tray and lit the candle, too. Perhaps Celestina smelled the soup, or maybe she smelled the match or saw the candlelight flicker, and it reminded her of *Maman*.

But, in any case, she gave out her cry of whales: *Welcome,* and *Come in.*

I crawled in willingly but gasped when I found her weak, her back turned slightly toward me so that she could rest her head on her clawed hands, which were stuck in the attic window slats as if she'd been there gasping for air. I edged my way around the side of the tray to rub the flattest parts of her twisted back, and she cooed weakly like dying songbirds.

Guiltily, I checked her dollhouse for diminished supplies, her skin for fever, her eyes for dilated pupils. I could find nothing wrong, but, *She knows!* I fretted and determined to think well of her while in the house. I forced mental images into the atmosphere around us of me on my bike, barreling to the grocery store and finding all her favorite treats, rushing up to the bathroom with a tray laden with goodies, and reading to her gaily for hours on end. *Not now,* I thought wildly, rubbing her back and petting her. *Don't die now.*

I still needed her.

Without Celestina, Professor Aaronson would not have admired me for my brilliant essay. And, to my dismay, I realized I would miss my sister terribly, if she weren't here waiting for me in the evenings. Needing me, in return. And she had never actually hurt me. She had done me a good turn when she found Professor Aaronson for me. And I wasn't ready for more misery and loneliness, not just yet.

After that day, things did change for the better for both of us. For, from the very next morning until the end of the semester, Professor Aaronson's Jeep pulled up outside our house every morning that I had classes, so that I needn't bike the long ride over ice or through snow to the university campus. Every afternoon after my classes, I lolled in his office in-between his appointments with other students, discussing assignments, until he found or made the time to take me from campus to my job at the public library. I soon began to think that perhaps I could survive this first semester at the university.

Because, best of all, most evenings before I got off work, Professor Aaronson also found or made the time to appear in Special Collections, waiting to be seated and gloved to look at a book of my choosing.

I loved these sessions and beamed under Professor Aaronson's praise of my choices. But the praise should not have been mine, for my choices were simple and unvarying. I always gave Professor Aaronson each of Celestina's Special Collections books, as she let me return them to the library. She would peruse her stack, select one, and drag it to me on the end of her claw. And I would flick on her bathroom light, stick the book in my backpack, and dust it and set it aside for Professor Aaronson, when I reached the library.

Except for *Sears' Travels through Russia and Mongolia.* Celestina might never finish reading and rereading that book.

But Celestina's other books gave Professor Aaronson the impression that I was smart, and I thanked my mother's spirit, or whatever else had stopped me from sealing Celestina in the attic. Without her, I could never have impressed him.

He began to say that he admired me.

Mrs. Willoughby stopped by my place, shelving Special Collections books, to ask if I were glad I'd started at the university. She said she was proud of me and smiled significantly.

And, as the semester closed on final exams, Professor Aaronson asked me if he might be invited to my home for dinner during the Winter Break.

We were parked outside my dark house when he asked. I studied his solemn face in the glow of the street lamps that filtered in through his Jeep's windows. *Oh no,* I thought. But, "Why?" was what I asked.

When he looked puzzled, I explained my question. "Why would you want to come have dinner with me?" And I thought of my chunk of day-old French bread dipped into a bowl of warm milk with leftover coffee, and wondered how far it would go if I had to split it in two.

Could one offer such a dinner to a guest? I doubted it. Maybe one of Celestina's favorite canned soups, instead?

Then I thought of *Maman*'s dinners. Maybe it was time I tried to learn how she had cooked them.

Professor Aaronson said soberly, "Because,

now that you have finished your semester and are no longer a student at my university, I can get to know you personally. Would that be all right with you, Ms. Beaulieu? Or have you decided to continue at the university? You're one of the most brilliant people I have ever known. Maybe you will continue for one more semester?"

I shook my head decisively. "No, I am done with the university." I smiled. "But I would be happy if we get to know each other personally, Professor Aaronson."

He smiled and blushed and turned from me to look out of his side window at the street, as if he were thinking.

It was just as well that he looked away, for I too needed to think. I thought, *Celestina will* know *if someone is in the house. How will she react?*

And then I shut down the next obvious, awful thought: *How will Professor Aaronson react when he sees Celestina?* Because he must not see my twin sister. *Of course not.* She would not leave her attic room or, at the furthest, our shared bathroom. *But he might hear her. The cry of whales. The trumpet of elephants. He will run from my house, screaming.*

"Leticia?" Professor Aaronson turned to me, calling my mind back to him. I looked to him. "Perhaps I can take you to see the community college during the Winter Break. As an educator, I shouldn't encourage you to give up on higher education, altogether," he added guiltily.

"We can do that," I agreed. "See the community college, I mean. And you can call me

264

Ticia." *If Celestina hears it, maybe he will remind her of Maman.*

Suddenly Professor Aaronson's fingers held my chin still, and he stared into my eyes. His were like silver starlight, his brows furrowed. I wasn't frightened.

But I pulled away and slid backwards out of my seat to stand on the sidewalk, facing him. "When will you ask me for my answer, Professor Aaronson?"

"Answer? Oh, dinner. Tomorrow," he said, rallying. Then, more shyly, "Ticia, may I come here to give you a ride to the library and ask you then?"

"Yes, tomorrow." I waved at him, smiling brightly, and turned and bounded up the walkway and the porch steps to the front door. I turned to wave at him one more time before I let myself into the house.

Celestina's coo reached me on the landing, as sweet as a morning whippoorwill. *What could have made her so happy?*

That very night, I poured out for her *Maman's* favorite breakfast of maple syrup glittering over a mound of grits. I pushed the tray toward her, on my knees. To my great relief, she hooked the tray closer to her in the dark of her attic threshold.

I flipped the university catalog from under my arm to show Celestina Professor Aaronson's photo. "May he come see us?" I asked gently, urgently. "May he come have dinner here in this house?"

Celestina startled me by uttering a cry I didn't know. *Hawks circling in the sky?* As the indecipherable cry drew out like a vulture's caw

265

across mountain ranges, I panicked. *Should I stop her? Take back my question?*

But I couldn't. I didn't want to give up on Professor Aaronson. *Tina, let me explain. Let me describe him to you. You found him. Let me keep him. Please.*

Celestina's hooked page-turning finger dropped to caress the photo of Professor Aaronson, right on the spot where his cheek would have been.

"I'll tell him he can come," I cried gaily to my sister and leaned over the catalog to throw a hug around her neck.

The next afternoon, I had barely biked back to the house with a basket of groceries and dashed upstairs to leave Celestina with a box of graham cracker teddy bears, a bowl of washed grapes, and several small containers of orange juice and chocolate soy milk, when Professor Aaronson's Jeep pulled up out front.

I tore back down the stairs, laughing with joy as I snatched up my emptied backpack to deplete it of my keys. Then I threw myself empty-handed, house keys dumped into my jacket pocket, onto the Jeep seat next to Professor Aaronson.

He handed me a steaming takeout eggnog latte and wrapped his cream-colored fingers around my golden ones, as I tried to take it from him. I was so happy, I didn't know what to do. So I threw my free arm around Professor Aaronson's neck to give him a squeeze, just as I'd done with Celestina the night before.

But Professor Aaronson was much stronger than my sister. I felt his resistance for just an instant

266

before he seized me with both arms and crushed me to his chest across the gear shift between us.

I jerked away and stared at him.

He stared back, surprised. "Did I-?" he began but obviously didn't know what to ask if he had done.

"No, no," I assured him, equally unsure what he had not, in fact, done to me.

"May I come to dinner, Ticia?"

I nodded, smiling above the steam of my delicious coffee. "Yes. When will you come, Professor Aaronson?"

He smiled and started the Jeep's engine.

It turned out that he wanted a few days to finish submitting all his grades before he came to dinner. He said he wanted not to worry and to have a clear mind for the evening. And he wanted me to have time to practice calling him Jeremiah.

I taught the name to Celestina. Though she would never exactly say it, she might want to *know* something about it. She had not relinquished the catalog with his photo.

"Thank you," I kept assuring her, "for letting Jeremiah come to dinner."

Celestina cooed.

And, too soon, Jeremiah stood under the porch light at the door with a bouquet of white roses, glowing out of the darkness behind him. "May I come in, Ticia?" he asked politely as I stared rudely, overwhelmed.

I'd worried about everything: the mismatched, dust-covered candles in the candelabrum, the bland recipe I'd found online for what should have been my deceased grandmother's spicy oven-fried catfish, keeping butter and sausage out of the cornbread and greens, in case Jeremiah was vegan or ova/lacto vegetarian, as Celestina was, and whether or not to put tofu into the creamed garlic salad dressing, in case he only ate raw foods, as my mother sometimes did when we could afford special groceries for her.

It turned out that I should have worried about none of those things and about something I never would have thought might happen. "I eat anything that tastes good, Tish. Ticia." Jeremiah laughed shyly as he stumbled through my baby nicknames. Then he cleared his throat and reached for one of my mother's vases on top of the kitchen cabinets, to fill with water for his roses.

After we congratulated each other with nervous pleasure over how the roses arced like a pearly peacock's tail from the vase, spreading their perfumed petals in a perfect fan, a noise on the stairs silenced us.

We turned, and I don't know how we didn't drop the vase between us.

For the noise was the drag of the curled legs like pale tentacles under Celestina's heavy hanging head and curved spiky spine as she struggled to grip the banister and not topple down the stairs.

I had never seen her entire body at a distance, like this, since we were small children and I went on my way to elementary school without her, mourning separation from my constant companion. I suppose, in my mind, she had remained the fetus as large as the seat of a rocking chair that I remembered her to be.

But she was not. Dangling on the stairs, her enormous head waving from side to side because nothing on her body was strong enough to anchor it, threatening to topple the whole of her down the steps to her death, I was at first stunned to see her.

Then I was appalled to see how she looked, a grand and awful creature raised from the primordial wastes, or fallen from the heavens, or tumbled like a flawed clay toy from the hand of an idle god.

And then I was ravaged by my love and pity for her.

"Oh, Tina!" I screamed and was suddenly up the stairs at her side, bracing her with my own body, her head a huge weightless mass like a balloon on my own shoulders. I struggled with my fumbling sweaty hands to clamp her claws more firmly on the banister and shove her backward up onto the landing, but her slight weight resisted me. Then suddenly Tina was above my head and over my shoulder and would surely hurtle to be dashed against the hardwood floor far below.

As Celestina sailed into the air, it was I who almost sprawled to the floor, spinning madly to grasp at her and clutch her back to me and save her life.

But she was safe in Jeremiah's arms.

Laughing a gallant introduction of himself, as though nothing untoward had happened at all, Jeremiah had lifted her from her desperate hold on the banister into his own strong arms and now backed carefully from me, to turn and carry my sister to safety.

I sank to the top step and wiped at my burning eyes.

In the parlor, out of my sight, I heard Jeremiah croon like a gentleman in a Jane Austen novel, "May I be so bold as to assume that you are the fair Miss Beaulieu's equally fair twin sister?"

And Celestina trilled nightingales to him and sent me whales softly singing for me to make my way down the stairs to join them.

I found Celestina tucked into a corner of the old-fashioned *chaise longue* that was our sofa. From this throne, she unleashed from her throat a perfect aviary in ecstasy at Jeremiah, who knelt at her formless feet. Though her beaked lips could not shape a real smile, she apparently wanted so to welcome him, to make him feel at home, that she had managed something quite close.

And Jeremiah gazed up at her, enchanted.

Standing alone, staring in at them, for the first time in my life I realized that I was probably beautiful. Of course, this was why boys and men had always smiled upon me and tried to protect me.

But it is true that I am not wholly myself without my sister, Celestina. She is my soul, my best self, as I used to know when I was small. It is also true that, beautiful or not, I am her monster, her beast, her ugly sister, and she is my fair maiden, and I must strive to be more like her, if I want to keep both her and Jeremiah. This is my lesson.

Jeremiah turned to me where I stood in the doorway and held out the book my sister had risked her life to bring down to him, in welcome. "Look, Ticia, what your sister has brought me," he said rapturously. "The only extant copy of *Sears' Travels through Russia and Mongolia* in the United States."

"Tina," I said softly. "Her name is Celestina. But she would want you to call her Tina."

He turned and beamed up at her half-lidded, lashless eyes, the dark orbs suspended inches from his face, and said, "Celestina-heavenly one. May I please call you Tina?"

Tina reached down her hook to Jeremiah to gently stroke his cheek, just as she'd done with his photo when she'd had me enroll in his classes. And she un-caged lovebirds.

The End

Alexis Brooks de Vita has published critical essays of literary and cultural studies, book reviews, poetry, and short stories and memoirs in such diverse publications as *Encyclopedia of the African Diaspora, Journal of the Fantastic in the Arts, Proverbium, English Language Notes, Candle in the Attic Window, Full Circle, The Griot, Absorbing Destruction: Poetry by Ten Women, Forced from the Garden: Poetry and Short Stories,* and *Safari: African American Stories, Parables and Tales.* She is the author of four novels published by Double Dragon/Blood Moon: *Left Hand of the Moon,* a stand-alone, and the *Books of Joy* series: *Burning Streams, Blood of Angels* and *Chain Dance.* Dr. Brooks de Vita, a Professor and member of the Regular Graduate Faculty at Texas

Southern University, is also the author of three scholarly books: her translation of *Dante's* Inferno: *A Wanderer in Hell* published by Double Dragon/Blood Moon, *The 1855 Murder Case of* Missouri versus Celia, *an Enslaved Woman* published by Edwin Mellen Press, and *Mythatypes: Signatures and Signs of African/Diaspora and Black Goddesses* published by Greenwood Press. She was co-editor with Lee Barwood of the Double Dragon/Blood Moon anthology, *Love and Darker Passions.* Please visit her website at www.alexisbrooksdevita.com.